D0093851

Wishing Upon the Same Stars

JACQUETTA NAMMAR FELDMAN

HARPER
An Imprint of HarperCollinsPublishers

Wishing Upon the Same Stars
Copyright © 2022 by Jacquetta Nammar Feldman
All rights reserved. Printed in the United States of America.
No part of this book may be used or reproduced in any manner whatsoever without
written permission except in the case of brief quotations embodied in critical
articles and reviews. For information address HarperCollins Children's Books,
a division of HarperCollins Publishers, 195 Broadway, New York, NY 10007.
www.harpercollinschildrens.com
This book is a work of fiction. Any references to historical events, real
people, or real places are used fictitiously. Other names, characters, places,
and events are products of the author's imagination, and any resemblance to
actual events or places or persons, living or dead, is entirely coincidental.

Library of Congress Control Number: 2021036826
ISBN 978-0-06-303438-9

Typography by Laura Mock
21 22 23 24 25 PC/LSCH 10 9 8 7 6 5 4 3 2 1
❖
First Edition

For L.P.F.—my Ayelet

One

Sometimes you don't know how much things have changed, until nothing's the same. Sometimes you don't know how much you belong, until you're without a best friend. And sometimes you don't know how much home feels like home, until your parents uproot you and drag you clear across the country a few weeks before seventh grade.

My parents make their big announcement during dinner at the beginning of August. I'm only half listening to the conversation they're having about the southern United States, about winters with no snow shoveling, about the strong housing market in the state of Texas.

I'm more focused on trying to eat my plate of mjaddara— a nutritious Arab dish that consists of yucky brown lentils, oily white rice with crispy fried onions, and a big helping of tart plain yogurt—for the second night in a row since my mother always makes enough for leftovers.

I look up when my father clears his throat. He sits up straighter and says in his formal way, "Children, we have breaking news—"

My mother interrupts him in her quick, thick accent. "Baba has taken a very important, *big* new job in San Antonio, Texas! It is a *dream* job. He will be a sales manager now!" She claps her hands, jingling her gold bangle bracelets.

I nearly choke on a bite of lentils. "Are we moving?"

Baba reaches over and pats my head. "Yes, Yasmeen, we will leave Detroit in just a few weeks, after we make all the arrangements and say our goodbyes."

My little sister, Sara, squeals. "San Antonio, really? My fourth-grade teacher told us about the Alamo! There was a battle with the Mexican army for freedom and the Texians fought to their *demise*. Hey! Are we going to live on a real Texas ranch with horses?"

"Yay, horsies!" my two-year-old little brother, Salim, cheers.

I sit still clasping my fork, my mouth suddenly too dry to swallow my food. The voices in the room hum, fuzzy in my ears. I can only half focus while my parents explain all the details.

They talk about selling the house I've grown up in and

packing our things. They talk about which items will be kept, and which will be left behind. They talk about our hilly new neighborhood, our excellent new schools, and the big new house that comes with my father's big new job.

I look around our cozy kitchen: at my father's nargila that always stands in the corner for smoking after dinner, at the brass lantern above our kitchen table that casts little star cutouts on our deep blue walls, and at the outline of the big crab apple tree I learned to climb outside our backyard window.

I can't believe my parents want to leave our home.

They tell us all about cowboys and rodeos. They tell us about San Antonio's rich Mexican culture, with traditional singers called mariachis, foods called elotes, and a candlelit fiesta at Christmastime along the river that winds through town. They smile and laugh, and the words come easily, like leaving Detroit someday was planned all along.

They don't notice how quiet I've become.

My mother looks at my father, and her honey-colored eyes soften. "Elias, to finally live someplace warm again . . . someplace a little more like home, habibi."

He smiles. "Yes, Myriam. A bit more like home, ayuni."

But Detroit is *home*, isn't it?

Home is where I was born and my siblings were born, with my best friend, Dina, across the street, and nice Mrs. Abboud next door, who comes over with powdered sugar–coated maamoul cookies and funny Disney movies when Baba and Mama go out.

But when my parents talk about home, they usually don't mean Detroit, Michigan. They mean the Middle East.

After dinner, I map the driving route from Detroit to San Antonio on Baba's laptop. It's 1,489 miles away. If my father goes an average speed of sixty-five miles per hour, it will take almost twenty-three driving hours and we'll have to pass through five states before we get to Texas: Ohio, Indiana, Illinois, Missouri, and Arkansas. Detroit is near the top of the United States by Canada, and San Antonio is all the way near the bottom, almost to Mexico.

Next, I map the route to the city of Jerusalem, where my father is from, which is close to the city of Beirut, where my mother is from. Jerusalem is all the way across the Atlantic Ocean, across Portugal and Spain, across the Mediterranean Sea and the southern tip of Italy. My map says: Sorry, we could not calculate directions to Jerusalem from Detroit, Michigan.

No wonder I've never been to the Middle East—it's so far away.

I don't want to move to San Antonio, Texas. I don't want to meet cowboys or watch rodeos or live in a big new house. I especially don't want to go to a brand-new school after I just spent all sixth grade making a few new friends.

I want to stay right where I am, with the stars dancing

on the kitchen walls, with nice Mrs. Abboud next door, and my best friend, Dina, across the street, with the big crab apple tree in my backyard—and even my dinner of leftover lentils.

Two

Our final weeks in Detroit fly by in a series of lasts: the last time Sara and I play Capture the Flag in the front yard with all our neighborhood friends; the last time my mother bakes her homemade pita bread, and fills our cozy kitchen with warm, homey smells; and the last time I climb our crab apple tree, even though I haven't done it in a while since I'm almost a teenager.

Salim holds his little hands in the air when I come down. "Up, Meenie?" he asks. I lift him to the lowest branch, and my heart squeezes tight. Helping my brother climb our crab apple tree is a first and a last at the very same time.

I sulk at the kitchen table in my church dress the Sunday morning of our last service at our Maronite church, where I was baptized as a baby.

Each and every last squeezes my heart harder and harder.

My mother doesn't seem to notice. She bustles around the kitchen preparing our breakfast. "Yasmeen, today is our family's going-away party after services!" she chirps. "It is very exciting, yes?"

I don't know what to say. I don't understand why our church is having a party for something that I'm not celebrating. Having a going-away party makes it sound like someday there's a chance we might come back. But Detroit wasn't enough like home for my parents, so I don't think that could ever happen.

Maybe our party should be called a leaving-forever party.

"Do I have to go?" I ask her in a small voice.

She tsk-tsks. "Yasmeen, what are you saying? Of course, you must attend our family's going-away party!"

We leave our house earlier than usual so we can sit up front in the first pew of the sanctuary. My mother doesn't want us to miss a single part of our last service.

When we get there, Dina and I ask our mothers if we can sit together if we promise not to talk. The whole service, we stay quiet and stiff with our legs almost touching and I try not to look at her.

I'm worried if I do, my heart will squeeze so tight it will stop altogether.

Our friend Nabil from school is an altar boy. He unhooks a brass incense holder on long chains from a stand near the wall and solemnly walks it to our white-robed priest. Then our priest swings the jingly container of burning incense forward and backward toward each corner of the sanctuary to bless our congregation.

I breathe in the strong, sweet smell that soaks into my skin and clothes, and say the prayers I've said so many times before, without even thinking about them. I run words into words, like a song I know by heart.

I add a few extra wishes here and there among the prayers: *Please let all the kids at my new school be nice like Dina and Nabil, please let me fit in, please let everything be okay for my family down in Texas. Please help me not feel this sad forever.*

At the end of the service when our priest says, "Go in peace," my mother finally starts to sniffle. All her church friends rush up to her at once and take turns giving her tight hugs until she smiles again.

From our pew, Dina and I watch the congregation file into the community hall for our party. Everyone seems excited—they're all talking and laughing like it's not even a leaving-forever party—everyone, except for us. We're the last to trail inside.

Mrs. Abboud baked a big chocolate cake with vanilla frosting and swirly writing that says: Good luck in Texas,

Khourys! I join my family standing next to her at a long buffet table in the front of the room while the congregants form a long, snaking line.

She cuts thick slices of cake and puts them on rainbow-colored paper plates, then we hand each person a slice as they get to the front of the line and say their goodbyes.

"Myriam and Elias, we will visit you!" one friend says.

"Lucky you, with no snow this winter!" another one says.

My mother's best friend, Claudette, tears up. "Little George and I will miss our long playdates with you and Salim while the older kids are at school, Myriam!"

Our priest shakes Baba's hand. "Congratulations on your big new job, Elias! As they say, everything is bigger in Texas!"

Nabil gets to the front of the line and faces me, frozen. He opens his mouth, but no sound comes out. A few seconds go by, then he blurts, "Yasmeen, it's been really nice knowing you!" and takes two slices of cake and runs away before I have a chance to say goodbye.

Dina is last in line. We offer her cake, but she shakes her head. "I'm not hungry," she says to my family. "I just wanted to tell Yasmeen I'll miss her."

I mumble, "I'll miss you, too, Dina . . . so, so much," and my heart squeezes even harder. I'm not hungry, either. I can't imagine taking even one bite of leaving-forever cake.

★ ★ ★

Monday morning, my father makes another run to the hardware store for more packing materials: boxes and plastic wrap, rolls of sticky tape, and thick Sharpie markers to label where each box will go in our new San Antonio house. All that's left to pack are the kitchen and our bedrooms.

While my mother starts on the kitchen, my sister and I take some boxes and tape to the room we've always shared. We fill them with our old stuffed animal collections, with our clothes and shoes, with the rolled posters we had thumbtacked on the walls next to our twin-sized beds.

We label the boxes *Sara* or *Yasmeen*, since Baba says that we'll each have our own bedroom and bathroom in our big new house. Our room looks bare without Sara's snowy poster of the mama and baby polar bears, and my big star map.

I unload my shelf of completed Sudoku books into a box. "Why are you taking those?" Sara asks. "Aren't they already done?"

I shrug. "They're mine and I like them, okay? I get to decide what I bring."

Something about finishing each book of puzzles and lining them on my shelf always makes me feel good. My mother got me two new Sudoku books for the car ride, and I bet I'll do a lot of them in San Antonio, since I won't have any friends. "Speaking of mine . . ." I reach for the speaker on the desk we share.

"Hey! That's *community* property! Who says you get that?" Sara says.

"I do. I'm older!"

She glares at me. "Mama!"

My mother hurries in, her high heels click-clacking. "Girls! What is this yelling?"

Sara points at the speaker. "Yasmeen says . . ."

My mother waves her dish towel at us and says, "Khalas!" then looks both of us in the eye.

We stop fighting immediately. But after she leaves, I slide the speaker into my box on top of my Sudoku books, and smile.

Sara sticks out her tongue.

After I'm done with my side of our room, I wander to the kitchen and my eyes grow big. My mother's packing food like we might get lost in the Arabian Desert on our drive down to Texas.

She's turning everything in our refrigerator into a picnic, she says.

I peer inside a big cooler full of ice—it doesn't look like a real picnic to me, at least not an American one. There are no egg or tuna salad sandwiches, or peanut butter and jellies, potato chips or lemonade. Our picnic consists of big plastic bags of pita bread, over two dozen hard-boiled eggs, glass jars of pickled cauliflower, turnips and beets, and at least twenty recycled yogurt containers filled with Arab foods.

"Mama, you know that there are lots of places to eat along the way," I say. "There's fast food. We can have American hamburgers. That's what people do on road trips."

She shakes her head and wipes her brow with the edge of her dish towel. "We are not taking chances! Fast food is not real food like my food." She smiles. "And your father says there are picnic tables at all the rest stops along the way!"

We never eat out at restaurants, so I'm not sure why I thought our road trip to San Antonio would be any different.

The movers come the next day to put my father's car on a big open carrier bound for Texas and load our moving truck.

They roll up our woolly rugs, leaving our wood floors bare. They take down the tapestries that blanket our deep blue walls. They plastic wrap our two big brass tray tables with their comfy beaded stools and carry them outside.

The home I've always known begins to disappear.

I can't watch. "Can I please go over to Dina's?" I ask my mother in a shaky voice.

She smooths my hair away from my face. "Of course, habibti."

Dina and I sit cross-legged on the floor of her room and play our favorite question game, What If, for the very last time. What if a boy tries to kiss you? What if your teacher catches you writing notes in class? What if you get asked to a dance?

"What if I hate it in San Antonio?" I mumble. "What if no one at my new school likes me?"

Dina's lip quivers. "What if I don't want to lose my very best friend?"

We both get teary. "Let's do something else on my last day," I say, and she agrees.

We decide to do our next favorite thing. Dina gets her mother's laptop so we can record a news skit. We sit up straight and put on our most serious faces. I'm usually the news anchor, and she likes to be the weathercaster.

This time, we feature the top headlines of the summer: Nabil got two hamsters that he thought were both girls, but one of them wasn't; Dina cut her long hair into a bob, so now she almost looks like an eighth grader; and I finally did one of Dina's *Just Dance* video games without ending up in a heap on the floor, since unlike her, I was born with two left feet.

There was lots of sunshine all summer, and hardly any rain.

The news segment is all good news, until I get to the very last part. I blurt, "This is Yasmeen Khoury signing off forever from Detroit, Michigan. Our programming has been discontinued until further notice since Yasmeen's parents are forcing her to move to San Antonio, Texas."

Dina sniffles and presses pause.

"Should we even save this one?" I ask.

She nods. "We'll want to watch it someday when we're back together."

When it's time for me to go, we stand hugging in her doorway. I don't want to leave my best friend behind. "My mother says I can have a phone when we get to San Antonio," I tell her. "We can text each other all the time!"

Dina frowns. "My mom says I can't have my own phone until eighth grade, but I can use her laptop to video chat you instead."

"Okay," I say. "That's even better since then we can at least . . . see each other. And maybe we can send some news skits so we'll know each other's headlines."

We talk for a few more minutes to draw out our time together, but I know if I stay here much longer, tears will come. So, I give Dina one last quick hug and whisper, "Bye."

Then just like Nabil, I turn and run.

Later, the last night in the house I've grown up in, our last night in Detroit, I lie awake in bed and can't help staring at the boxes stacked high in the corners of my bedroom and the empty walls. Hot tears run down my cheeks in little rivers and soak into my pillow.

"Aren't you excited, Yasmeen?" Sara whispers in the dark.

I open my mouth, but no sound comes out. So I squeeze my eyes shut and pretend I'm asleep.

I try to imagine what our new life will be like in a place my parents say will feel more like home. I try to imagine making new friends clear across the country. I try to imagine a place that is bigger, and better.

But I don't try too hard. I can't imagine any place else ever being near this good.

Three

My father drives our minivan on the first leg of the Khoury family road trip to San Antonio at an average speed of around fifty-five miles per hour.

I do a quick calculation in my head. At his extra slow speed, the trip that might take another family two days will take us three. We'll arrive Friday night, right before our new schools start the very next Monday.

We drive all day Wednesday through Michigan and Ohio, only stopping for gas and our rest stop picnics. Then in Mount Vernon, Illinois, my parents rent a hotel room with two lumpy queen-sized beds and an outdoor pool.

Sara, Salim, and I play games in the pool until our fingers look like raisins, and even after long, hot showers, we still smell like the chlorine that has seeped into our skin.

I fall fast asleep that first night, despite sharing the lumpy bed with Sara, despite Baba's loud rhythmic snores and Salim's waking whimpers. I dream about cowboys on horseback galloping alongside us on the highway, kicking up big dust clouds around our minivan.

Thursday is nearly the same. Baba still drives slowly, and we stop for gas and picnics. But the air gets hotter and hotter as we make our way farther south.

At our lunch break, my mother complains she's lost her appetite. She dabs her runny mascara with a wad of napkins, and repeats to no one in particular, "It is so hot, you cannot believe!"

My father hikes his slacks up and his black socks show above his loafers. He wipes at his sweaty forehead while trying to reassure her, "We will get used to the heat again, habibti."

By afternoon, we've all had enough of our road trip, and there's still one day to go: my mother snaps her fingers at us from the front seat when Sara and I start to bicker; Salim whines and squirms in his car seat between naps; and Baba blasts the air conditioner since we're all sweltering.

Finally, it's decided—we'll stop early.

My father takes a small detour to Hot Springs, Arkansas, and we pull into a giant water park. My mother turns around and winks. "We could all use a little, how do they say . . . pick-me-up, yes?"

Sara and I cheer, and Salim joins in.

We eat dinner at picnic tables outside the entrance, then my parents spend the evening fanning themselves under an umbrella while my siblings and I splash in the cool, refreshing pools. As the sun sets, we're the last family to leave the park.

Everyone oversleeps on the third day, so we start the last leg of our road trip late.

We finally enter Texas at a town called Texarkana at lunchtime and pull into a rest stop. My father unloads our cooler from the trunk again, but now it's much lighter. "Myriam, I am afraid that dinner tonight will have to be fast food."

She furrows her brow and protests, "But fast food is not real food, habibi!" Then she tries to ration our lunches before Baba puts a stop to it.

When we're just south of Dallas, my mother finally admits we don't have enough food left in our cooler for a family of five. Sara and I chant, "American hamburgers! American hamburgers!" until my father pulls off the highway into a fast-food parking lot.

My mother crosses her arms over her chest as we stand at the back of the line in the restaurant. She looks at the choices on the screen above the cash registers and complains to Baba in Arabic.

A big man near the front of the line spins around. "Hey!

What did y'all say?"

My father stares at him and blinks. His voice gets quieter than usual. "We are discussing the menu," he tells him.

The man moves out of line. He points his finger at Baba. "We speak English here. You understand me?"

The woman next to the man lifts her chin and puts her hands on her hips. A girl about my age cups her hand and whispers to her friend, whose eyes grow big.

My mother picks up Salim and moves behind my father. Her gold bangles jingle together as her hands shake. I scoot close to Sara and grab her hand. Some of the other people in the line turn around to look at us, too. My eyes rush over them.

One man drops his head and focuses on his shoes. An older woman clutches her purse and clears her throat. A young man wearing mud-caked boots stares at the big man and clenches his fist, and the young woman with him unfolds it.

The big man's face turns red and the younger man steps in front of him. He says, "Sir, I think they're just getting some dinner, so maybe—"

"Maybe . . . ," the big man interrupts him and glares at Baba. "Maybe it's best *they* leave."

So we do.

My father nods to the younger man, then hurries us out of the restaurant. We leave without getting any food at all.

He drives down the highway gripping the steering wheel with stiff arms and tight knuckles.

Sara sniffles and Salim whines and rubs his belly. My mother blows her nose with a tissue. My father's jaw clenches and clicks. No one says anything.

I want to ask my parents why this happened, but I can't seem to catch my breath. My chest puffs in and out in big quick bursts. Finally, I squeak, "Does that man hate us?"

My mother looks back at me with teary eyes and shakes her head. "Hate is a very strong word, Yasmeen . . . but he did not seem to like us very much."

I don't understand. That man doesn't know us at all.

My father gets off the highway at the next exit and pulls into the drive-through of another fast-food restaurant. He looks at my mother. "Myriam, we will eat our American hamburgers in the car."

Before we met "that terrible man" at the restaurant, as my mother now calls him, my parents' excited conversation filled our car. My mother scrolled through the pictures of our new house over and over on her phone and grilled my father about the details since he chose the house without her.

Was the wall-to-wall carpet in the bedrooms soft, as she liked it? Did our house have central air-conditioning for the hot Texas summers? Was there a good place in the backyard for a new swing set for Salim? Had Baba met any of the neighbors? Were any of them Middle Eastern, like us?

But after our fast-food dinner, my parents are tense and quiet. My mother stares out her window as the miles tick away.

Sara's constant chatter fills the void. "Is that a real Texas ranch?" she asks as we pass a dusty road with tall metal gates marked *J Bar D*.

No one answers.

She points to the next sign. "That one's a ranch for sure, right, Yasmeen?"

I nod, but I'm quiet, too. What happened in the restaurant replays in my mind. I remember the big man's angry words and his glare. I hear my mother's jingling bracelets and my father's soft voice. I see the young man's fist as the young woman unfolds it.

I ask my parents again, "But why? Why didn't that man like us?"

A look passes between them and my father says, "Because we came to America from another country, Yasmeen. That is all."

I nod my head, but I still don't understand. Other than Native people who've always lived here, didn't everyone in America's family come from somewhere else once?

The sun drops below the horizon and short metal mile

markers with yellow reflective tops whiz by in our head-lights. I fall asleep in the back row of the minivan counting them in the dark.

When we finally stop, I'm jolted awake.

My parents open their doors and warm, heavy air fills our car. I can barely make out the shapes of my sleeping siblings in front of me in the faint glow of an overhead streetlight—Salim's curly-haired little head resting on his shoulder, Sara's long, crossed legs with her book resting in her lap.

I unfold myself from the back row and slide around them. When I step out into the near blackness, I can barely see my feet.

My mother reaches inside the car to gather Salim into her arms and somehow, he stays asleep. But Sara pops wide awake and resumes chattering where she left off. "Are we in San Antonio?" She peers out the door. "Is that our new house? It's huge!"

My mother shushes my sister. "Sara, you will wake our new neighbors!" But her eyes flash as she looks up at our new two-story home. "Everything is bigger in Texas, just as they say!"

We follow Baba up a long, stone walkway to our new front door, and he flips on the lights. With his extra slow driving, the movers beat us to San Antonio. Rows of boxes line the halls, and our old furniture is placed haphazardly against freshly painted walls. The inside of our house is shiny and new.

"Let's explore, Yasmeen!" Sara squeals.

Baba holds up his hand. "We will get to know our new home tomorrow, my children. But tonight, it is late, and we must rest."

We trudge upstairs with our suitcases, and my parents show me to my room, where a brand-new, queen-sized mattress has somehow been made up on the floor. Then they say good night and stumble down the hall to settle my siblings.

I look around the room at all the boxes marked *Yasmeen*. Tomorrow, I'll open them one by one and unpack my old life into this unfamiliar, new place, but tonight—I could use just one thing.

I find the tube with my star map in the biggest box, but I can't find any thumbtacks to put it up on my wall. So, I smooth it out on the floor next to my bed and trace the patterns with my finger.

Most people like the Big Dipper the best, since it's easy to find in the night sky with its bright, open pattern, but not me. I like the Little Dipper, because it has my favorite star in it, Stella Polaris, the North Star.

No matter where you are in the United States, if you look to the north, you can always find it.

I change into my pajamas and flip my lights off, then lie

down on my stiff mattress all alone in my room. I try not to cry again.

I look through my curtainless window at the huge night sky—darkness stretches in all directions, and the North Star seems farther now than ever.

When I finally fall asleep, I dream I'm floating in the expanse like the distant stars, trying to find my place in the big wide world, trying to figure out how I can float back home again.

Four

I wake up Saturday morning to hot sunlight streaming through my window and familiar kitchen noises carrying up the staircase. I head downstairs for a first daylight look at our brand-new house.

My mother, makeup applied and dressed for the day, already in her high heels, furiously digs through boxes marked *kitchen* while Salim plays in the overflowing packing peanuts at her feet. The rest of my family sits sleepily at our old kitchen table.

I peel a yellow sticky note with an attached photo off the refrigerator. It says: Hi, y'all! Welcome to San Antonio, Texas! The Jones Family.

"Who are they?" I ask, pointing to the photo.

"The Jones family live in our new neighborhood," Baba

responds. "They let our movers in since we were running late, and even made our beds for us! Mr. Jones is my new colleague at work."

My mother smiles at my father. "This is the Texas hospitality we have heard so much about! Please give Mr. Jones our thanks next week at the office!"

When she opens the refrigerator, there's even everything we need for breakfast, American style: eggs and packaged English muffins, small containers of strawberry yogurt with cereal mix-ins, and pale yellow orange juice in individual-sized plastic bottles. Another sticky note on a platter covered in aluminum foil reads: Some leftovers from last night's neighborhood potluck. See you next time!

My mother lifts the foil and crinkles her nose, then turns to my father and asks, "What is this . . . potluck?"

He shrugs.

I examine the photo of the Jones family—they look nothing like us.

The mother and a daughter about my age both wear white jean shorts, bright-colored tops, and trendy metallic sandals. They have the same stick-straight golden hair tucked smartly behind each ear, and the same big blue eyes. The father grins despite a lobster-red sunburn beneath his summery shirt and khaki shorts.

I notice their family beach vacation group hug, their arms wrapped tightly around each other. Our family photos look stiff and formal in comparison.

While we eat breakfast, Baba tells us all about our new neighborhood, Oak Forest. He says it's filled with rolling streets and circular cul-de-sacs, unlike our neighborhood in Detroit where long, flat streets crisscrossed the suburbs for miles and miles.

My sister perks up and starts combing through the dictionary she always carries around. She slams it shut and announces, "Did you know a *cul-de-sac* is a dead-end street?" Then she scribbles her new word and its definition on a fresh flash card with a purple sparkle pen.

Sara can be really annoying with her big dictionary, her long spelling lists, and slippery stacks of know-it-all flash cards. She's always using big words like she's a genius or something. She even thinks she can win San Antonio's regional spelling bee next February at the Jewel of the Forest Auditorium that our parents told her about, since she almost won last year's regional spelling bee in Detroit.

After we eat, my father and I walk into the living room and look out a big front picture window; there's no forest I can see. Instead, short, bent oak trees grow in rocky-looking soil at the edges of all the yards.

"It looks so different here, Baba . . . than Detroit," I say.

"Yes, Yasmeen, San Antonio is part of the Texas Hill Country." He smiles. "The rolling hills and limestone rocks remind me of Jerusalem."

I nod like I understand, even though I don't. *How could I?* San Antonio is the farthest place I've ever been. My parents have never taken me to their home across the ocean.

I scan the length of our street. Mirrored rows of plastered, cream-colored houses with stone-accent walls stack one after the other, blindingly bright in the morning light. Long, front walkways dissect green yards that meet wide, concrete sidewalks. Each box house shares a brown-stained backyard fence with the one right next to it.

And every single one is way bigger than our old house in Detroit.

"Baba, all the houses look the same," I mutter.

He follows my gaze and frowns. "This Hill Country style is very popular in Texas. And our house is special. There is a secret beyond our backyard."

My father takes Sara and me out our back patio door to look at our secret—a place he calls the wide-open space.

We walk to the corner of our yard and he pushes a sprawling green vine aside to reveal a narrow wood door in an old rock wall. We walk through it, and I gasp. "Wow, Baba! There are no houses on the other side!"

He smiles as his eyes sweep over a big grassy field with hills in the distance and a trickling creek that runs through it. Tiny trees struggle to grow along its banks, and here and there, sparse clumps of grass lie flat like a whooshing force trampled them. The night expanse has been replaced by the biggest, bluest sky I've ever seen.

"A long time ago before our neighborhood was built, all of this was ranchland," my father explains. "Now this area forms a giant reservoir to catch the water when it rains."

I close my eyes and imagine this place as a ranch with cowboys and horses, before the cream-colored houses lined up like dominoes along the cul-de-sacs. I imagine the wide-open space filling in everywhere, the little creek winding through other ranches, flowing into bigger streams to join the giant Gulf of Mexico.

We walk back inside to tour the rest of the house and find my mother in a full-on Myriam Khoury frenzy. She's flitting from room to room across the hard beige tiles in her click-clacking heels, opening all the windows to air things out since our new house smells like a brand-new car.

In addition to my and my siblings' bedrooms upstairs, our first floor has a small office for Baba and a big bedroom my mother calls her suite. It has a luxurious bathroom with two sinks and a big marble soaking tub that she can't wait to use. There's another bedroom right off the kitchen with a stiff, new, queen-sized mattress that she calls our guest room.

"Who's going to sleep there?" I ask her.

My mother answers me with a wave of her hand. "Your grandmother, when she visits us from Jerusalem." But I haven't seen my father's mother, Sitti Khoury, since she came to Detroit when Salim was first born.

My parents spend the rest of the day arranging our furniture from Detroit in the new rooms. Baba pushes our worn sofa to different walls in the living room as my mother instructs. He drags our two brass tray tables with their comfy stools to different corners to try them.

My mother slumps in the middle of the room, distressed; our old furniture and my family's Middle Eastern decor look funny in our shiny Hill Country–style house.

It looks just like I feel—out of place.

Finally, she kicks off her heels and announces, "I am retiring to my suite!"

Sara giggles and leans close. "Yasmeen, this house is perfect. A fancy suite is exactly where Mama belongs."

I take my mother's place slumped in the middle of the room until my father asks me to help him in the garage. He pries open big moving crates and unloads their contents while I gather packing peanuts into big black trash bags. "What's in this one, Baba?" I ask as he opens the very last crate.

His eyes twinkle. "Something we could not leave behind, Yasmeen."

He uncovers our brass kitchen lantern with the little star cutouts, and my eyes well up. I thought that just like so many familiar things, our lantern had been left behind. My father gives me an extra long pat on the head, and we carry it inside.

Baba takes down the iron chandelier that came with our house and hangs the lantern above our old kitchen table instead.

I flick the switch on, and the freshly painted kitchen walls light up with tiny dancing stars, 1,489 miles from Detroit. I reach up to touch them, and our new house instantly feels a little more like home.

Five

By Sunday morning, we all have cabin fever.

Salim races around our new house as fast as his little legs will carry him, until he melts down in a heap on the floor. Sara and I take our bickering to a whole new level—if it were a contest, I'd say we're about neck and neck since she's a quick study. My mother heads to her suite every few hours, and even Baba seems a little short-tempered; he claims a new favorite spot on our living room sofa and stays put, flipping through channels on the TV.

I'm all unpacked: I've thumbtacked my star map on the wall next to my bed like in my old room in Detroit; I've taped pictures of Dina and me to the mirror above my dresser; I've lined my Sudoku books neatly on a shelf and added the two new ones I finished on our ride down to San

Antonio. And I've put my old stuffed animal collection in the closet—it's the one thing that I should've left behind in Detroit.

But my room still feels like I'm just visiting here and instead of bringing a suitcase, I've somehow brought all of my stuff.

My sister, on the other hand, practically leaps up the stairs to her new room. She already seems perfectly at home.

I pop my head through her doorway and narrow my eyes. "Thank goodness I got the room at the end of the hall so if Salim wakes up and cries at night, I won't hear a thing."

She glares at me. "Mama! Yasmeen's being mean again!"

My mother calls up from the kitchen. "Khalas! Come down at once. We are going on a family outing."

Sara lights up and grabs her latest book for the car ride. She skips past me, first down the stairs. "Yay! Are we going to the Alamo or the River Walk?" she asks our parents in the kitchen.

Baba shakes his head. "We are taking a stroll around our new neighborhood to see the lay of the land."

He opens the front door and steps outside, and a humid blast of heat enters our house. My mother gives him a worried look, grabs an old sheet of newspaper from one of the packing boxes, and follows him down the walkway.

We start up the hill to the top of our street, and I notice we're the only family on this kind of outing, for good reason. It must be over a hundred degrees outside!

I imagine how we must appear to our new neighbors, with our wide-eyed looks: Baba in his slacks and loafers; my stylish mother click-clacking along in her heels, fanning her melting makeup with some newspaper; a wiggly boy with a sweaty head of dark curls pulled along in a red plastic wagon; a whistling girl with a book tucked under her arm; and me—a shorter-than-average, soon-to-be seventh grader trailing behind her family, pretending like she's not even with them.

To make matters worse, my parents pause in front of each house and debate which ones have the best location, the most attractive accent walls, or the nicest gardens. I want to run back down the hill and hide in my unfamiliar new room.

We pass by several neighbors out in their yards, and my mother waits for a hint of a smile before she shyly waves hello. I've never seen her act this way; at our church back in Detroit, she was always surrounded by her large group of friends. Sara and I agreed—our mother held court like a queen.

But here, she seems different. We seem different.

We walk around several long blocks, then my father stops pulling Salim for a minute to catch his breath.

Even though the houses look almost the same, I figure we're almost back where we started. If I walk to the end of the street and turn left, I should see our minivan parked in our cul-de-sac at the bottom of the hill.

I'm tired of seeing the lay of the land with my family. We've been stuck together nonstop since Baba's big news flash, but no one has noticed that I'm miserable, that this move is an exciting adventure for everyone but me.

I pick up my pace and walk off. My mother calls to me but I ignore her.

At the next block, I stop and look left. There's no hill. There's no minivan. I don't know where I am after all. *Why did I think I did?* So, I wait on the corner for my family to catch up with me and take my place trailing behind them again.

Sara peppers our parents with questions as we walk back toward our cul-de-sac. "Where's our new church? Why is it so far away? Do we have any Arab neighbors? What about Mexican neighbors?"

She stops in her tracks when she sees a woman gardening in her front yard who has dark hair and brown skin like ours. "I wonder if she's Mexican, Mama!" she says, a little too loudly.

My mother's face flushes. She whispers, "Habibti, you cannot assume this neighbor has Mexican heritage because of her looks. Perhaps she is Arab!"

Baba gapes at the woman's flower garden; it's the most beautiful one on our cul-de-sac by far. "Perhaps she is!" he says. "Some of her plants grow in Jerusalem you know, like the thistle and sage."

The gardening woman waves to us and we wave back. A girl about my age stands in the big picture window of her house. Our eyes meet for just a second, and she smiles. And I can't help feeling hopeful—maybe I'll have a neighbor friend in San Antonio, just like I did in Detroit.

We cross to the other side of our cul-de-sac and follow my father up a walkway. He reaches for the front doorknob, then looks down at the doormat. It says: Welcome Home, Y'all!

I can't believe it! We're at the wrong house!

He snaps his hand back with a small "ugh!" and runs it through his dark wavy hair. Then with a flustered half smile, he pretends to show my mother our neighbor's plant choices.

But it's obvious—my father's having a hard time telling which of the nearly identical houses in our new neighborhood is home, just like me.

Sara and I team up that afternoon. We complain to our parents that our walk around the neighborhood didn't count as a real family outing. They finally give in after dinner and drive us across town to see what one of the city's main attractions—the San Antonio River Walk—is all about.

The river is amazing! Just below the street, colorful little shops and restaurants line both sides of its banks and long barges filled with smiling sightseers float by. It's even a few degrees cooler under the dense canopy of trees that soars over the water.

We file into a tight stream of people, winding our way around stone walkways and over low bridges, until we stop in front of a small, lit stage where a group of men with wide-brimmed hats and fancy embroidered suits sing in Spanish.

Sara lights up. "Are they the mariachis you told us about?"

My father smiles and nods. He lifts Salim onto his broad shoulders to get a better look as the crowd happily sings along.

Sara taps her foot and tries to mouth the words. "I need a new dictionary, Baba!" she says. "So many people here speak Spanish and I want to know what they're saying!"

He pats her head.

As we continue to weave through the crowd, my mother stops at each little shop and peeks inside. There are bright-colored dresses and beautiful hand-painted pots; there are cowboy boots and hats, some of them small enough for babies and toddlers.

She smiles and gestures to the dresses in one of the windows and tells Baba something in Arabic, then another quick look passes between them.

She glances at the shoppers around us and switches to her accented English. "Elias, these dresses are hand-embroidered with colorful cross-stitching just like traditional Palestinian thobes! Please treat the children to ice cream from the shop we passed while I take a closer look."

Then I realize—my parents haven't been speaking in Arabic on our outing to the River Walk, and they didn't speak in Arabic on our neighborhood walk, either.

My mother disappears into the shop, and we walk with Baba to get ice cream. As we sit on a low stone wall and lick our cones, I search the faces of passersby for anything familiar but find nothing. Everyone seems so different here.

A lump forms in my throat. "Baba, are there any Arabs here in San Antonio . . . like us?"

He looks around and digs his hands deep into his pockets. "Yasmeen, San Antonio is not like Detroit, with a large Arab community. But next week, we will begin attending St. Anthony's, the Maronite church that your mother found. She even made some new friends from the congregation on video chat before we left Detroit!"

I nod, scoot closer to Sara and Salim, and keep watching the crowd. Before I know it, my ice cream melts down my hand.

★ ★ ★

Later that night, my mother passes out gifts from the San Antonio River Walk shops. "For your first day at your new schools tomorrow!" she tells us, clapping her hands.

Sara gets bubble gum–colored pink leather cowboy boots and Salim gets a brown suede cowboy vest with a gold star pinned on it that says: Texas Sheriff.

I get a long white Mexican Puebla dress cross-stitched with a bright pink, yellow, and blue flowery pattern. "The woman at the shop told me all the San Antonio girls wear them!" my mother says, and waits for my reaction.

The girls here wear dresses to school? I have serious doubts.

But I force a smile since she's so excited about her gift for me. "Shukran, Mama!" I lie. "It's perfect for my first day!"

Six

My mother's makeup routine persists no matter where we're going or if she has time for it.

I pop into the bathroom of my parents' suite for the second time the next morning, just as she douses herself with a cloud of spicy perfume. "Mama, please hurry!" I cover my mouth and cough. "I . . . I can't be late for my first day of school!"

She smooths my hair away from my face and flashes me a big smile. "Do not worry, habibti! You always worry! I mapped it with my new cell phone application—we have plenty of time. It is a piece of cake!"

My mother has always loved American sayings, but since our move to Texas, she's been trying them out more often.

Too often, if you ask me.

She looks at me in the mirror, clucks her tongue approvingly, and adjusts my new dress, which keeps sliding around on my shoulders. Then she applies a sheer coat of lipstick and brushes out her long, shiny hair. "Please start Baba's morning tea," she says while I wait. "I will be ready to go in a jiffy!"

I head to the kitchen and measure fragrant tea leaves and a few sprigs of mint into a big teapot, then I fill another pot with water and turn on the stove. When the water boils, I'll pour it over the tea leaves to steep, and our kitchen will smell just like it does every morning. Almost like home.

While I sit jittery at the kitchen table—crossing and uncrossing my legs, waiting for the water, waiting for my mother—Sara springs down the stairs with her nose stuck in the middle of her book and slides into the seat across from me.

Unlike me, my little sister doesn't seem fazed about starting a new school today. She doesn't seem to have an anxious bone in her ten-year-old body.

She's wearing stretchy blue jeans tucked into her new pink cowboy boots and a T-shirt with a picture of a polar bear on it that says *Chill Out*. She's pulled her hair into a side ponytail and even put a smiley face decal on the back of her hand.

Sometimes, I can't stand her.

I get up from the table and pour the boiling water into

the teapot, then I head back and wait some more. I tug at the scratchy cross-stitching that cascades down the front of my dress and my face gets hot. I feel anything but chill.

Sara notices. "Is that new dress comfy?" She glances under the table. "My new boots are super comfy. Being itchy on my first day of school would be *excruciating*."

"It's perfectly fine!" I snap. "And are you really wearing that ratty old T-shirt on your first day of school? It's got a polar bear on it and it's not even winter!"

She takes a piece of our mother's homemade pita bread from a basket in the middle of the table and slathers it with soft butter, then she cuts a thin slice of sweet sesame halawa to make a quick sandwich for breakfast. She twirls her side ponytail and reads while she munches away.

I hate it when she doesn't answer my questions! I clear my throat.

Sara looks up and shoots me a calm, cool *whatever* glance.

My voice gets loud and tight. "Don't give me that . . . that *whatever* look!" I'm not calm at all.

She raises her eyebrows, then saunters to the shelf where she's stashed her big dictionary next to our mother's recipe binders. She walks back to the table and flips through it until she finds what she's looking for.

"A better word choice than *whatever* would be *blasé*, Yasmeen . . . from the French, meaning *indifferent*. Maybe you'll use it next time."

I shoot up from the table with my hands on my hips and I'm about to snap something else at my sister when my father's happy voice booms from the stairwell. "Sabahelkher, my daughters!"

He's carrying Salim, whom he'll drop off at preschool on the way to Sara's new elementary school before heading to his new job.

I sit back down and take some big breaths. I adjust my dress on my shoulders again and avoid looking at my sister. "Sabahelnoor, Baba," I respond to him in the little Arabic I know.

Though I'm technically Arab, I barely speak Arabic. I only understand what my parents are saying some of the time, and I can't write the complicated-looking, flowing letters at all.

Sara's the same, but of course she'll hardly admit it.

Most of the time, when my parents speak to me in Arabic, I answer in English even if I know the Arabic response. But Baba seems so happy this morning, I want to make an effort.

I pour him a steaming cup of tea and take my little brother into my arms. "Shukran, habibti!" my father says, and sips his tea.

"Hi, Meenie!" Salim hugs my neck. He giggles as I plant quick kisses all over his sleepy little eyelids. I bury my face in his curly hair, which somehow always smells fresh like baby shampoo, and my anxious feelings start to fade—but not for long.

Baba puts his empty teacup in the sink. He pats Sara and me on our heads, and says, "My daughters, today you will start your new schools and inshallah, everything will be wonderful."

My anxious feelings bubble up again. *Wonderful? Probably not.* That's just not how it usually goes, starting a new school clear across the country.

When my mother's finally ready, we speed out of our neighborhood in the minivan. Her cell phone mapping app's "Don't Get Lost, Lady," as she calls her, expertly guides us to Forest Hills Middle School.

Almost: her phone actually guides us all the way past my school to a gas station.

"We missed my new school, Mama!"

She stops and stares at her phone for a second, then tosses it in her purse. "Oops, I may have put it in wrong. My badness?" she says, and turns the car around.

I was relieved when our parents offered to drive us to our first week of school, but now I'm wondering—maybe it would have been better if I'd taken the bus. "It's *my bad*, Mama," I mumble, right as we turn into Forest Hills.

We pull into a parent parking space and my stomach lurches—the others are empty. The bell has rung, and school has started without me, exactly as I feared. We hurry through the parking lot and into the front office, my mother's jingling bracelets and click-clacking heels announcing our arrival.

One of the office ladies is talking to a fidgeting boy who's sitting alone. "Tommy, the student helper you've been assigned to should be along anytime to take you . . ." She notices us and stops mid-sentence. "Can I help you?"

The change in my mother happens right away. She places her purse on the counter and clasps her hands together. She lowers her eyes, and her voice gets quieter. She says each word slowly and carefully, "It is my daughter's first school day here in Texas. We are sorry we are a bit late."

I don't understand why *she* would be nervous this morning like me. She's not the one who's starting a new school!

The ladies shift forward in their chairs, taking in my mother's strong-smelling perfume and accented English, her perfect makeup and long black eyelashes. My mother would usually smile and toss her shiny hair with this kind of attention like she does at church, but she doesn't today. Her face flushes at the ladies' questions and she fills out my paperwork as fast as she can.

I hide behind her the whole time. It's almost like I'm not in the room. If the office ladies peered around her to look at me, they'd be disappointed—I'm nothing like her.

I've inherited what my mother calls the Khoury *stronger*

features from my father's side, unlike Sara. I have unruly jet-black hair, a prominent nose, and dark brown almond-shaped eyes. I have a constant sprout of hair on my upper lip and between my eyebrows that I already have to wax, and a year-round summer tan that my mother diplomatically calls an olive complexion.

But I'm not really olive colored. I'm brown, like lentils.

And unlike Sara, who's been blessed with our mother's height, and is almost as tall as I am, I take after Sitti Khoury, who's barely five feet tall.

I shift from foot to foot behind my mother while she hurries through each page. I stare at a big State of Texas flag in the corner of the room with its gleaming, single white star. I watch Tommy leave with his student helper. I pinch myself over and over to make sure that starting at a new school today isn't just a bad dream.

But today is real—we've left Detroit forever.

My mother signs the last page and turns to me. She looks me over head to toe one last time, straightens my dress again, and pushes my hair away from my face. "Now I can see you better," she says.

But she doesn't really see me.

If she did, she'd see how miserable I am starting a new school. She'd see that everything is different here—too different. She'd see that our move to San Antonio was a big mistake, and that Baba's big new job as a sales manager wasn't worth leaving our home in Detroit.

Once she's satisfied that I'm presentable, she loops her purse back over her arm and gives the office ladies a small, shy wave. Then she's gone—off to meet some new church friends, to replace the ones she left behind.

And I'm left sitting in Tommy's chair waiting for my student helper at my new school in my new town, all alone.

A few minutes later, the same girl from the sticky note photo on our refrigerator bounces through the office door. "Welcome to Forest Hills!" she drawls in a sugar-sweet Texan accent, extending a hand for me to shake. "My name is Waverly Jones."

I can't believe she's standing in front of me. My mouth goes slack for a minute, then I recover. "Hi, I'm Yasmeen," I mumble.

"I know who you are! Our dads work together! And funny story, I made your bed before you moved into your house."

Now I'm really tongue-tied. *The girl from the photo has been to my house? She's been in my room?* I'd thought her mother made my bed.

One of the office ladies hands me my schedule and turns to Waverly. "She has Mrs. Shelby for first period math class, dear. Thanks so much for helping out this morning."

Waverly flashes her a sunny smile, and says, "Any time!" Then she leads me out of the office.

I steal glances at her as we walk down the hall. Up close, her stick-straight hair shimmers in the overhead lights, and her big eyes are blue like the Texas sky. And her nose isn't a stronger feature like mine—it's a perfect miniature slope.

Waverly chatters the whole time she's walking me to my class, but I barely say a thing. My mouth isn't working again.

She tells me seventh grade has eight periods and that the period right before gym class each afternoon is called advisory. "Advisory is kind of like homeroom," she explains. "And once a month, all the advisories go to the cafeteria for assembly, which is really great since you know, Principal Neeley makes announcements and gives out kudos."

I nod like I know what advisory, assembly, and kudos are about, even though I don't.

Right, left, right. We walk down one long, windowless hallway, then two others that look exactly the same. My new school is huge, unlike the middle school I left in Michigan. I look around and realize I'm already lost. I could never find my way back to the front office on my own.

We arrive at Mrs. Shelby's room. "You're super lucky to be here," Waverly says. "Forest Hills is the best middle school in San Antonio! We have the nicest teachers, the best hot lunches, and of course, the nicest kids." Then she shakes my hand again and leaves me at the door.

I finally manage to call, "Thanks!" but she's already disappeared down the hall.

Seven

I suck as much air as I can into my lungs, knock lightly, and step inside.

I imagined what the other students would look like at this school, and I'm right—most of the kids in my class have light complexions and light hair, and there's just a sprinkling of brown skin and dark hair like mine.

And none of the girls are wearing Mexican Puebla dresses today.

Mrs. Shelby stands up from her desk and waves me inside. She wears a crisp white shirt and a tailored navy skirt like a daily uniform. Bright red reading glasses hang around her neck on a silvery chain below her smiling eyes.

"You must be our new student," she says, and I nod.

All eyes turn to me as Mrs. Shelby introduces me to

the class. "This is . . ." She puts on her reading glasses and squints at her class roster. "Sweetie, how do you pronounce your name?"

"Yasmeen Khoury," I squeak. I know what's coming next.

"Your name is so unusual. Where are you from?"

"I—I'm American," I stammer, "from Michigan."

She smiles. "But where is your family from?"

"My father is Palestinian, from Jerusalem. But my mother is Lebanese," I offer, as though this detail matters.

Mrs. Shelby's eyes grow big, like she's never met anyone like me. "Class, please welcome our new student, Yasmeen Khoury."

I'm used to people not being able to say my name, like at the doctor's or dentist's office, or once when I met some of Baba's old coworkers. But there were lots of Arab kids at my old school in Detroit. I wasn't even the only Yasmeen or the only Khoury.

Here in San Antonio, I can already tell—I'll have to get used to correcting how people say my name for a while.

Mrs. Shelby assigns me a seat in the middle of the room.

"Nice dress." A girl with strawberry-red hair and lots of freckles snickers when I shuffle past her.

Mrs. Shelby peers over her reading glasses. "Hallie? Do you have something you'd like to tell the class?"

"No, ma'am," she drawls, but when Mrs. Shelby starts

flipping through her lesson book, she snickers again.

Another girl near the front of the room whips her head around, and her thick, dark brown ponytail whips along with it. She glares at Hallie. "Stop it!" she says, and miraculously, Hallie does.

Mrs. Shelby raises her eyebrows at the girl with the ponytail. "That is quite enough, Esmeralda," she says. "And Hallie, this is your last warning."

I try to sit down at my desk as quietly as I can, but my backpack comes down with a *thud*. Everyone looks at me again. I wish my seat was in the very back of the room, where it would be harder for the other kids to examine me. Or better yet, I wish my seat was in Detroit.

"Class, we'll continue with some probability review problems from last year before moving ahead," Mrs. Shelby says while passing out some thick packets. She gets to my desk and whispers, "Sweetie, you've got me for advisory every day, so if you need any catching up in math, we can work on it then."

I nod and look around the room at all the unfamiliar faces and do my own calculation: the probability of me not fitting in here is close to 100 percent.

The same kind of introduction repeats in my next three classes, and by lunchtime, I'm tired and hungry.

I follow my fourth-period classmates to the cafeteria and stand in a long, hot-lunch line holding a heavy plastic tray. It's a miracle my mother's letting Sara and me get school lunches sometimes, since I'm sure she thinks they aren't real food.

One of the ladies serving food sees my Puebla dress and lights up. "¡Qué linda niña! ¿Cómo te llamas?" she says, passing me a turkey sandwich.

"I'm so sorry." I smile and shake my head. "I don't speak Spanish."

When I get out of line, I scan the cafeteria for an empty seat, and my mind starts to wander. Maybe I should tell people my family is Mexican, not Arab; maybe I should sign up for Spanish; maybe I should at least change my first name to something easier to pronounce.

There's a familiar first-day-after-summer buzz in the air. Everyone's excited to be back together again. They're already grouping at the long tables into distinct sets like Venn diagrams. I examine each set, but it's not immediately obvious where I might fit in.

There's a table of dark-haired girls speaking Spanish: no. Not yet at least.

There's a table of tall, leggy girls wearing athletic clothes: no. Not with my two left feet.

There's a big table of about twenty girls that includes the snickering girl from my math class, Hallie: definitely, no. Not unless I want a repeat of earlier.

My eyes settle on a girl who looks friendly and familiar,

and I feel a little hopeful.

I think she's my neighbor across the cul-de-sac from my new house in Oak Forest, but I've only seen her that one time through a window. She's sitting with just one friend, their heads bent together, and she's giggling uncontrollably. I start smiling because she's smiling.

She looks up and sees me, and waves. So, I wave back.

Right then, Waverly Jones makes a beeline toward me with her tray. "Hey there! Remember me?"

How could I forget? She's the only girl I've actually talked to since we moved to San Antonio.

She flashes me one of her sunny smiles and says, "How do you say your name again?"

I shift my tray between my hands. "You say *yeah* with a soft *s*, then draw out the *meen* at the end for Yasmeen," I tell her. "And my last name Khoury is pronounced with more of an *h* at the beginning even though it's spelled with a *k*."

She nods. "Cool! I've never heard those names before. How do you like Forest Hills?"

"It's okay." I scan the room again. All the tables are filling up. The girl who lives across the cul-de-sac from me isn't looking my way anymore. Her head is bent together with her friend's again. "This is such a big school. My mother says everything's bigger in Texas."

Waverly laughs. "Come sit with me, Yasmeen!" she says,

and walks off without waiting for an answer.

I follow her halfway across the cafeteria and realize she's taking me to Hallie's table.

So I slow down and look for a different place to sit. But other than the girl who lives across the cul-de-sac from me and Waverly, everyone at my new school's completely unfamiliar.

Waverly sits down and calls, "Over here, Yasmeen!" and I speed back up.

But when I get there, the table's full. "I'll just find another place to sit," I mumble.

"You'll fit!" Waverly says. "Hey, everybody, scoot down!"

I stand there while the girls make room for me a little too slowly, but she doesn't seem to notice. Then I set my tray down and squeeze in.

Waverly introduces me to a few of her friends. I officially meet Hallie, her *best friend forever* since preschool, which seems a little strange because Waverly seems so nice and Hallie just . . . doesn't, and two girls named Chloe and Kayla who look alike and say "Hi" at the exact same time.

All the girls at the table have silky, tame hair; smooth, powdered faces; and shiny pink lip gloss. Whatever genetic trait gives you perfect hair like these girls, I don't have it. I reach up to touch my hair that always springs out of barrettes and falls into my eyes, and try to push it out of my face like my mother does.

But it just springs back.

Waverly's friends spend a few minutes trying to say my name in their singsongy accents: Yezz-mine, Yazz-min, Yess-meen. Chloe asks, "Hey, is your name like Princess Jasmine from *Aladdin* or something?" and Kayla cracks up. Hallie cups her hand and whispers something to the girl next to her.

Waverly pipes up, "It's not hard, guys! It's *yeah* with a soft *s*, then you draw out the *meen* part, right, Yasmeen?"

I nod my head and don't bother teaching them how to say my last name.

The girls at our end of the table ask me a few questions about where I moved from, then pick up talking where they left off like I'm not there. But Waverly chats with me the whole time she eats her sandwich. She asks me question after question, like I'm the most interesting person she's ever met.

What was my old school like? (Well, I had two friends.) *What are my hobbies?* (Umm, doing *Just Dance* videos and making news skits?) *What's my favorite subject?* (Easy, math!) *Have I ever had a boyfriend?* (No! My mother thinks that's for high school or even college, or maybe never.)

We look at our schedules and we don't have any classes together, but we're both in Mrs. Shelby's seventh period advisory. "We're destined to be study buddies, Yasmeen!"

Waverly gushes, and my mouth spreads into a ridiculously big smile.

She tells me that all the girls at the table are part of the Forest Hills drill team—the Sapphires—and that Hallie is their new team captain.

"Basically, Yasmeen," she says, "our drill team is a dance team where we do complicated routines in unison for competitions. It's super fun since we're really, really good. Hey! Do you play a sport?"

I shake my head.

"That's too bad," she says. "Because if you don't have sports practice you'll have to run or walk the track during gym class, yuck." Then she grabs my arm and looks at Hallie. "Oh my gosh! We have an open spot on our team now, right? Can Yasmeen try out for you?"

Hallie shoots her a dirty look just as I'm about to explain that I didn't exactly master any *Just Dance* video games at Dina's house. She says, "If you want, I guess."

Waverly ignores the look and smiles at me. She leans in and whispers, "Since you missed tryouts over the summer, I'll tell you which videos to watch so you can practice some routines."

My eyes run up and down the table, mesmerized by the girls. I watch the way they laugh at each other's jokes and whisper and roll their eyes. I watch the way they toss their hair and walk around the cafeteria with their chins held high.

I'm not the only one. Other girls in the cafeteria watch them, too.

By the end of lunch, I can tell that the Sapphires are the most popular girls in middle school. I can also tell that besides Waverly—who's probably just being nice to me today since she's my student helper and our fathers work together—there's no way they're ever going to be my friends.

Unless somehow, I figure out how to dance and try out for the empty spot on the team. Maybe if I make it, Waverly's best friend, Hallie, will be nicer to me, too.

My mother picks me up that afternoon, and I slide into the passenger seat. "You had a good first day like your sister?" she asks, but it's not really a question.

"No one wears dresses to school," I mumble.

Sara pipes up from the back seat, "My boots got lots of compliments today, Mama."

I whip around. "Be quiet, Sara!" My mother snaps her fingers at both of us.

I'm sure my sister had a great first day. I'm sure that all the popular girls already want to be her friends. I'm sure with her common name and honey-colored eyes like our mother, Sara blended in at school just fine—unlike me.

We ride home in silence, and I ignore my mother's worried glances. When our minivan stops in the driveway, I jump out and run inside. I fly up the steps to my room and slam my door.

I feel so out of place in Texas.

The people here who look most like me are from countries you could drive to over the Texas border. Their families aren't from a place far across the ocean that I've never even been to, a place people here might not even know about.

I don't want to have a hard-to-pronounce name. I don't want to have unruly jet-black hair. I don't want to have the Khoury stronger features. I want to blend in at school like Sara—somehow.

I want to belong.

My mother knocks at my door. She sits on the bed next to me and waits for me to talk. Finally, I ask, "Mama, why don't I look more like you and Sara? Why do I have to look more . . . Arab?"

She looks at me with tender eyes. "Someday, habibti, you will realize your features are so very beautiful."

My bottom lip quivers. "Can someday please happen tomorrow?"

The tears I've been holding inside all day build up in the corners of my eyes and slip down my cheeks. My mother stays with me and wipes them away until I'm all cried out.

Later that night after I finish my homework, I record a quick news skit on my phone to tell Dina about my first week in San Antonio. I try to focus on the positives.

I report on the amazing San Antonio River Walk and the singing mariachis. On my new room with my brand-new, queen-sized bed and our spacious Hill Country–style house. On the wide-open space with its trickling little creek and the bright stars in the dark Texas night.

My voice starts shaking when I get to the news about my big new school with its maze of halls, where everyone seems so different from me.

I end with, "This is Yasmeen Khoury, signing off from Texas, all alone without her best friend."

I think about pressing delete for a while, but I email my skit to Dina anyway and hope she sends one back.

Then I think about all the different sets in the cafeteria again, the distinct groups of kids that don't include me. I can't imagine how an Arab girl from Detroit could overlap with even one of them.

I take a pencil and cross the name *Yasmeen* out at the top of my homework. I practice writing new names like Yvette, Yvonne, and finally a Spanish name—*Yolanda*.

Yolanda is a name that blends in, that the girls at my school could pronounce. I feel good trying out this new name.

Y is for *Yolanda*. Yolanda can be a girl from San Antonio, Texas, but Yasmeen—probably not.

Eight

Friday afternoon, I hear loud news coverage through my bedroom door. I'm supposed to be finishing my homework before the weekend, but I'm on my phone watching the drill team videos Waverly told me about instead.

No matter how many times I try the routines, when I look in my dresser mirror—I'm doing them all wrong. When the dancers kick, I stomp. When their hands fly to the air, mine flap by my sides. When I'm supposed to step left, I step right.

It's no use. I'm an absolutely awful dancer. If I try out for Hallie, I'm just going to embarrass myself.

Downstairs, I find a familiar scene: Baba's on the living room sofa watching TV, his eyes glassy and his brow knit together, while my mother sits tense beside him patting his hand since he's so upset.

I tiptoe behind them to see what they're watching—it's news coverage of the Israeli-Palestinian conflict again.

My father has always looked for news from *home* each day after work. I don't know why I thought that might change in San Antonio with his new job and our new life.

But it hasn't. He sits on the edge of our sofa and mutters in Arabic as the scary images of the conflict scroll over and over, then he clenches his fists and yells.

Doesn't he understand? No one is listening.

My parents came to the United States to attend the University of Michigan. They met their very first semester at a Middle Eastern cultural dinner. Baba says the moment he saw our beautiful mother, every face in the room disappeared except for hers.

My mother tells us that my father was the handsomest and kindest man she'd ever met. It didn't matter what her Lebanese family back home thought—she knew that Baba was the one she'd been waiting for. Her eyes always soften when she says, "Perhaps for each other, we have made an exception."

My father's mother was unhappy about their relationship at first just like my mother's family was, since Palestinians and Lebanese don't always get along. But when she visited them from Jerusalem, my mother's charm won her over in no time.

The Israeli-Palestinian conflict is a part of my father's life even though we live a world away. We live in America, but sometimes, when the news coverage from home gets bad, Baba is not really here.

He sits on our sofa, but his mind and heart fly far away, back to Jerusalem.

My parents notice me and flip the TV off. "The news from Jerusalem is terrible today," my father says as I join them on the sofa. "It is even worse than last month."

My mother looks at me with nervous eyes.

My thoughts immediately race to my grandmother who lives on the edge of the city in the house where my father grew up—a house I've never been to, but only seen in photos.

I ask for the millionth time, "Baba, can we go with you to check on Sitti when you visit her in Jerusalem next month . . . please?"

I know the answer before he shakes his head from side to side—no. It always is. My father visits my grandmother every fall for a few weeks, but he never takes us with him.

A tense look passes between my parents. Baba reaches over and pats my head. "Things are not good for Palestinians in Jerusalem since the Nakba, Yasmeen. You know the Nakba?"

I nod. Of course, I know about the Nakba, since I've been hearing about it my whole life. But my father always asks me the same question anyway—maybe he wants to make sure that I remember as well as he does.

The Nakba is a catastrophe for Palestinians like my father. It happened in 1948 when the land of Palestine became the country Israel. Some families, like mine, managed to stay in the new country, but most did not.

Most Palestinians lost their homes and ended up in lots of different countries. Baba calls it a diaspora, which is a Greek word for *scattering*. He says that after their mass exodus from Palestine, they became refugees.

I hate it when my father talks about the Nakba: his face hardens, his broad shoulders slump, and his voice sounds tight, like he's breathing through a small crack in a nearly shut door.

"But I want to see Sitti's garden and the house where you grew up, Baba," I protest.

My father shifts in his seat. His jaw clenches just like when we met the man at the fast-food restaurant. My mother reaches for his hand again. He stares at the floor and says, "We have talked about this, Yasmeen. I cannot take my family where we are not *welcome*, where we are not *wanted*."

But Baba has two passports in his sock drawer—I've seen them. He has an American passport that says he's from Jerusalem, and he also has an Israeli passport written in Hebrew, a language I've never heard him speak but my mother says he knows just as well as Arabic and English. She says he only speaks Hebrew when he must.

"I don't understand, Baba." I won't let it go this time. "Why aren't we welcome? Aren't you from Israel?"

"Yes, Yasmeen." He nods. "I am from Israel. But I am really Palestinian."

My mother has told me that Baba wants to share Jerusalem with us more than anything, that he dreams of taking his family there all the time.

The way he describes the city—with its blooming gardens and spice-shop-filled stone alleyways—Jerusalem seems like paradise. My mother has said he wants to show us the place he dreams about, not the place that exists today.

Maybe she's right. Tonight's not the first time I've snuck up behind my parents while they watch the news coverage of the conflict, and the Jerusalem I see on TV is not what Baba describes. What I see is this: soldiers line the streets everywhere, and people yell and cry and run.

Maybe once, Jerusalem was the paradise that Baba describes, but it's not anymore.

After dinner, my mother stands at the big picture window in our living room making what she calls *helpful observations*. Ever since my family's first walk around Oak Forest, she's been applying her expert-level reconnaissance skills to figuring out all our cul-de-sac neighbors.

She finds out that the couple on one side of us has triplet boys—she looks exhausted just telling us about them—and she says that an older couple with a fluffy, yapping dog live on the other side of us. But she's most curious about the dark-haired woman who lives across the cul-de-sac who's tending her beautiful flower garden again.

Sara sits at the brass tray tables organizing her spelling bee flash cards, and Salim plays with his Hot Wheels collection on the windowsill. My father has finally calmed down. He sits on the sofa reading the local San Antonio paper, which doesn't seem to have any upsetting news from *home*.

I sit next to him, working my way through a brandnew Sudoku book. The puzzles aren't math problems, even though they use numbers—they're logic problems. Each time I fill in a square, I feel hopeful that things that might start off a little shaky or confusing can eventually come out right. With moving to Texas, starting a new school, and stumbling around my room trying to be a dancer, the line of finished books on my shelf is growing fast.

My mother claps her hands, and I look up. The door to the gardening woman's house has opened, and a darkheaded boy about Sara's age hands his mother a tall glass of something to drink.

"Elias!" she exclaims. "What if they *are* Arab?"

My father looks up from his paper and peers out the window. He shrugs, then flips the page and continues to read.

My mother keeps watching. Finally, she has to know. She runs to the kitchen and returns with a plate of freshly baked maamoul cookies and carefully reapplies her lipstick in the hallway mirror. Then she gives Baba a big, bold smile and heads across the cul-de-sac to introduce herself.

I put down my book and stand at the window.

My mother hands the woman the plate of cookies. Her bold smile wavers as they talk. Then she turns on her heel and hurries back to our house.

She rushes through our front door, jolting my father from reading the paper. Her gold bangles jingle. "Elias, this woman speaks Arabic, but her family is not Arab! Their last name is Cohen!"

It turns out the neighbors are from Israel, just like Baba, but they're not Palestinian—they're Jewish. Their daughter's name is Ayelet and their son's name is Tal.

My father tries to calm my mother down. He says, "It will be all right, Myriam. We cannot hope to be friends with all of our neighbors."

I clear my throat, remembering their daughter in the school cafeteria. How she waved and I waved back. How her smile made me smile, too. "We haven't even met them," I point out. "Maybe they're nice."

But my parents ignore me.

My mother announces she's developed a headache, then she click-clacks down the hall to her suite to lie down. Baba folds his newspaper and shuffles after her.

I stand at the window and watch our Israeli neighbors, just like my mother.

I think about Sitti Khoury in Jerusalem, living in the *home* I've never been to. I think about Baba searching the news coverage every night on our TV, and all the things I still don't understand—about Palestinians and Israelis and the Nakba.

Our neighbors' front door opens and the girl my age joins her mother in their front yard. She takes a cookie off the plate as her mother gestures to our house. The girl bites into the cookie, and her eyes light up.

I say her name aloud—Ayelet. It's a name I've never heard before. It's a name from someplace far away, just like mine.

Nine

Sunday morning, my family drives across town for our first service at St. Anthony's Maronite Church.

At the edge of the parking lot, we join a group of dark-haired congregants on their way to a big, white-plastered building surrounded by a green lawn dotted with the same bent oak trees as our yard. A row of arches stretches along a walkway that leads us to an interior courtyard with a water fountain and blooming pink flowers.

Strong incense immediately fills my nose when we step through the wooden doors of the main sanctuary, just like at my old church in Detroit, just like the incense we burn at my house.

Tall, narrow, stained-glass windows line the walls, and a burnished wood crucifix hovers from a domed ceiling above a stone altar. Sara's eyes grow big—the thorns on Jesus's forehead and the real nails in his hands drip dark red sap.

The same tiles from the courtyard cover the sanctuary floor, and tapping shoes echo from wall to wall. During services, you probably have to think twice before getting up to go to the bathroom—the noise your shoes will make means all eyes will turn to you.

Going to church is really important to my mother, unlike my father. My father says he's a lapsed Catholic, whatever that means, but he goes to church for my mother's sake. Most Palestinians aren't even Christians—they're Muslim. My Christian Palestinian family was part of a small minority, even in Jerusalem.

During services, Baba always sits stiff like he's watching the news coverage. His lips barely move at all. But sometimes, early in the mornings at home—I catch him praying at a window, his eyes and hands raised to the sky. Then, he looks like he's praying with his whole heart.

My mother says he feels most comfortable praying in private.

The San Antonio congregation is an interesting mix. Some of the families speak less Arabic than I do, some speak French, and some speak English with a Texan drawl. Sara and I notice that some men even wear cowboy boots with their suits!

A few of the families must be recent immigrants from Lebanon. They look a little lost during the parts of the service that are in English, and not in Syriac or Arabic. Sometimes I'm a little lost during services, too. Even though I can say all the prayers, I don't always know what they mean.

Some of the families seem just like us, with immigrant parents and kids who were born in America who answer them in English instead of Arabic, like I do.

My mother sits next to me during the service and makes more helpful observations, despite the fact that she always says church is for praying, not talking. We watch the older girls parade in and out of the pews, ignoring the echoing sound their shoes make and the disapproving glances of their mothers and fathers.

My mother tsk-tsks and whispers, "Some of these girls are very *showy*, yes?"

I shrug.

"Their mothers must be very concerned, yes?"

I shrug again, but I can't take my eyes off the girls—it's hard for me to even follow the service.

One girl especially catches my attention during services; her friends call her Nadine. She has honey-colored eyes like my mother and long, dark eyelashes. Her makeup is near perfect and her shiny hair reaches down to her waist. She wears a shimmery dress and real high heels.

She passes our pew again and I glance around the sanctuary. I'm not the only one who's watching her. It's almost like Nadine's performing on stage.

At the luncheon after services, you would never guess that we'd only been in Texas for just over a week, and this was our first Sunday at St. Anthony's, since here at church my mother is back to her usual, outgoing self.

The new friends she met for tea last week all come over to introduce themselves, and Sara and I watch them compete for our mother's smiles. One lady corners my mother a second time this morning. "Myriam!" she exclaims. "Have you decided if you can attend my party next week?"

My mother bats her eyelashes. "My sweet new friend," she says, "you will know my plans just as soon as I know them."

Sara and I giggle. We're both thinking the very same thing: at St. Anthony's, our mother is already back to being queen bee.

Right before we leave, one of the ladies looks me over. "Your oldest daughter can join St. Anthony's Magic Is the Night dance troupe, Myriam!" she exclaims. "Practice starts in December, and all the middle and high school girls are invited. They perform along with the boys' dabke troupe every June at the annual Texas Folklife Festival!"

"Yasmeen would love to join the dance troupe, right, habibti?" my mother says, clapping her hands together.

But it's not really a question.

As soon as the lady walks away, I say, "I'm not a very good dancer, Mama."

Sara agrees. "I watched Yasmeen do a *Just Dance* video at Dina's house once. She's a little *uncoordinated*."

I nod and start mumbling about the empty spot on the Sapphires drill team at school. I say, "I'm trying to learn some dance steps so I can try out for the team captain, but I can't do them very well. I don't think I can be in the St. Anthony's dance troupe, either."

My mother looks at me for a minute, then waves my words away like a pesky fly. She says, "Thank goodness there are no tryouts here and there is plenty of time to learn. You will be an expert dancer by next June!" Then she click-clacks off to find Baba and Salim so that we can drive home.

Sara tries to make me feel better. "Maybe you just need more practice, Yasmeen. Maybe you'll get it. Magic Is the Night sounds really fun."

But just like my mother, I wave her words away, too.

Monday morning, I wait with my sister in silence at the bus stop with our Israeli neighbors, Ayelet and Tal Cohen.

We sit on one side of some tall stone mailboxes, and the Cohen kids sit on the other. Every once in a while, we steal glances at each other. Sara or I lean over to look at them, and we catch them doing the same.

I wonder if their family had a worried conversation like ours did Friday night after our mothers met for the first time. I wonder if they decided they couldn't be friends with everyone in our neighborhood like we did.

The long, yellow elementary school bus arrives first, and Sara and Tal get on. Two girls near the front of the bus jump up to hug my sister right before it pulls away.

I keep waiting with Ayelet. Neither of us makes a peep. We look anywhere but at each other, and minutes feel like hours.

When our bus comes, Ayelet rushes on ahead of me. She sits in the very first row, places her backpack on the bench next to her, and stares straight ahead. So, I brush past her and sit a few rows back by myself.

I guess we won't be friends with all our neighbors, after all.

Two stops later, Waverly hops on the bus and flashes her sunny smile at the driver and everyone else as she moves up the rows. The first few days of school, I thought she was just being nice to me because she's my student helper, but she invited me to sit at her lunch table every day last week!

She throws air kisses to two Sapphires from our neighborhood who are sitting at the back of the bus—Chloe and Kayla—but then stops short when she notices me. "Hey,

Yasmeen, it's your first day riding the bus! Can I sit with you?" she says, then slides in next to me without waiting for an answer.

She blows a big bubble with her chewing gum and it pops on her face. She giggles and peels it off and starts chewing again. Ayelet turns around to examine us, and frowns. But I'm not sure who she's frowning at—Waverly or me.

Waverly chatters nonstop during the ride to Forest Hills, just like she did the first morning I met her.

She tells me that the Sapphires perform in the Elite Showcase in Dallas every spring break, and they usually win first place, but last year they got second. She tells me that the girl who messed up and cost them the win transferred schools right before seventh grade started, which Hallie said was really for the best. She even takes my phone out of my hands and adds me to the Sapphires' group chat. "Now you'll know what's going on since you're trying out for our empty spot!"

I stare at the group chat for a second and scroll through a few entries. They say things like, *OMG! He really said that?* and *I SO hate it when that happens!* and *Team sleepover next Saturday!*

I want to read them all, but if I tell Waverly I can't dance so I shouldn't try out for Hallie, I won't be able to be on the chat. I won't be able to follow along.

And maybe Waverly won't even sit with me on the bus again.

The whole time we're riding to school, I watch her closely and hang on every word. I breathe in her fruity hair conditioner and bubble gum smell. I memorize the way her nose crinkles when she tells me something exciting, and the way she tucks her stick-straight hair behind her ears when it slips out.

Of all the Sapphires, Waverly's the prettiest, with her big Texas-sky eyes, creamy skin, and golden hair. She's the kind of pretty everyone agrees about—like the pretty I see on teen magazine covers in the grocery store.

But she doesn't act pretty the way other girls sometimes do, like being pretty makes them better than everyone else. Maybe girls with Waverly's kind of pretty don't need to act at all.

She says, "Yasmeen, it's positively kismet that I was your student helper and now you're trying out for my drill team! And that our dads work together, and we live in the same neighborhood! We're just meant to be friends, don't you think?"

My mouth pops open and I nod. *Waverly thinks we're meant to be friends?*

Kismet is like fate—it means all our stars align!

We get to school, and I ignore the cool stares Chloe and Kayla give me as we file off the bus. I follow Waverly

Jones up the steps, and right then I know: I'd follow her anywhere.

I'm still daydreaming about the ride to school at the end of first period math class. As I'm walking to the door, Mrs. Shelby pulls me aside to her desk.

She puts on her glasses and shuffles through some papers. "Sweetie, is this your handwriting? Do you sometimes go by the name Yolanda? Because I have a paper here that looks like your writing but . . ." Her voice trails off.

Little sweat beads instantly prickle my neck. I glance around the room as the last student left in class, Esmeralda, shoots me a strange look and hurries into the hall. "Just sometimes," I say. "I mean, I used to go by Yolanda, but I don't anymore. I just forgot. I'm just Yasmeen now."

She lowers her glasses and smiles. "Okay, then, that's settled. And by the way, take a look at your grade. You didn't miss a problem!"

I smile. "Thanks, Mrs. Shelby. Thanks so much for figuring out—"

She shakes her head. "It's all good, and I'm glad we had this little chance to check in. Is everything else going okay for you at school?"

I nod. Mrs. Shelby's so nice! Plus, she loves math like I do.

She waves me out the door, but as I'm rushing down the hall to my next class, I hear Esmeralda cackle to the girl she's walking with. *"Yolanda?"*

And my neck gets prickly all over again.

Ten

The next Sunday after church, I change out of my dress and head downstairs to Baba's office to video chat with Dina on his laptop.

My father's urgent Arabic filters through a small crack in the door. His voice gets louder and louder until, *bam!* Something slams on his desk.

I run to the foot of the stairs and wait until I hear him trudge down the hall toward the kitchen, then I tiptoe back to his office to call my best friend.

Even the funny-sounding ringtone knows how far apart we are—it sounds hollow like it's hopping along a big distance. Dina's mother answers the call on her laptop just as I'm about to hang up. "Hello, Yasmeen!" she says. "I will get Dina straight away."

Within minutes, Dina's smile fills Baba's screen.

"H-hi!" I stammer. "Did you get my news skit? I—I thought maybe you'd send one, too, so I could see what's going on back home."

She nods. "I'm so sorry, Yasmeen! I thought about making you one, but there's no news here. Nothing's changed much since you left! But your new life sounds really exciting."

We fall into talking just like always, and twenty minutes fly by.

I tell her my exciting new life is actually pretty confusing. Then I work up the nerve to ask, "Dina? Do you ever not feel very American? You know . . . because you're Arab?"

"What are you talking about, Yasmeen? We *are* Americans! We're citizens of the United States of America. Our country is a melting pot. Remember from social studies class?"

"Yeah, I remember," I say, pulling at a thread at the bottom of my shirt. "I know we're citizens. But do you *feel* American since our families act so different . . . at home?"

"I feel like I always did, Yasmeen, except you're not here anymore. Don't you?"

"I don't think so." I pull the thread all the way out. "I'm starting to feel really different from everybody else."

We talk until Dina's mother calls her for dinner, then we promise to video chat again soon.

My father's outside firing up our backyard grill, his shoulders slumped forward. I step out our back patio door and join him. "Hi, Baba, what's for dinner?"

His eyes look sad and far away, and the corners of his mouth droop. He slowly scrapes the grill back and forth with a wire brush. "Your mother is making hamburgers."

"Are we having *American* hamburgers?" I'm trying get him to smile, but it doesn't work.

My mother only makes one kind of hamburger, of course—the best kind, she says—the Arab kind. They don't even look like real hamburgers. They're long, skinny kafta patties heavily seasoned with cinnamon and allspice and stuffed with crunchy vegetables.

You don't put them in a fluffy white bun, you don't melt American cheese on them, and you don't slather them in ketchup and mustard, which we don't have in our refrigerator anyway. You put them in a pita pocket with pickled turnips and tart tahini dressing.

I head to the kitchen, and sure enough there's a big pile of chopped parsley and onions on the counter. "Mama, can you please leave all that out of my burger?" I say. "I'd rather have an American hamburger."

She looks at me and tsk-tsks. "American hamburgers are not real food, Yasmeen." She lowers her voice to a whisper. "And that terrible man at the restaurant was a *racist*."

Baba barely speaks during dinner. He pushes his

unfinished plate toward my mother to wrap up for later, then he shuffles to the living room and flips through TV channels until he finds what he's looking for—more news from home.

Sara and I follow him. She sits down at the brass tray tables with her stacks of flash cards to practice for the spelling bee, and I sit down on the sofa. This time, his eyes are so far away that he doesn't even notice that we're watching the news coverage of the Israeli-Palestinian conflict right along with him.

Just like last week, things are still bad in Jerusalem. The violence has escalated out of control. A newscaster says, "House demolitions have reached an all-time high this month. Palestinians have taken to the streets to protest."

We watch a family run from their little stone house right before a big bulldozer knocks it to the ground. The mother clings to a little boy Salim's age whose tear-streaked face is covered in thick, gray dust. The boy's father throws his hands to the sky.

My father shakes his head. "Where will they go now?"

I lock eyes with Sara. The flash card in her hand is shaking; her eyes are welling up.

Baba hangs his head and whispers over and over, "He who has no land has no honor. He who has no land has no honor."

I don't understand my father when he talks this way,

in cryptic Palestinian proverbs. They're like riddles I can't solve. Sometimes, when I ask him to explain them, his explanation only leads to a different proverb.

I inch closer to my father on the sofa and pat his hand the way my mother does as the news coverage shifts to two other places he says Palestinians live where the fighting's even worse—the West Bank and the Gaza Strip.

Baba told me that the West Bank gets its name since it's the land on the western bank of the Jordan River, which starts in the mountains on the border of Lebanon and Syria and flows all the way down into the Dead Sea, a super-salty body of water that has the lowest elevation on earth.

He also said that even though the West Bank isn't technically part of Israel, it's occupied by the Israeli government and their military roams the streets. He says most of the people who live there are Palestinian, but more and more Jewish people move to the West Bank all the time.

The Gaza Strip, he told me, is a separate sliver of land where Palestinians are packed in tight, like sardines in a can. The top and right sides of the strip are surrounded by Israel, and the left side meets the Mediterranean Sea. Egypt lies at the bottom.

My father says the West Bank and Gaza Strip aren't inside a modern-day country Palestine, but they aren't inside of Israel, either. He says that Palestinians who live in these two places aren't citizens of anywhere at all.

"It is becoming apartheid now," my father mutters. "Palestinians have no rights."

"Apartheid?" My sister wipes her wet face with the back of her hand. She grabs a sparkle pen, scribbles the word down, then leafs through her dictionary. She reads aloud, "Apartheid comes from a language in South Africa called Afrikaans. It means apartness; segregation or discrimination on the grounds of race."

She takes a deep breath and blinks at Baba. "What a powerful word," she says, and he nods.

Suddenly, the confusion that I've felt since we moved here erupts. I've had enough of cul-de-sacs filled with Hill Country houses, in a neighborhood where we don't fit in. I've had enough of the riddles I can't solve. I've had enough of my parents' obsession with what happens in a faraway home that was never *my home*.

But most of all, I've had enough of my little sister's know-it-all flash cards.

I jump up from the sofa and walk by the tray table where Sara's alphabetizing her new word—apartheid—and placing it into a neat stack. I push the stack off the table.

My sister suppresses a cry as her cards flutter to the floor. My father's eyes stay fixed on the TV, unaware of our commotion.

I shake my head and say, "I'm so sorry, Sara," and help her pick the cards up. I know I shouldn't take things out on her—but the Palestinians, the Israelis, and apartheid—it's all just too much.

My father's faraway sadness fills the air in the room and the air in my lungs.

I rush to the stairs and take the steps up to my room two at a time, trying to breathe it all out. When my door closes behind me, I finally exhale. Then I crawl into my bed and pull my comforter tight around me.

Before I go to sleep that night, I stand at my window and look up at the Texas night sky.

Tonight, it's filled with more stars than I've ever seen—there are way more than our brass lantern with the little star cutouts can cast on our kitchen walls.

I search the heavens for the Little Dipper with my favorite North Star, and my heart filled with wishes calls out to it, hoping it might answer.

I wish for a new best friend like Dina in Detroit. I wish that Baba weren't so sad all the time, worrying about my grandmother in Jerusalem. I wish my family could be more American like the other families in our new neighborhood, so that we can fit in.

And I wish more than anything that somehow, we'll all find a way to be happy in San Antonio, Texas—our new home.

Eleven

Mrs. Shelby asks me to step into the hall during math class a few days later.

She lowers her reading glasses to hang around her neck, and smiles. "Yasmeen, I just graded last week's math homework, and you didn't miss a single problem. Actually, you haven't missed a problem on any of your homework so far. Math must be easy for you!"

I smile and nod.

"So, I checked your math grades from your old school, and all I can say is . . . wow! You made perfect scores there, too."

I smile bigger.

"Forest Hills has a math club for advanced students called the Math Lab. Each May, they compete in a city-wide competition. The team was chosen at the end of sixth grade, but I think they could really use you, so I'm prepared to make an exception. Would you like to join?"

"Yes, Mrs. Shelby! Thank you so much." I don't even have to think about it. I love math! It always makes perfect sense, unlike a lot of things.

"Great! Our club coach is Ayelet Cohen's dad. He's a mathematician, and we're so lucky that he can work with our students again this year." She winks. "I also think he wants to spend a little more time with that sweet daughter of his."

My breath catches in my chest.

I don't tell Mrs. Shelby that the Cohens are our neighbors across our cul-de-sac, who my parents don't want to be friends with. And I don't tell her that's because it's a big deal to them that they're from Israel, like my Palestinian father. And I especially don't tell her that Jewish Israelis and Palestinians have been fighting over the same homeland for more than seventy years, and there's no end in sight.

Instead, I ask, "When does practice start?"

Mrs. Shelby leads me back into class. "Math Lab's first session is next week. They'll meet for an hour on Monday and Thursday afternoons."

The rest of the day, I think about our neighbors, the Cohens. I think about how Mrs. Cohen speaks Arabic, but she's not Arab like us. And I think about how Ayelet's name and my name are both from the very same place, all the way across the ocean.

There's just so much about Baba's *home* that I don't understand. But joining Math Lab with Ayelet Cohen seems like the perfect way to find out.

All weekend long, I try to work up the nerve to tell my parents about Math Lab. I rack my brain for some way to present the idea where it will seem okay for Mr. Cohen to be my after-school math coach, but I can't think of anything.

By Sunday evening, I'm about to lose my chance.

After dinner, I clear my throat. "Mama, Baba . . . guess what?"

They don't seem to hear me. My father's sitting on the living room sofa flipping through channels on the TV again and my mother's alternating between patting his shoulder and his hand. They're both glassy-eyed and far away.

I clear my throat a second time. "I was invited to be in an after-school math club for *advanced* students. They're making an *exception* for me since Mrs. Shelby thinks they need me on the team. There's a city-wide *competition* at the Jewel of the Forest Auditorium in May."

My parents perk up. Apparently, I've said all the right

words: *advanced*, *exception*, and *competition*. They immediately stop what they're doing; I have their full attention now.

My mother's face breaks into a wide smile. "Elias, did you hear this good news? Yasmeen was invited to a math club for advanced students, already!"

Baba nods his head and says, "Of course she was, Myriam. Sara has a way with words, as they say, and Yasmeen multiplies faster than any calculator. Both of our daughters are experts. No, more than experts! They are geniuses." Now he's smiling, too.

It doesn't take much to be a genius in the Khoury home, I've discovered. I'm a math genius, Sara's a spelling genius, and little Salim—I'm sure that our parents will identify what kind of genius he is soon enough.

A car door slams outside, and we look out our big picture window. The lights inside the Cohens' house flip on. My mother's smile fades, and I know—there's no way they'll ever let Mr. Cohen be my after-school math coach.

"I'm so excited!" I say. "Mrs. Shelby's my favorite teacher and I'd love to spend more time with her after school. Plus, you know how much I love math. So, can I join?"

The lie about who my math coach will be rolls off my tongue like a runaway train.

I tell myself it's just another little white lie, so my parents won't be upset. After all, they're really proud I was invited to a math club for advanced students. It's just the good news they needed.

My mother smooths my hair away from my face, and beams. "Of course you can, habibti."

Then we decide that my parents will wait for me in the school's parent parking spaces after each Math Lab session, so they won't have to come inside.

I walk into the first meeting of Math Lab the next afternoon and a tall man with glasses and wispy sandy-brown hair greets me in Arabic. "Marhaba!"

I give him a tiny wave. "Hi . . . Umm, I really don't speak much Arabic."

He reaches up to wipe invisible sweat from his brow and chuckles. "Neither do I. I'm Mr. Cohen, the Math Lab coach." He extends his hand for me to shake and pumps it up and down. "And you must be Yasmeen, our new neighbor."

He gestures to a desk in the back of the room. "You know my daughter Ayelet from the bus stop?"

She looks up from texting on her phone for a second, then looks back down. Mr. Cohen shrugs. "Charmed to meet you, Yasmeen. Please take a seat."

Just as he's about to close the door to the classroom, Esmeralda rushes in. She slides into the desk next to me, and when she sees me, her eyebrows shoot up in surprise.

"Now that our Math Lab wizard, Miss Esmeralda Gutierrez, has bestowed us with her presence," he says, "the twelve of you can begin this year's spellbinding adventure!" He walks over to the chalkboard and writes "MATH IS MAGICAL!" in big letters all the way across.

I turn around and look at Ayelet. Her face flushes deep pink like she's sunburned.

Mr. Cohen paces the room and tells us all about the exciting new math we're going to learn this year, and how we'll achieve our big goal—to win the Math Lab city-wide competition next May. "I have high hopes since we missed winning last year by . . . just a hair!" he says, pointing to the top of his head and chuckling again.

"Plus," he says, looking straight at me, "we have a new student this year who I hear has a *potent* combination of math skills." He walks back to the board. "Okay, class! Let's make some magic!"

I turn around and look at Ayelet again. She's giggling uncontrollably. With her same sandy-colored hair, when she laughs, she looks just like her dad. Our eyes meet, and she smiles.

So, I smile back.

Mr. Cohen passes out a packet of challenge problems. He explains that mastering these puzzles will require way more ability than our seventh-grade math skills alone. They'll require keen logic.

Right away, What Ifs start to bubble up in my mind, even though I've been doing my Sudoku books every chance I get.

I can't seem to help it. I can't push them back. And this time, they aren't just a silly game.

What if I can't work any of the problems? What if I don't belong in a special club like the Math Lab? What if I'm not the math genius my parents think I am?

I open the packet and focus on the first problem set. I catch my breath and push my worries away. *I can do this*, I tell myself. And once my breath steadies, I know exactly how to begin.

The instant I write the first few numbers down in a neat row, there's a familiar shift. Everything else fades away, and I'm not worried anymore—about anything at all.

I'm not worried about Baba's sad news from home, and his mind and heart flying far away; I'm not worried about fitting in at a new school, where there aren't any Arabs like me; I'm not worried about the best friend I left behind or finding a new one.

I complete problem after problem, lining the numbers up, carefully checking my work, and drawing crisp, satisfying boxes around the answers I know are right.

And I remember—when I'm doing math problems, all the pieces of the puzzle fit together perfectly. I fit.

Nothing feels confusing like Baba's riddles.

I whip through the problem set and put down my pencil, then I stretch my arms above my head and glance around the room. Everyone's still working—everyone but me.

I smile wide, and Mr. Cohen catches my smile and returns it.

Esmeralda watches us, shifting and fidgeting, furiously erasing her paper. Her brow knits together, and I know exactly what she's thinking: she's not the only wizard in Math Lab.

Twelve

The last two weeks of September fly by, now that my life in San Antonio has settled into a familiar routine.

I ride the bus to Forest Hills with Waverly each day and sit with her at the Sapphires' table at lunch; I go to Math Lab twice a week where Ayelet and I steal glances at each other and Esmeralda squirms if I finish a challenge problem before she does; I watch Nadine and the older girls parade around St. Anthony's on Sundays; and the rest of the time—my mind wanders like never before.

I daydream in my room for hours—playing What If—all by myself.

When we lived in Detroit, I never wished I were different. But now, in San Antonio, I find myself wishing for a whole different life.

What if my family ate real American hamburgers with french fries, instead of mjaddara? What if we went to restaurants like other families in our neighborhood? What if we even joined a Protestant church instead of our Maronite one, where some of the service isn't even in English?

I follow the Sapphires' group chat, but I'm not brave enough to chime in. I walk the track by myself during gym class in my baggy gym uniform and memorize their routines. I practice them in front of my dresser mirror, but I never get them right.

Just like with Dina's *Just Dance* video games, I'm horrible; I spend most of the time tripping over my two left feet.

Try out and make the Sapphires drill team? Become an expert Magic Is the Night dancer by June?

There's no possible way.

I stick my tongue out at myself in the mirror: even with all my daydreaming, the person I see is still just—me. No amount of pretending or silly What Ifs can change that.

"Yasmeen!" My mother cracks the door open to my room. "I have been calling you from the kitchen. Is your head stuck in a cloud?"

I didn't even hear her. "Sorry, Mama, what did you need to tell me?"

"Please come down for dinner. It is the last time our family will eat together before Baba leaves tomorrow for his yearly visit with your grandmother in Jerusalem," she says, wringing her hands together. "It will be a very difficult trip, so we are having his favorite, mjaddara, to cheer him up."

Waverly sits down next to me in the cafeteria during assembly the very next week. Even though it's the beginning of October, and even though I've only been in San Antonio a short while, it's beginning to feel like we're long-lost friends.

We're listening to Principal Neeley's announcements and kudos, which I now know is a word he uses to congratulate Forest Hills students on their finest achievements, when she fixes her blue eyes on me and frowns. "I'm so, so sorry, Yasmeen. I feel awful."

Right away, I know why she's sorry, since it was all too good to be true: she doesn't want me to sit with her at the Sapphires' table at lunch anymore; she doesn't want to ride with me on the bus to school; she doesn't think we're meant to be friends.

None of it was kismet.

But that's not it at all. She takes a big breath and rattles, "Hallie changed her mind! She filled the empty spot on the Sapphires with someone who tried out over the summer! I told her you should get to try out, too, since you weren't here then, but she said no!"

A wave of relief washes over me. "That's okay, Waverly,"

I blurt, then pout a little. "I mean, I'll just try out for eighth grade. It'll give me more time to learn the routines."

She nods. "Thanks so much for understanding, Yasmeen."

Then her eyes well up. "Can you come over to my house after school to study today, since you're in that special math club now? I couldn't finish my math homework last night and I was even more lost today."

"Really? You want me to come over to your house?" I glance away for a second to hide my smile. "I'm happy to help. Math is my favorite subject!"

I can't tell Waverly that math's really easy for me, that it makes perfect sense, or that doing math problems helps push my worries away. Not when it seems just the opposite for her. "I'll ask my mom right after school and text you!" I say.

Now she's the one who seems relieved.

"Thanks, Yasmeen. I could really use a friend like you as a study buddy," she says, blinking the tears from her eyelashes. Then she plasters on a sunny smile, gives me a few air kisses, and flits away.

"Mama!" I yell as I walk through the front door later that afternoon.

My mother's in the kitchen as usual, furiously stirring steaming pots of spicy food while Salim zooms around her feet with his new ride-on fire truck.

"Meenie, look! I has big fast truck now," he says.

I bend down and peck his soft little cheek.

My mother doesn't look up from her pots. Since Baba left for Jerusalem, she's been in another full-on Myriam Khoury frenzy. She bustles around the house, cleaning and cooking nonstop; she marshals us to school and St. Anthony's with military precision; she says she's "holding down the fort."

"Can I walk over to a friend's house to study today?" I ask.

My question spins her around. She wipes the steam from her forehead with her dish towel and assesses me carefully. "A *girl*friend? Someone from school?"

"Yes, Mama! Of course, a *girl*friend! You know—the Joneses' daughter—from the photo. Can I go now? She's waiting for me."

My mother lights up and repeats, "The Joneses' daughter?" Then she covers her pots, takes off her apron, and turns off the stove. She fetches Salim's shoes, and yells to the top of the stairs, "Sara! Come at once, we are taking Yasmeen to a *girl*friend's house!"

It takes me a second to realize what's happening. "Mama, I'm in seventh grade and Waverly Jones lives in our neighborhood—walking distance—and her dad and Baba work together. Not everyone has to come!"

"Yasmeen, what are you saying?" she asks, but she doesn't wait for my response. She digs in her purse and runs a comb through her shiny hair and freshens her lipstick. Then on our way out, she checks herself in the hallway mirror and practices another bold smile.

I sulk and drag my feet. I should have known that my mother wouldn't let me go by myself; my study buddy date with Waverly is the perfect excuse for her to finally meet Mrs. Jones.

I text Waverly to give her the heads-up that my mother wants to meet her mom, but that of course, she's not staying. Then Sara and I help redirect Salim from his ride-on fire truck to a miniature Hot Wheels version he can carry with him in the car.

Waverly's house is just a few minutes' drive toward the inside of our neighborhood, not bordering the wide-open space like my house. Each backyard on her cul-de-sac smacks right up against the next one. From the outside, her house looks just like mine.

My mother turns the car off and reaches over to smooth my hair down. "Yasmeen, habibti! You have made your first Texas friend!"

"Stop, Mama!" I squirm away from her. "We're just study buddies!"

She gives me a hurt look, gets out of the car, unbuckles Salim from his car seat, and slings him on her hip. Then she click-clacks up the walkway to the Joneses' front door while Sara and I trail behind her.

Their door opens before she knocks.

Waverly stands next to her mother, who's dressed in a crisp pantsuit like she works in a fancy office. They look so much alike, with the same straight golden hair and sky-blue eyes. And just like Waverly, Mrs. Jones is the kind of pretty everyone agrees about.

She smiles wide and drawls, "Hey there, it's so nice to finally meet y'all!"

I glance at my mother. She shifts Salim to her other hip and sinks into her heels a bit. Her face freezes. She's acting a little like she did at my school with the office ladies—not like herself—quiet and shy.

"Hi, Waverly," I say.

My mother recovers. She clears her throat and introduces us, saying each syllable of our names slowly and carefully. "This is my older daughter, Yasmeen, my younger daughter, Sara, and this is my son, Salim. I am Myriam Khoury."

"What lovely names you have, and your accent is delightful!" Mrs. Jones gushes. "I'm just so grateful Yasmeen can help Waverly with math—the program's so difficult this year!"

My mother smiles and puffs up a bit. Her face relaxes. "The subject of math is not difficult for Yasmeen since she is a real math expert," she rattles. "She is likely a genius!"

Sara snorts and covers her mouth. I want to reach over and pinch her. I want to hide.

"Yasmeen, you will text me when you are done?" my mother asks.

But Mrs. Jones shakes her head. "No need, Myriam. I'll run her home. My husband told me Elias was overseas on a family emergency, so you've got your hands full. I'm just so sorry."

My mother's eyes dart from me to Sara, and her face flushes. Her bangles jingle. She stutters, "It—it is not really an emergency! My husband is just visiting his m-mother, attending to m-matters of great importance!"

I look at my sister, and she shrugs.

Before I can ask my mother about the emergency and the matters of great importance, which I've heard absolutely nothing about, she thanks Mrs. Jones for having me and turns on her heel. Then she grabs Sara's hand, shifts Salim on her hip, and click-clacks back to the car.

I step inside Waverly's house, and my nose fills with the delicious smell of baked apples. I forget all about my mother's embarrassing comment on the front porch. My father's emergency flies out of mind. I'm so excited to finally be invited over to another girl's house—even if it's just to be study buddies.

And whatever happened in Jerusalem can't be that bad, or my parents would've told me.

"What are you baking, Mrs. Jones?" I ask.

Waverly grins. "My mom, baking? Not a chance!"

Mrs. Jones laughs and leads us into the kitchen, where a big red candle burns on the center island.

She asks, "Are you hungry, sugars? What are you fixing for?"

I raise my eyebrows for a split second, then will them back down. I'm not exactly sure what Mrs. Jones asked. I guess my mother's not the only one with a thick accent!

Waverly rummages through the freezer and pulls out a box of Hot Pockets. "Do you like these, Yasmeen?"

I look at the bright red box with its thin layer of frost. It's exactly the kind of thing my mother classifies as *not real food*. "Umm, I've never tried them," I say, setting my backpack on the floor.

"Really?" She crinkles her nose and slides two into the microwave. "They're super yummy. You'll love them."

And I do.

After our snack, I follow Waverly to her dad's office to do our homework. It's way bigger than Baba's small office at my house: rows of thick leather books in tall glass cases line the walls, and a big oval table with plush leather chairs sits in the center of the room.

I scan the books on the shelves; they have funny titles like *Contracts* and *Torts*.

"My dad's the company's lawyer," she says. "I sure wish

I had a brain like his. Let's do math last, Yasmeen."

We work our way through all our other subjects, then I open my math book. Waverly's face immediately falls.

She slides her math homework over, and I read through the last problem she was stuck on. "See, Waverly," I tell her. "Just think of it this way, that x and y are actual numbers. Equations are like mysteries to solve."

"All math problems are mysteries to me, Yasmeen. Why can't we just use regular numbers again? Why do we have to use fake numbers?"

"You'll get it, Waverly." I try to reassure her. "Math just takes practice."

"It's just that . . . I'm not sure why it's so hard for me." She starts to tear up.

I notice a tissue box on a shelf, and I walk over to get one for her. Her nose honks when she blows it.

Waverly's acting really different at home than she does at school. When she's surrounded by Hallie and the big group of Sapphires—she acts so sure of herself, like she's got everything down. But right now, Waverly seems anything but sure.

"Thanks for helping me, Yasmeen," she says. "You're super nice, and I can just be myself around you because you're just so . . . real."

Me, real? I think of all the time I spend daydreaming What If, pretending to be someone else, pretending to be someone more like Waverly.

She checks her next answer in the back of the book and frowns.

"That's okay, just start that problem over," I say. "Practice makes perfect, right?"

She nods and erases her mistake.

Maybe I'm not the only one who's pretending.

Thirteen

I hop off the bus after school the very next week to find a large blue shipping container parked in our driveway. Two men ferry its contents through our front door as my mother paces in her apron and high heels, directing them.

"Mama, what's going on? What is all this stuff?"

"Thank goodness, Yasmeen! You are finally home to help me!" She sounds panicked. "Your grandmother Khoury sent *everything*!"

The men pass us with dollies loaded with a large, carved olive wood trunk inlaid with mother-of-pearl shells; a giant, table-sized nargila; and a long, rolled-up red and black rug.

Sara pops out of the container, holding a little brass lamp and rubs it hard with the corner of her T-shirt.

"Yasmeen, there's so much treasure in here! Look what I found! Maybe there's a magic genie in this lamp!"

I walk up the driveway and peer into the shipping container, confused.

My jaw drops—inside, it looks just like the pictures I've seen of the souk in the Old City of Jerusalem. It bursts with stacks of bright-colored embroidered cushions and fabrics, dark carved furniture, and more shiny brass than I've ever seen in one place.

"What do you mean, Mama, she sent everything? Is Sitti finally visiting us again? Why did she ship all this stuff?"

My mother wrings her hands in her apron. "Yasmeen, we did not want to worry you. But when Baba comes back from Jerusalem next week, he is bringing your grandmother to San Antonio with him. She is coming to live with us!"

I blink. "Sitti's leaving Jerusalem to live with us? Why?"

My mother's words run together. "She got an eviction letter a year ago from the Israeli government . . . your father appealed in the courts . . . he thought he would win . . . he thought she would keep her home . . . he thought that surely at her age, they would not . . ." Her voice catches in her throat. "But it was no use, habibti! They took her home a few weeks before he arrived!"

I think back to all the worried looks that passed between

105

my parents recently, to my father's slumped shoulders and his angry voice in his office. I've only been half focused on what's happening at home since I've been so busy trying to fit in at my new school.

I squeak, "Is Sitti going to be American now, like us?"

My mother tsk-tsks. "Yasmeen, becoming a citizen of the United States of America will take your grandmother many years, but at least your father had the foresight to fill out her paperwork when she got the eviction letter. At least we have a guest room in this big Texas house!"

I peek inside the container. My grandmother's Jerusalem things look so strange—so foreign—compared to the nearly identical Hill Country–style style homes on our cul-de-sac.

My mother dashes into the house to direct the men, and I trail behind her.

Sitti, evicted? Baba's trip to Jerusalem was not like all his others. It was a matter of great importance, an emergency.

My grandmother's house is not hers anymore—just like that—and she's coming to stay with us forever. And what's left of her life in Jerusalem sits in our driveway in a big blue shipping container.

I'll never see where my father grew up now.

I head upstairs to my bedroom. My mother calls after me to come back down to help her once I'm settled, but her words fade, fuzzy in my ears.

I know I shouldn't feel the least bit selfish right now, but

I do. I shouldn't feel angry that I'll never see Sitti's house or her garden. I should only feel grateful that my grandmother can come live with us in San Antonio, since now, she has nowhere else to go.

But with the contents of my grandmother's shipping container filling our house with more Arab things, I'm worried about something else now, too. We're becoming even less like our San Antonio neighbors, less American.

It's clear. My pretending days are over. There's absolutely no chance of my family—or me—fitting in here, after all.

When Sitti Khoury walks through our front door almost a week later, she looks like an older, plumper version of me. Even from the outline of her body underneath her long, cross-stitched Palestinian thobe, I can tell that we share the same compact figure.

I immediately spot the Khoury stronger features I've inherited: my prominent nose, my dark brown almond-shaped eyes, and my year-round summer tan. We're exactly the same height, and when I face her in our kitchen, we meet eye to eye.

She drops her big bag, and bright-colored balls of yarn and thread spill to the floor along with clinking knitting needles. Then she throws her arms around me and plants quick crimson lipstick kisses all over my forehead as tears stream down her cheeks.

I freeze. I've always loved my grandmother, but I've mostly loved her from afar. Now she holds on to me like there's no letting go.

"Ahlan, Sitti," I manage to say, gasping for air.

She starts speaking to me in rapid-fire Arabic. I shake my head and my mother reminds her I won't understand very well if she speaks too quickly. Her lips quiver.

She lets go of me and repeats the same teary greeting with Sara, then she pries bewildered Salim from my mother's hip and smothers him with more lipsticky kisses.

"Salim . . . it is your grandmother!" My mother smiles wide and nods furiously, trying to reassure him that it's all okay, but he doesn't remember her since he was a baby the last time she visited. He wails in Sitti's arms.

Baba comes in from the garage, his arms loaded with heavy suitcases. Dark circles ring his eyes, and his face is cut in hard lines and angles. He moves tensely around the kitchen and doesn't meet anyone's gaze, not even my mother's.

She walks over to him and gently touches his cheek, then her worried eyes follow him as he carries my grandmother's suitcases down the hall to our guest room.

A few minutes later, his office door slams shut.

My grandmother's tears turn into loud, ragged sobs, and my brother cries with her. My mother puts him back on her hip and takes Sitti's hand. "Girls!" she says. "Let us show your grandmother our big Texas house!"

Sitti shuffles from room to room while we point out all of the things my mother carefully arranged from her shipping container. When she sees her big brass coffee service displayed prominently in our living room, she dries her eyes with the long sleeve of her dress, revealing a tall stack of gold bangle bracelets just like my mother's.

"There, there, it will be all right," my mother tells her. "You will see."

She hands Salim to me and whisks the brass cups to the kitchen so that she and Sitti can prepare Arabic coffee together after my grandmother's long journey.

My father's voice rises behind his office door, louder than ever before.

I look at my sniffling grandmother, and my mother takes Salim from me and puts him on the kitchen floor to play with his cars. Then she pulls me into the hallway.

Tears well up in the corners of her eyes and she pats them away, but they keep coming. "It is much worse, habibti. Your grandmother's little stone house has been torn down . . . demolished," she explains, her bangles jingling on her shaky wrists. "The house your father grew up in is gone."

"What?" I say. "Their house in Jerusalem is gone?" Now I'm shaking, too.

She takes my hands to steady me. "Bulldozers came

right before your father and grandmother left Jerusalem. Baba watched, helpless, as his childhood home disappeared. A block of tall apartments will be built on your grandmother's lot."

She looks around the corner at Sitti, who slowly stirs black coffee in a pot on the stove, and she shakes her head. "Getting evicted was hard enough, but bulldozing? Even her prized garden is gone! All that is left of her home is the key she wears around her neck."

That night, I lie awake on my stiff mattress, unable to sleep. Ice-cold currents rush through me, chilling me from the inside out.

I close my eyes and see Baba's dark circles and hard face. I hear my grandmother's sobs echoing through our house. Baba's proverb plays over and over in my mind—he who has no land has no honor—and I wonder: could the proverb be true?

When I finally fall asleep, I dream of thousands of keys jingling together like gold bangle bracelets. I dream of an army of bulldozers smoothing the Jerusalem hills pancake flat. After every little stone house is gone, every tree and every garden, tall white towers rise to the sky—as far as the eye can see.

Until there is no land left for anyone.

Fourteen

The last two weeks of October pass by in a blur.

Each morning, I wait for the bus with Ayelet in silence, wondering if her family is like the Israelis who demolished Sitti's house. At lunch, I sit with Waverly at the Sapphires' table and pretend like I belong.

I go to my classes. I raise my hand. I smile in the hallways.

No one at school knows my grandmother's little stone house became rubble far across the ocean. No one knows that my father stood by watching, unable to stop it. No one knows that his heart and mind have flown farther away from us than ever.

They don't know because I don't tell them.

At school, it's easy to pretend that things are okay, but

at home, pretending gets harder and harder.

I walk through the door after school the day of Halloween and hear the TV on in the living room. My heart sinks—my father's back from work early again, searching for news from *home*.

At least he's out in the house now. The first week after he came back from Jerusalem, he holed up in his suite or in his office, and sometimes, he didn't even come out for dinner. But a few mornings when I'd woken up early, I'd caught him by a window again with his hands raised to the sky. His face had been streaked with tears.

"Hi, Baba," I say, standing next to him by the couch. "How was your day?"

He sits nearly still, his face frozen like stone. His eyes slowly shift from the TV to me. He doesn't look like the Baba who sat tall and proud, telling us the exciting news about his San Antonio dream job over the summer. *Will that Baba ever come back, or is he gone forever?*

My father doesn't answer my question. He mumbles, "How are you, habibti?"

A lump forms in my throat. I choke out, "I'm okay, Baba," even though it's just another little white lie. *How can I be okay, when things are so sad at home?*

"I'm doing really well in my special math club!" I hope this will get a small smile, but it doesn't.

It's like we're caught in one of my news skits that plays

over and over, but it's all bad news: there's no sunshine, only rain.

My mother whisks in from the kitchen and hands him a tall drink. His watery eyes hold hers for a second. "Shukran, ayuni," he says, and returns to what he's watching.

"Habibi, is there something special you would like for dinner, to bring your appetite back, to bring your spirits up?" She takes a deep breath, smooths her apron down, and stands next to me, waiting. But my father doesn't answer her question, either.

I step into the hallway with my mother again. The lump in my throat expands and makes it hard to speak. "Mama," I ask, "when Baba prays by a window early in the morning, what does he pray for?"

She smooths the hair away from my face. "Yasmeen, his childhood home being demolished is the straw that broke the camel's back. I think he is praying for the life he lost in Jerusalem. It will take time for him to adjust."

I want to tell my father that his home here is just as important as the one he lost. I want to tell him that San Antonio is where he lives now, with us, not Jerusalem. I want to tell him that he should try to leave his sad story behind, that it should just be—history.

But I can't seem to tell him any of this; the words in my heart won't rise to my lips. I'm frozen just like Baba, like stone.

And I'm beginning to wonder if my father thinks his proverb is coming true. That when he lost his home in Jerusalem, he lost his honor, too.

I follow my mother into the kitchen, and find the entire room plastered with yellow sticky notes for my grandmother. She's written words like *pan, teakettle, refrigerator, oven, toaster, knives,* and *spices,* and stuck the notes on the items.

Our kitchen looks like it's been toilet papered in yellow notes.

"Mama, what *is* all this?"

"Your grandmother is so very sad, like Baba. I thought practicing English might distract her a bit. . . ."

I open the refrigerator to pour a glass of milk and several sticky notes fall to the floor: *refrigerator, cold, electricity, stay shut.* My mother has somehow even managed to stick a note on the ceiling's light fixture: *light on,* it says.

I look around the kitchen. "Where's Sitti?" After school, she's usually helping my mother make dinner or playing with my brother.

She looks at all the sticky notes. "Your grandmother is lying down in the guest room with a headache."

I don't doubt it—the sheer amount of paper usage suggests that my mother's idea for helping Sitti feel better by improving her English has gone a bit extreme, like a lot of her good intentions.

I look at the floor, and mumble, "Was she any . . . happier today?"

The first few days after my father brought my grandmother to San Antonio, she bustled around our house redistributing the contents of her shipping container that my mother had so carefully arranged before her arrival. But once Sitti arranged everything as best she could, she didn't know what to do. She seemed lost in our big Texas house.

My mother blinks. "Perhaps a little," she says. "Your grandmother has been through so much, habibti . . . it is not easy for her to *begin again* so far from home. It will take time for her to adjust, just like Baba."

I dump my backpack on the kitchen table, and head down the hall to check on my grandmother. As I near her room, giggles float through the air.

Sara stands on a stool in the middle of Sitti's room, dressed in one of our grandmother's intricately embroidered Palestinian dresses. Her two fifth-grade friends from the bus, also in my grandmother's clothes, appear just inside the doorway.

"Marhaba, Yasmeen!" Sara says. "Keef halek?"

I storm inside.

"Sara, you don't speak Arabic any better than me! And how could you play with our grandmother's clothes? She wouldn't . . ." My voice trails off when I see Sitti propped up on her bed cross-stitching, surrounded by colorful threads. She's smiling ear to ear.

One of the girls says, "We're trying on your grandmother's clothes for Halloween tonight! We're thinking of going as Scheherazade from *The Arabian Nights*, or maybe Princess Jasmine from *Aladdin*. Who do you think we should we be?"

I'm speechless. For the first time since arriving from Jerusalem, Sitti seems really happy; my little sister has somehow cheered her up.

Sara and her friends sift through the big pile of "dress-ups" that they've thrown on the bed and change outfits again. My grandmother tosses a beaded scarf to my sister, who dramatically wraps her face so only her honey-colored eyes show. Sitti clucks her tongue and whistles.

I can't believe how pretty my sister is in our grandmother's traditional clothes. I can't believe how happy it makes Sitti to see her wearing them.

Sara walks to our grandmother's dresser and digs in her jewelry box to find her gold bangles, then slides the deep yellow bracelets up her arms. She bats her long eyelashes through the narrow slit of her scarf and admires herself in the dresser's mirror. "Don't I look *exquisite*?" she asks.

She seems excited about wearing our grandmother's thobes. She seems happy speaking Arabic. Why is it so easy for my little sister to be an Arab girl, but it's not for me?

"Oh, Sara!" one of her friends exclaims. "You look just like Princess Jasmine!"

Princess Jasmine? I'm not dressing up for Halloween this year since Waverly says seventh grade is way too old for that, but if I did—I wouldn't want to go as an Arabian princess.

I'd want to go as a Sapphire.

I shoot Sara my meanest *whatever* glance and stomp out of the room. I fume back to the kitchen and slip across the floor on a bunch of sticky notes that have fluttered onto the hard tiles. I want to scream.

I grab a yellow note from the stack on the counter. Then I scribble my words down, put it front and center on the refrigerator, and hope everyone will see it.

sticky notes = annoying

But with all my mother's words floating around the kitchen, I doubt anyone will notice mine.

Fifteen

The first week in November in Math Lab, Mr. Cohen waves a piece of chalk like he's waving a magic wand.

He writes on the board: *Five houses of different colors are inhabited by wizards from five different countries. They each have a pet creature, a favorite drink, and a favorite activity. Who owns the unicorn and who drinks the potion?*

Then he turns around. "Okay, class! I have an enchanting new challenge problem for you today. It's one of the hardest ones we've had yet, a serious logic problem, so I can see how your magical minds do their sorcery. You'll have forty-five minutes to complete it, then we'll see how you did!"

He hands out a problem with a long list of clues, and Esmeralda shoots me a worried glance. I pretend to ignore her as I read through the list carefully.

1. The wizard from England lives in the red house.
2. The wizard from Mexico owns the black cat.
3. Coffee is drunk in the green house.
4. The wizard from the United States of America drinks tea.
5. The green house is immediately to the right (your right) of the ivory house.
6. The wizard who casts spells owns a dragon.
7. The wizard who tells fortunes lives in the yellow house.
8. Punch is drunk in the middle house.
9. The wizard from Canada lives in the first house on the left.
10. The wizard who flies a broom lives in the house next to the wizard with a pet rat.
11. The wizard who tells fortunes is in the house next to the house where the owl is kept.
12. The wizard who dances drinks fizzy water.
13. The wizard from Japan likes to juggle.
14. The wizard from Canada lives next to the blue house.

I love this kind of logic problem! I map out all the details in neat columns, make a matrix, and get to work.

After about thirty minutes, Mr. Cohen walks around the room to check our progress. He stops at my desk first. I put my pencil down and look up. He examines my matrix and winks, then moves on to the next student.

I must be on the right track.

"Do you have it?" Esmeralda whispers. She must be frustrated by the problem, from all her noisy erasing.

I whisper back, "Almost. I think the key is sorting the colors first."

Fifteen minutes later, Mr. Cohen says, "Time's up, wizards!" and Esmeralda slams her pencil down on her desk and hangs her head in her hands. He asks, "Who among you has used your wands successfully to figure out our problem? Who owns the unicorn and who drinks the potion?"

No one makes a peep.

I keep my eyes focused on my desk. I think my answer's right, but I don't want to risk feeling embarrassed.

"No one?" he asks, walking up and down the aisles. "Did anyone get close? You are my best magicians, err, math students!"

Esmeralda nudges my arm. "Yasmeen, raise your hand!" she says, but I shake my head.

"Miss Gutierrez! Do you have something to share? Perhaps a solution to our problem?" Mr. Cohen asks.

She gives me a sly smile. "I don't have it, but Yasmeen might."

"Then come on up, Yasmeen," Mr. Cohen says, "and write your answers on the board!"

Esmeralda mouths, "You're welcome."

I half-heartedly glare at her, then grab my paper off the

desk and shuffle to the board. I take a deep breath, pick up the chalk, and slowly write my answers: *The wizard from Japan owns the unicorn and the wizard from Canada drinks the potion.* I exhale and turn back around.

Mr. Cohen bows. "Ta-da! Yasmeen's answers are . . . correct! Very well done. We are so excited to have a wizard of your caliber in Math Lab! For the rest of you, a hint . . . the key ingredient of your spell is the matrix."

Then he winks at me again.

After class, Esmeralda stuffs her unicorn and potion problem in her backpack and bolts out the door behind Mr. Cohen, who says he's heading down to the office to fill out our competition paperwork before the office ladies head home.

I'm about to leave, too, when I hear, "Are you like some kind of math genius?"

I spin around to face Ayelet. I detect the hint of an accent in her voice on the word *genius*, but otherwise, her English sounds almost like her dad's.

She glances out the door. "*She* sure took off fast. I guess she has a little competition this year."

I laugh. Maybe Esmeralda does. I just hope it turns out to be friendly competition. "My parents think I'm a math genius, but you know how that goes. Their children are exceptional, of course."

Ayelet laughs with me, then bites her lower lip. Her green eyes examine me closer, now that we're at arm's length instead of on separate sides of the cul-de-sac mailboxes waiting for the bus.

I'm surprised she's talking to me after all this time.

"You're Arab, right? And your dad's Palestinian?"

I'm defensive right away.

"So?" I say. "You're Israeli, right, and your family is Jewish?"

She bites her lower lip again. "Yes, as a matter of fact, and we live across the cul-de-sac from each other." She raises an eyebrow. "Don't you think that's kind of ironic? Israelis and Palestinians? Here we are in America, the land of the free, so we're finally neighbors."

I hadn't really thought of it that way, but I guess it *is* kind of ironic—that over in Israel, Ayelet and I probably wouldn't have anything to do with each other.

Maybe we'd even be enemies, fighting like everyone else.

But here in San Antonio, we live in the same neighborhood and we go to the same school. Her dad's even my Math Lab coach—not that my parents know that.

"So, you didn't really answer my question, Yasmeen."

Her green eyes flash mischievously. She seems just as curious about me as I am about her. "Are you a math genius or not?"

I laugh, my guard coming back down. "I guess that's what the Math Lab competition is for, right? You'll have to wait until May to find out." I mimic my mother's technique with the ladies at church. "You'll know when I know."

"Well, my dad sure is impressed." She bites her lip again. I can tell it's a habit. "Fun fact, I don't even like math that much. I write for the Forest Hills paper, and someday I'm going to be a reporter or maybe a newscaster."

"Being a newscaster would be really fun . . . as long as the news is good," I say. "Wait, then why are you in Math Lab?"

"Hello? My father's the Math Lab coach, remember?" Ayelet looks out the window. "And I don't want to let him down, since you can probably tell he has a great time coaching."

"Your dad's really funny," I say, "with all the wizards and wands and potions stuff."

She nods and laughs. "I was super into magic when I was little, but my dad stayed seriously hooked. I've tried to tell him his jokes could use a little update, but there's really no way to . . . break the spell."

I smile. Like her dad, Ayelet's funny, too.

In the span of five minutes, I've learned more about Ayelet Cohen than our nearly two months at the bus stop. I've learned that her dad is funny and embarrassing, but that it doesn't really bother her. I've learned that her little white lie is that she doesn't like math. And I've learned that she thinks about the Israeli-Palestinian conflict, just like me.

Maybe neither of us has a choice.

As we walk down the hall, I tell her about the news skits I used to do with Dina. Then she tells me about the time she got to tour a San Antonio news station. She doesn't seem like the Israelis I've seen on TV. She doesn't seem like the kind of person who would be happy about someone's home being bulldozed to the ground to make room for apartments.

And after all the weeks that Mr. Cohen's been my Math Lab coach, I've decided—neither does he.

Sixteen

Waverly Jones has invited me over to her house after school to be study buddies six times since school started, but who's counting? It's been a dream come true, especially right now since my house is the last place I want to be.

"I'm sick of studying at my house," she announces at lunch. "Let's study at your house tomorrow."

"No!" I yelp, then clap my hand over my mouth. Her eyes widen in surprise and Hallie smirks at the opposite end of the table.

Inviting Waverly over to my house would be a disaster. It might ruin everything good that's happened since I got to San Antonio. What would she think of me, if she knew that even though my house looks exactly like her

Hill Country–style house on the outside—on the inside, it's not the same at all?

That on the inside, everything's different—with our full-to-the-brim Arab decor, with my grandmother who barely speaks English, and my father who's obsessed with sad news coverage from home, with my mother who mixes up all of her American sayings in her thick, jingly accent.

I know what she'd think—nothing good at all.

My mouth feels scratchy-dry like sandpaper. I swallow hard. "I mean, umm . . . there's just so much going on at my house since my grandmother moved in with us."

"That's okay, Yasmeen! My mom has to stay late at work, and you know I absolutely hate being alone. So, text your mom to ask."

I fish my phone out of my pocket and slowly tap out the words.

With any luck, my text will get lost in cyberspace, or my service will suddenly die. With any luck, my mother will say no.

> **Me:** Can Waverly Jones come over to study at our house tomorrow?
> **Mama:** Your first Texas friend? Of course! She will stay for dinner.
> **Mama:** Yasmeen? Habibti?
> **Me:** OK. Thanks, Mama.

Mama: 🖤 🖤 🖤 🎉 🎉 🎉

My luck's run out. "My mother says she'd love for you to stay for dinner after we study but of course, you don't have to! I mean, umm . . . all we eat is Arab food. We don't have any food you'd like." I'm queasy the minute I've spit it all out.

Hallie grins like I've just made her day again. She tosses her strawberry-colored hair, cups her hand to Kayla's ear, and whispers, "Yezz-mine thinks . . ." and I can't hear the rest.

I'm sure *Hallie* can tell how uncomfortable I am right now, even if Waverly can't. I'm sure *she* can tell that I'm pretending that everything's okay, even though it isn't.

"Great, Yasmeen!" Waverly says. "Thanks so much for inviting me!"

The next day after school, Waverly and I hop off the bus at my stop and walk the short block to my house. I brace myself and open the front door.

As I flip on the hall light, her big Texas eyes grow even bigger. "Wow, Yasmeen," she says, looking around.

"I know, right?" I say. "Welcome to Jerusalem!"

"Jerusa . . . where?"

"Never mind." I lead her into the kitchen.

"What's that?" She points to my father's nargila, which

stands in the corner of our new kitchen just like it did in Detroit.

"It's for smoking after dinner."

"Wow," she says again. "My dad holds his breath when we walk by people with cigarettes."

Waverly takes in all the sticky notes next. "We're trying to teach my grandmother more English," I explain.

"Wait, she doesn't speak English? What does she speak?"

"She speaks Arabic."

Her jaw drops for a second. "Do *you* speak Arabic, too, Yasmeen?"

"Just a little," I say, and change the subject. "Are you hungry?"

I rummage through the refrigerator for an after-school snack, but I only find the usual recycled yogurt containers full of Arab foods.

"Would you like some baba ganoush and pita bread?" I offer.

Waverly hesitates, then scoops some of the roasted eggplant dip with her pita like I do. She gobbles it down and scoops some more. "Yum! It's really good, Yasmeen. This bread is amazing. Is it homemade?"

I nod and finally relax.

We're still in the kitchen when my mother breezes in from shopping with Sitti and Salim. Her eyes dart to her phone. "We are late!" She tosses her purse on the counter.

"That 'Don't Get Lost, Lady' does not know where she is going!"

She rushes up to Waverly and hugs her tight, like she's known her forever even though she's only met her once. She says as she squeezes, "Habibti! We are so happy Yasmeen's new best friend can join us for dinner!"

Habibti? My new best friend? I can hardly breathe—what is my mother doing?

Waverly whispers, "What's habib—"

"It means, 'my love,' " I say with a nervous little laugh.

But she grins ear to ear, like she's just gotten the biggest compliment ever. In that moment, I know we're more than just study buddies. She *is* my first Texas friend.

My mother introduces her to my grandmother in Arabic, and Sitti breaks into a wide smile. She kisses her forehead like she does with her grandchildren, leaving a deep crimson smear. Apparently, she's decided Waverly is part of the family now.

I'm next. Sitti wraps her arms around me and plants a kiss on me, too.

Waverly and I laugh at the lipstick on each other's faces. "There aren't any air kisses with my grandmother!" I say. "Come up to my room." I know from experience we'll have to scrub for a while to remove the near-permanent color.

We do our homework while my mother and grandmother swirl in the kitchen, making dinner to loud Arabic music. The sound of Salim's smashing Hot Wheels cars carries up the staircase, too. He yells, *"Vroom, vroom!"* over and over, and my grandmother laughs and laughs. In just a few short weeks, he's become her little prince. She dotes on him nonstop, and now he reaches for her almost as much as he does for my mother.

Waverly and I come downstairs right after my father and Sara arrive home from a meeting about this year's regional spelling bee. Sara's already at the kitchen table combing through her new spelling lists. She gives Waverly a quick nod and turns back to them, hyper-focused.

Baba seems less sad today, a little more like himself. "How do you do, Waverly?" He shakes her hand. "We are glad you can join us for dinner."

"I'm great, Mr. Khoury. It's so nice to meet the rest of Yasmeen's family," Waverly says. "My dad told me he missed you around the office when you were away for your family emergency."

My father smiles and stands a little taller.

In the short time we've been upstairs, my mother and Sitti have worked their magic in the kitchen again. They've made baked chicken with oregano and lemon, and fluffy rice with tiny browned noodles. I'm grateful that our dinner looks more like a normal American dinner than some of the other family favorites, like stuffed grape leaves or diamond-shaped meat kibbi.

But I didn't need to worry about having Waverly to

dinner at my house, after all. She shovels big bites into her mouth over and over, and gushes, "So! Super! Amazing!"

We all laugh.

Sitti watches her clean her plate. When she sits back to rest, my grandmother grabs it and piles more food on it, then pinches her cheek. Waverly flashes her a big sunny smile.

I look around the table at my family—we're the happiest we've been since Baba and Sitti arrived from Jerusalem. My first Texas friend has won my family's heart, just like she's won mine.

Maybe things aren't so bad in San Antonio, after all.

Seventeen

The next week, a rapid succession of texts sounds from my phone while we're eating dinner.

Ding, ding! Ding, ding!

I smile and know right away—it's the Sapphires' group chat.

After Hallie filled the empty spot on the team, I thought for sure she'd delete me. But I checked my phone each day and it never happened.

It's a really big chat so no one seems to notice me. I'm a fly-on-the-wall, as my mother would say. *Ding, ding! Ding, ding!*

"Can I please be excused?" I ask my mother. "I have so much homework tonight!"

She gives my father a satisfied look—their older daughter

is such a great student. "Of course, habibti."

I leave them beaming at the table and rush to my room to look at the texts.

I kind of like being a fly-on-the-wall, I've discovered. I like knowing which girls are in or out this week, which boys the Sapphires think are cute, or who has a crush on whom. It doesn't matter that I'm not really a part of the conversation, since Waverly and I are friends. She's all I need.

The last text in the thread is from Hallie: *Waverly, if u c this, text us back ASAP! I want her out!*

The skin on the back of my neck prickles. *Her* could mean anyone, right? I'm just feeling overly sensitive, since Hallie's been mean to me since I started at Forest Hills.

As I scroll up to find the start of the thread, my hand starts shaking and the screen looks fuzzy. I struggle to focus on the swimming words.

> **Kayla:** Where is she from again?
> **Hallie:** Who cares? She's NOT like us.
> **Chloe:** She's Arab or something like u c on the news.
> **Hallie:** My dad says they r terrorists!
> **Chloe:** OMG! Like they hurt people?
> **Kayla:** Scary! I don't want to be around her!

Hallie: Waverly, I know ur just being a school helper, but c'mon, she might b dangerous!

Kayla: Hey, could she b on this group?

Chloe: OMG, she is! Waverly added her!

Hallie: Waverly, if u c this, text us back ASAP! I want her out!

They're talking about me. How could they think I might be like the dangerous people you see on the news? How could they be scared of someone like me?

I know there's terrorism, but my family and I would never hurt anyone. We're American—Arab American.

I sit still on the edge of my bed and break out in a cold sweat. The details of my room start to fade. My pink comforter looks gray, and so do my matching curtains. My desk in the corner looks far away. I try to focus on the little loops in the rug under my feet, but everything starts spinning. I feel like I'm being carried away.

I try to suck air into my lungs, but I can't. Big choking sobs fill my throat. My stomach cramps like I'm getting punched over and over until I'm going to be sick, then I scramble to my bathroom and my dinner comes up.

When there's nothing left, I look in the mirror.

Before we came here, I liked my face. But now, I have

a wish list a mile long: I wish my dark brown eyes and my prominent nose away; I wish for pale skin that's not olive or lentil-colored; I wish away the dark hair that sprouts above my lips and between my eyebrows.

I wish I weren't an Arab girl.

The Sapphires didn't want to know me, but I pretended it didn't matter.

I pretended I didn't notice their cool stares on the bus, their side-eyed glances in class, or their snickering as I walked the track. I pretended I didn't notice their cupped hands and whispers at lunch, or how Hallie started mispronouncing my name on purpose.

I thought that if Waverly was my friend, things would get better, wouldn't they?

But now I know the answer—no. And Hallie's taken my name-calling to a whole new level.

My mother knocks on my door a little later and I turn the shower on to disguise my shaky voice. I tell her I'm tired and turning in early, then I stand in the shower until the steamy water turns my brown skin pink.

The Sapphires' mean words swirl in my mind as I cry into my pillow that night: *terrorist, scary, dangerous.* How could they think those terrible things about me, when they barely know me at all?

I wish I were back in Detroit, with my best friend Dina right across the street, a friend who's more like me. It was silly to think I could somehow blend in at my new school. It was silly to think my Arab family could belong here in Texas.

It was silly to think that my What If daydreams would somehow come true.

In the morning, I stay in bed with my comforter pulled up tight. When my mother finally knocks at my door, I can't help it—my tears start all over.

"Mama, I think I have the flu!"

She rushes to my bedside and touches the back of her hand against my forehead. "You threw up?"

I clutch my stomach and nod.

She hurries from my room. "Do not worry! I will be right back with soda water and bread."

I reach for my phone when the door shuts. *What if the texts didn't really happen? What if it was all just a bad dream?*

The texts are still there. The mean things they called me are still there. Hurt floods over me again as I read through them.

But Waverly never responded last night. She doesn't think those awful things about me like the others. She knows how mean Hallie can be. I'm sure all the girls do. So she'll take my side—since she's my friend.

My mother calls Forest Hills to tell them I'm not coming today, and I curl up on the sofa in my pajamas while she and Sitti pamper me all morning.

I can't tell her the real reason I don't want to go to school, what the Sapphires did to me. She'd be in Principal Neeley's office in a split second if she knew what happened. There would be a meeting and the Sapphires would be forced to make apologies through their fake tears. Then my mother would go home, and I would have to deal with the aftermath at school on my own.

I spend the afternoon watching movies, and the sharp pain begins to dull. I call Waverly when school lets out and she doesn't pick up, but there are no more mean Sapphires texts. Things must be blowing over.

The rest of the day, I go back to pretending—that things are fine, that things haven't really changed, that they'll go back to the way they used to be just as soon as my friend Waverly Jones clears everything up.

The next morning, it's obvious things are different the instant she gets on the bus.

Waverly's eyes meet mine and slide away, then she walks right past me to sit with Chloe and Kayla. They talk and joke the whole way to school like nothing's happened— like today's any other day.

But for me, it's the day my worries come true.

When we get to school, I get off the bus and wait for her near the steps. I grab her arm as she breezes past me.

A big lump forms in my throat. I choke out, "Waverly, did you see the texts? We're still friends, right? You don't think those awful things about me, too, do you?"

Chloe and Kayla stand behind her looking uneasy, shifting from foot to foot. Hallie appears out of nowhere. "Let go of her!" she snaps. "She doesn't like you anymore, get it? She's *my* best friend. We don't want you to sit with us anymore! Go find your own friends!"

Waverly's sky-blue eyes hold mine for a split second and I plead to her one last time. "Can we just talk . . . away from them?"

She looks away and her lips tremble, but she doesn't answer.

The bell rings and I let go of Waverly's arm. Then she follows the other Sapphires up the steps, and I'm left standing there, all alone.

I run behind the school to call my mother. "Mama! I feel like I'm going to throw up again! Please, please come get me! I need you to come and get me right now!"

Eighteen

Gossip travels fast in middle school. By the next Monday, whispers float down the hall past my locker. People who never noticed me before look me over as they pass.

I dump my books into my backpack and hurry to first period math, which used to be my most favorite class, but now it's my least—since Hallie's in it.

I keep my eyes to my desk the whole period. I don't look at my teacher, Esmeralda, or any of my classmates. I especially don't look at Hallie, but I can feel her eyes on me, satisfied.

The Sapphires' mean words keep flooding my mind. Now that they've said them, I can't dam them up. I can't pretend anymore.

Mrs. Shelby catches me as I'm about to leave for second

period. "What's going on, sweetie? You look upset today. You're just not yourself."

My voice cracks. "I can't talk about it. Things just . . . aren't easy for me here."

She reaches her arms out to give me a quick hug, and all the feelings I'm holding in overflow. The dam bursts. My voice shakes and my eyes well up. "I'm so, so sorry." I back up. "I just need . . ."

I just need to leave now!

I race down the hall through the passing students to the bathroom to hide. As soon as I burst through the door, my tears overflow.

But I'm not alone. Ayelet stands at the mirror putting on some lip gloss. She sees me, and her face falls.

Great. I rip a paper towel from the dispenser. *Just great.*

What if she's afraid of me, too?

I mop up my blotchy, wet face with the stiff paper, but it's no use. My tears just keep coming.

Ayelet locks eyes with me and says, "I heard what happened."

Of course, she did.

The bell rings, and I look away. I rip off a few more paper towels. I don't care if I'm late to my next class. I can't go back out into the hall looking like this.

Ayelet digs through her backpack and slides a mini packet of tissues to me across the counter, then she zips her lip gloss into a front pocket and slings her backpack over her shoulder. She stands there, locking eyes with me again. She's going to be late, too.

She bites her lower lip. "I'm so sorry they did that to you, Yasmeen. They're such bullies. Try to keep your chin up . . . okay?"

I don't know what to say. She's being so nice to me again. I nod my head, and she's gone.

By lunchtime, it seems like everyone in seventh grade is talking about how the Sapphires pushed me out. Who did I think I was, anyway, a new girl trying to run with the popular crowd?

I keep my eyes focused on my tray as I move through the hot-lunch line to get my pizza. "¿Qué pasa, mi niña?" one of the nice ladies behind the counter asks, the same one from my first day at school. "¿Por qué la cara triste?"

I look up. I'm not sure what she says, but her eyes are so kind. I force a half smile to reassure her that I'll be all right. But I'm not so sure.

Now that I'm not eating lunch with Waverly, I don't know who to sit with. I don't know if there's a Venn diagram at this school that could ever include me.

I scan the room for friendly faces, and notice Esmeralda sitting with a group of dark-haired girls. But after our unicorn challenge problem, I'm not exactly sure she's a friendly face. I take my chances and sit down next to her, but she's speaking in Spanish with her friends, so I start eating lunch in silence.

She finally turns to me and gives me a sympathetic look. "Hi, Yasmeen, rough time, huh?"

My lips quiver. "Hi, Esmeralda, I guess you could say that. This school's . . . more than a little rough."

She nods and opens up a yogurt container, then puts a sugary pastry on a napkin and slides it in front of me.

I look at the container and suppress a small smile, my first of the day.

"Try it. My dad's pan dulces are really good," she says. "And you can call me Esme for short."

Right then, a deep voice echoes across the cafeteria: "Prima!" A goofy-smiled boy wearing a soccer jersey brings his tray over and plops down. He gives Esme's ponytail a tug.

"Stop it, Carlos!" She squeals and turns to me. "My cousin is *so* annoying."

"Hey." He gives me a quick nod and looks at Esme. "Aren't you going to introduce me to your friend?"

"Who? Her?" she says, pointing at me.

"I'm Yasmeen," I say. "Yasmeen Khoury."

He stares hard at his cousin. "Yasmeen? *Someone* told me you called yourself Yolanda. Oh well, where are you from, anyway? You don't exactly have a Spanish accent." He waits for an answer.

"I'm from Detroit, Michigan, but, umm . . . I'm Arab. Like my family is from the Middle East, on the Mediterranean Sea. Do you know where that is?"

He shakes his head. "Nope! I know where our family is from near the border, and I know San Antonio. I've never been anywhere else."

How can I explain that I've never been to the Middle East, either? That where my family's from has everything to do with me, and at the same time, it has nothing to do with me. I say, "My dad is from Jerusalem, you know, from the Bible."

He opens his eyes wider as he takes huge bites of his pizza. He practically inhales his food. "Like where Jesus died? Man. Cool."

Cool? After what happened with the Sapphires, being Middle Eastern seems anything but cool.

Carlos and Esme look a lot alike. They both have the same shade of dark brown hair, the same athletic build, and they're both around my height, which means they're not very tall. And they both speak with an accent just like my family does.

I'm about to ask them how long they've lived here when Carlos jumps up. "See ya!" he says, then he throws his plate on his tray and walks away.

Esme tells me they're from a small town in an area near the Texas border with Mexico called the Rio Grande

Valley. She and her dad came to San Antonio right before sixth grade after her mother passed away, and they brought her cousin along, too.

I swallow my bite of pizza and push my tray away. "I'm so sorry about your mom, Esme," I say.

"Thanks," she says, giving me a small smile. "She was sick for a really long time. I miss her."

I nod. "What about Carlos?"

"He lives with us during the school year since his parents travel for work. They're migrant farmers. He's almost like a brother, so it's great having him around . . . except when he's being annoying."

"What's a migrant farmer?" I ask.

Esme's eyes look like they're going to pop out of her head. "Yasmeen, don't you ever watch the San Antonio news? Migrant farmers move from place to place and follow the harvest."

I can't imagine what it's like to move to a new city after your mom passed away or what it's like moving without your parents.

I clear my throat. "Wow, all that sounds pretty rough, Esme."

She shrugs. "Yeah, moving was hard for both of us at first. My dad says it takes a while to get used to a new place."

Does it ever. I stare across the room to where Waverly

144

sits with the Sapphires. "Maybe it takes a while for this new place to get used to me, too."

Esme follows my glance. "Yasmeen, why do you even care what they think? You're way better off without them."

I work up the nerve to ask, "Esme, have any of the Sapphires ever said anything mean . . . to you?"

"Yeah," she says. "That freckly girl Hallie and I had a few words. Let's just say she won't be calling me anything other than my real name ever again."

The girl next to Esme asks her a question in Spanish, and she turns away from me.

And I can't help it—I look back over to the Sapphires' table. I do care what they think, even after what they said about me. I especially care what Waverly thinks. I really thought we were friends.

How could I have been so wrong?

"Your mother has a surprise for you, Yasmeen!" my father says a few nights later when I come downstairs at dinnertime after finishing my homework.

Sara slams her book shut and raises her hands in a finish line cheer. "Finally! Are we going to a real restaurant for dinner?"

I follow them from the living room to the kitchen, where my mother's in another full-on Myriam Khoury frenzy, whisking foil-covered platters onto the table.

She smooths the hair away from my face and nods to Sitti. "Yasmeen, habibti, we think you can use a little . . . pick-me-up, so I have prepared a very special dinner for you." She peels the foil back on one of the platters. "We are having American hamburgers!"

All the adults in the kitchen look at me with wide, forced smiles. They seem overly eager to see my reaction to my special dinner. I'm instantly suspicious.

I eye the platter of hamburgers; at least they're flat and round this time, not long and skinny-shaped like kafta patties. My mother's even bought iceberg lettuce and condiments—ketchup, mustard, and mayonnaise—and real hamburger buns. She's only missing a jar of sliced pickles, which has been replaced of course by a jar of pickled turnips and beets.

But still, I have to admit—I do feel a little bit better.

Since I faked the flu last week and called my mother from school sobbing the very next day, she's been watching me out of the corner of her eye and fawning all over me, trying to cheer me up. She even wants to take me on a shopping spree over Thanksgiving break in the teen clothing section at the mall. Usually, she tries to squeeze me into kids' clothes, since she thinks they're less showy.

She said, "Seventh grade is time for a new wardrobe, habibti," and actually winked.

But tonight, my mother is trying extra hard. I know

how difficult it must've been for her to put bleached-white hamburger buns in their see-through plastic bag into her shopping cart, since store-bought bread falls into her category of *not real food*.

Sara's ecstatic about our mother's attempt at a normal American dinner. She assembles her hamburger and explains while chewing, "Hamburgers are not only delicious, they're also *economical*. Lots of Americans *subsist* on them."

Salim is excited, too. "Yummy! Yummy!" he chants with his ketchup-streaked little face. "You like hamburgers, too, Meenie?"

I smile at my little brother. "Yes, Salim, I like hamburgers, too," I say, and my mother looks relieved.

Our oven dings, and she whisks out another platter. She's also made french fries for us. They almost look like fast-food fries but smell curiously like spicy Arab food.

I put a hamburger on my plate and spread ketchup on my bun, then take a cautious first bite. Sure enough, it tastes just like a kafta patty, flavored with cinnamon and allspice.

My mother wipes her brow with her dish towel and looks at me expectantly. I say, "Mama, these burgers are just the pick-me-up I needed."

Nineteen

Somehow, my mother knows about the Sapphires' texts without me telling her anything at all.

I'm taking a pop quiz the very next day in my Texas history class. We're finally studying the Texas Revolution, which has been my favorite unit so far.

The year started with Texas geography and its Native peoples, then moved on to the early exploration of Texas by Europeans and the Spanish Colonial era, and then to the Mexican National period when Texas was actually a part of Mexico.

Now we're focusing on the War of Texas Independence and the famous Battle of the Alamo. It's really exciting, so just like Sara, I want to go there sometime soon.

The intercom buzzes just as I'm filling in the last

question on my quiz. One of the office ladies says, "Can you please send Yasmeen Khoury to see Principal Neeley?"

My pen suspends in midair. My mouth goes dry.

Principal Neeley?

I've never actually met him. He probably doesn't even know who I am.

I look at my teacher, and he nods. Then I move in slow motion while my classmates whisper around me: stuffing my papers into my binder, zipping my pens back into their case, dropping my books into my backpack. I can't look at anyone.

I leave my quiz on my teacher's desk and shuffle into the hall. As I make my way to the front office, there's only the dull hum of the overhead fluorescent lights and my shallow bursts of breath.

What could the principal want with me?

When I get there, one of the ladies points to an open door and I hear the sound of my mother's determined high heel tapping on the hard floor, even before I see her.

My mother is here—at school.

"Hello, Yasmeen," Principal Neeley says, waving me inside. "Please shut the door and take a seat next to your mother."

I avoid looking at her and focus on the principal. He looks a little scared, with dark sweat rings forming under his armpits. But I can still hear her—the sound of her jingly bangles has been added to her tapping foot.

My stomach lurches and sour juices sting the back of my throat like I might throw up for real this time.

What's my mother doing here?

She leans over to give me a reassuring squeeze, but I stay stiff as cardboard. "Principal Neeley," she says, "now that my daughter is here, we can get started."

I finally turn my face to her. I know the look in her eyes well: it's the look that makes Sara and I stop bickering, the look that makes our whole family throw on our church clothes and jump in the car, the look that even makes my father do the dishes after dinner sometimes.

Principal Neeley pulls his tie away from his neck and clears his throat. "Very well. Now, Mrs. Khoury, when we talked on the phone this morning, you said that some of the girls were err, texting your daughter in an anti-Arab . . ."

How does my mother know about the texts?

She takes her phone from her purse and scrolls through it with her painted red index finger. She finds what she's looking for and slides the phone in front of him. "I downloaded a very helpful new application to my phone yesterday and look at what I found!" she says.

He reads through her phone, shaken. "Mrs. Khoury, Yasmeen . . . I assure you. This kind of mean behavior is not allowed—"

My mother interrupts him. "Of course, you mean *racist*

behavior, yes? They called my daughter a *terrorist*. It goes beyond just being mean. It is completely *unacceptable*."

A chill moves through my body. My mind goes numb.

My mother can read my text messages on her phone, too?

I always knew she had expert-level reconnaissance skills, but I never thought she'd use them on me. My stomach lurches again as it dawns on me—*she's been spying on me!* Apparently, she's way more tech-savvy than I thought.

Principal Neeley clears his throat again. "Yes, err, I suppose the texts *are* a bit racist, and err, we won't tolerate that kind of thing at Forest Hills. We're a top middle school and I assure you, err, we'll get to the bottom of this."

I glance at my mother again. Her piercing eyes and set jaw say it all: she's not the Mama whose hands shook behind Baba at the fast-food restaurant; she's not the soft-spoken Mama from my first day of school; she's not the Mama who waits for a neighbor to wave first.

She means business, and she's ready to stand up for me.

The only problem is, I'm worried that since she's standing up, I'm going to be pushed farther down.

She stares at Principal Neeley long and hard, until he averts his gaze and pulls at his choking tie again. Then she drops her phone in her purse and rises from her chair, satisfied. "You'll keep me informed about these racist girls and their punishment, yes?"

I slump in my chair and stare straight ahead, unable

to move a muscle. But inside, I'm jumping up and down, screaming, *How could you spy on me, Mama? It's none of your business! I don't need you!*

"Yasmeen, would you like to spend the remainder of the day at home?" the principal asks.

I open my mouth, but no sound comes out. Then I pick up my backpack, brush past my mother, and run back to class.

I know my mother thought she was doing the right thing, standing up for me against the Sapphires and their mean-ness, calling out their racism. But just as I worried, she only makes things worse.

By the next week, the whole school's talking about what happened, even the teachers.

Everyone on the group chat gets called into Principal Neeley's office—Hallie, Chloe, Kayla and even Waverly, whose name is mentioned in the texts though she didn't respond to them.

The Sapphires stick together and cover for each other. They play innocent and smooth over their behavior. Every-one leaves crying, except for Hallie.

Hallie leaves the principal's office meaner than ever.

Everyone but Waverly gets punished with after-school detention starting right after Thanksgiving break for the whole month of December. That means instead of extra rehearsals for the Elite Showcase, Hallie, Chloe, and Kayla will have to sit in the school cafeteria for two hours every afternoon thinking about how much they hate me.

It doesn't help that Principal Neeley schedules an emergency assembly with a special counselor who's an expert on cyberbullying, which is bullying over electronic devices like your phone or laptop.

I sit still as stone during assembly and imagine every set of eyes in the cafeteria fixed on me. When it's over, I dash through the halls to gym class, where I can at least walk around the track to clear my head.

But as I near the Sapphires' practice on the far side of the field, I learn I have a new name now, one that Hallie's comfortable saying right to my face: *snitch*.

Twenty

During Thanksgiving break, the screaming inside me quiets. I go silent, at least where my mother is concerned.

It's not like I intended to give her the *silent treatment*, at first. It's just that after all my screaming, I don't have any words left for her.

Sara's chatter fills the sound void. She comments on everything and anything with sheer abandon, now that she isn't competing with me. She talks so much that at first, my mother doesn't seem to miss my voice in the room.

When my mother finally notices I'm not speaking, her explanation for my silence is obvious; of course, I'm quieter than usual—I've been through so much at Forest Hills. I've been seriously harmed by those "terrible mean girls" and their racism.

She gives Baba and Sitti knowing looks, and proclaims more than once, "I am telling you! It has been proven! Children learn these terrible things from their parents!"

Eventually, my silence wears on her and she begins to chatter like Sara.

"Yasmeen, habibti, what would you like for breakfast?"

Silence. (And I make myself a pita and halawa sandwich.)

"Habibti, would you like to go on your shopping spree now?"

Silence. (But I walk toward the car since I *could* use some new clothes.)

"Yasmeen, did you enjoy our American Thanksgiving dinner? It was another little pick-me-up, yes?"

Silence. (The turkey tasted like cinnamon and allspice.)

By the Saturday after Thanksgiving, she finally catches on that my silence is reserved for her. "Yasmeen, why are you not talking to me?" she demands, heel tapping.

I keep my mouth sealed shut.

Sara grins at me. With a look of admiration on her face, she informs our mother, "Yasmeen's giving you the *silent treatment*, Mama, since you know, you kind of violated her *privacy* by reading her texts."

My mother's heel taps faster. "*Privacy?* What privacy?"

I know I'm not exactly being fair to her, but I don't care. She didn't have to keep tabs on me like I couldn't be trusted. She didn't have to come to my school. She didn't have to be a spy.

I glare at her and reach for the stack of yellow sticky notes she still keeps on the kitchen counter. Then I write my note, smack it on the refrigerator, and run to Baba's office.

spying = silence

I try to video chat Dina, 1,489 miles away. Her mother's picture pulses larger, then smaller, then larger again. *Please pick up, please be there. I could really use a friend right now.*

No one answers and her mother's picture fades with a *pop!*

Moving to San Antonio has been great for my parents, with Baba's big new job and my mother's fancy suite. It's even been great for Sara, who blends in since she barely looks Arab.

But San Antonio is terrible for me. It's worse than I

ever thought it would be. Just like I worried while playing What If with Dina on my last day in Detroit, no one here likes me.

I've lost Waverly, my first Texas friend, and now I've been labeled a snitch at my new middle school.

Sunday during St. Anthony's services, I sit next to my mother in the pew while she makes more observations. My silent treatment morphs into one-word answers.

"Yasmeen, habibti, your new dress from our spree looks just like the older girls' dresses, yes?"

"No!"

"Habibti, today is a good day for you to start taking Communion again since I noticed you have stopped, yes?"

"No!"

After the priest concludes the service, one of my mother's new friends gets up to make announcements. "Today is the day we've all been waiting for," she says, smiling at my mother. "The Magic Is the Night dance troupe sign-up!"

Great. That's just what I need right now.

My mother claps her hands. "It is very exciting, habibti, yes?"

"No!" I snap and slide out of the pew.

All the middle and high school girls at St. Anthony's sign up for Magic Is the Night, and apparently today, so will I. I'm not really being offered a choice.

I watched a video on the internet from last year's Folk-life Festival since we didn't have a dance troupe at my old church in Detroit, and their performances are nothing like the Sapphires' routines.

Instead of cute drill team uniforms, Magic Is the Night dancers wear sequined tank tops and long, billowy chiffon skirts with jingly coined belts. Instead of waving pom-poms, they wear bell-sounding finger cymbals. Instead of dancing to pop or hip-hop, they dance to Arabic music.

And the Magic Is the Night dance steps look even more complicated than the Sapphires' routines I couldn't figure out.

Americans think of our dancing as belly dancing, but for my mother—it means much more. She sees the troupe as a way for me to connect to my cultural heritage and make some nice new church friends here in San Antonio.

But I would rather do almost anything else.

After services, we head into the community hall for lunch. My mother practically sprints to the sign-up sheet, which is all too conveniently located on the dessert table next to the flaky baklawa pastries, which I love.

I follow her the whole way, miserable.

"I am telling you! Everyone loves this style of Arab dancing!" she says, sweeping her red-fingered hand from one side of the community hall to the other. "You will like it, you will see. Such beautiful music and costumes! So much fun!"

Finally, I've had enough of her not noticing how I feel. I've had enough of her making choices for me without even asking.

The words I've been holding in since she came to my school spit out of me. I yell loud enough for everyone to hear, "I can't even dance, Mama! And if I could, I'd want to be on my school's drill team! I told you I don't want to be in our church's dance troupe! Why can't you ever understand? I just want to be A NORMAL AMERICAN GIRL!"

But there's no talking my mother, Mrs. Myriam Khoury, out of anything.

She puts her red fingertips to her cheek, like it's been slapped, but regains her composure in a split second. Her eyes dart around the room to see if any of her new friends are within earshot. Fortunately for her, it's just our family watching us fight, sulking nearby. The skin under one of her eyes twitches wildly, and her nostrils flare as she signs my name on the list with a flourish.

Then my mother turns on her heel and click-clacks toward the exit. As she passes our family, she motions for them to fall in behind her.

So, they do. Baba and Sitti exchange worried glances and hop up from the table with Sara and Salim. They leave their desserts unfinished and follow my furious mother outside. I stand at the table by myself for a minute, staring at my name on the list, then I burst into tears and run after them.

My parents tell me that being citizens of the United

States of America is really important to them. They tell me we're living a dream in our big new Texas house. But what I've figured out that they don't seem to understand is this: to be a real American, you have to act like one.

Twenty-One

The first day back at school after Thanksgiving break, it's almost like I'm new all over again. It's almost like my friendship with Waverly never happened, like it was just one of my daydreams. Except, it did happen.

We were friends, until Waverly decided we weren't.

Sara and I wait at the bus stop with the Cohen kids that morning in our usual silence. Things feel really awkward since I ran into Ayelet in the bathroom during the Sapphires mess. We're back to stealing glances at each other, neither of us brave enough to make the next move.

In math class, Mrs. Shelby keeps a close eye on me, and watches Hallie, too. Each time my teacher turns her back to the class, I wait to hear the new name I've been given—snitch—but the name never comes.

Mrs. Shelby catches me as I'm leaving class. She says, "Yasmeen, I'm just checking in with you after the break. How are you feeling, sweetie . . . after what happened?"

I can tell she really cares. "I'm fine," I say. "I'm sure it's all blown over."

"Very well . . . ," she says, but she doesn't seem convinced at all.

Neither am I.

I go through the motions before lunch, and I stick to myself. I'm still a fly-on-the-wall, but now, there's no fun inside information to learn since I've been completely pushed out.

Esme's table is full at lunch. In a brave second, I look for Ayelet, but she's eating with the friend she sits with all the time and they're engrossed in conversation.

So, I take a seat in the far corner of the cafeteria by myself. I can't watch the Sapphires whisper and laugh or shake out their long, shiny hair and parade around with their chins held high.

I especially can't watch Waverly act like she never met me.

The noisy room hums around me.

"Why the long face?" A deep voice cuts into my thoughts. I look up—I'm not sure how long Esme's cousin Carlos has been standing beside my table.

He slides in next to me like I invited him for lunch, and my face flashes red-hot. I glance around the cafeteria to see if anyone's watching. Us sitting together with Esme seemed okay, but the two of us sitting alone in the far corner of the cafeteria—that seems like something else.

Carlos doesn't seem to notice as he shovels food into his mouth, just like the first time I met him. He says between bites, "So are you all the way over here because that girl Waverly's not your friend anymore?"

I lower my eyes and nod.

"And you actually liked hanging out with those drill team girls?"

I nod again, but when he says it like that, I'm not exactly sure. I liked being on the inside, even just a little. I liked pretending I belonged.

"Hey, charro!" one of his soccer teammates calls from across the room.

Carlos turns around and waves, then he stands up with his tray and kicks at the waxed floor tiles for a second. "Well, if you ask me, you're way better off without them . . . and you can come sit with me and Esme anytime."

Then he smiles his goofy smile and says, "Later, Yolanda!"

The next day after school when I get home, my mother says, "Yasmeen, yallah! Run upstairs and put on a dress! We cannot be late!"

I blink at her, confused for a minute, but then I

remember—my Magic Is the Night costume fitting is today at Mrs. Haddad's house.

My stomach instantly twists into a knot.

Both my mother and grandmother are smiling ear to ear, all dressed up and ready to go. My mother wears a sleek skirt and an elegant, tailored blouse, and Sitti wears one of her fanciest embroidered Palestinian dresses. And they're both wearing their gold bangles, all of them, extending up their arms.

My grandmother gets up from the kitchen table and wraps her arms around me, then she slides four bangles off one of her wrists and puts them on one of mine.

I don't know what to say. I sputter, "Shukran, Sitti, shukran!" and hug her tight.

She kisses my forehead while my mother beams. Right then I realize—me dancing in the Magic Is the Night dance troupe is hugely important to both of them. It means way more than I thought.

I throw on a dress and we speed out of our neighborhood across town. My mother's "Don't Get Lost, Lady" app expertly guides us to Mrs. Haddad's house.

Almost: her lady actually takes us on a slight detour. I notice in the rearview mirror that the skin under one of my mother's eyes starts twitching again.

We're a few minutes late. The yellow sticky note on the front door says: Min fadlik—come on in! So we head inside.

Mrs. Haddad's house bustles with excitement.

Two young women stitch away at loud sewing machines under the dining room chandelier surrounded by bright bolts of fabrics stacked against every available wall space. Young girls and their mothers stream in and out the front door, scheduled for costume fittings all afternoon.

I walk over to a mannequin in the corner of the room that models one of Mrs. Haddad's elaborate creations, a shimmery gold-sequined top and a long, violet chiffon skirt with a jingly band of coins at the waist.

I have to admit—it's beautiful.

My mother greets Mrs. Haddad as she hurries from the kitchen to welcome us, and cuts to the chase. "Nothing *showy* for Yasmeen, like some of these girls," she says, eyeing a curvy high-school-aged dancer who's parading around with her navel exposed.

Mrs. Haddad puts my mother's worries to rest. "Mrs. Khoury!" she says, taking her hand. "Here, we are modest! But what can I do with these older girls? They can sew! If they adjust a little at home, well . . ."

She winks at me and my mother tries to ignore it.

I run my hands over the silky bolts of fabrics, mesmerized by the rainbow of colors. I especially like the pale peach one.

"Habibti!" My mother notices the fabric that catches my eye. "That one would be very nice with your olive complexion."

Mrs. Haddad grabs the bolt and corrals us to the kitchen. "Sit down, sit down," she says to my mother and Sitti, and gestures to the kitchen table. "My home is your home! Would you like some tea, pastries?" She winks at me again. "We are all women here, no men allowed. It is almost a party!"

Sitti greets her favorite church friend, who's at the table with her granddaughter. The girl looks fairly miserable. She tells me that her fitting's been done for a while and she and her grandmother are just socializing now. It may be a party for our mothers and grandmothers, but for us, I'm not so sure.

Mrs. Haddad checks my name on her clipboard and tells me to head to her laundry room to change out of my dress to be measured for my costume. The girl at the table gives me a sympathetic look.

Change out of my dress into what? I wonder as I head down the hall.

When I open the door, her laundry room has been transformed into a dressing room complete with a tall three-way mirror, a row of chairs to sit on and wait your turn, and a long rack of sparkling Magic Is the Night costumes.

Two girls are inside: Nadine, the girl my eyes have been glued to all these months during church services at St. Anthony's—the girl who acts like she's on stage—and a girl about my age.

I gulp. Both of them are in their underwear and bras, so I guess I'm not really going to change into anything.

Nadine sits on one of the chairs and waits while Mrs. Haddad's assistant runs a measuring tape over the younger girl's chest and hips in front of the mirror and scribbles her dimensions on another clipboard. I notice both girls have long dancers' legs and graceful necks.

"You must be Yasmeen," the assistant says, turning the younger girl around and measuring from her collarbone to her waistline. "Take a seat, and you can get undressed in a minute when I'm finished with Sylvie."

I shut the door behind me. I run my hands over the costumes on the rack on my way to the chairs. They're so, so soft. I wish I could stand in the middle of the rack and let them fall around me.

Maybe everyone would forget I'm here.

Nadine raises her perfectly shaped eyebrows and looks me over. She combs her long, shiny hair with her fingers and says, "You're new."

I nod and can't help staring at her lacy panties and full bra. I don't know where to look. Her figure is already womanly like my mother's—it's nothing like mine.

"Can you dance?" she asks, jiggling her foot on the floor.

I mumble, "Umm, not very well . . . my old church didn't have a dance troupe like St. Anthony's."

She uncrosses and recrosses her long legs. "Well, you'll

dance for me at our first practice on Sunday and we'll see."

The door cracks open and one of the seamstresses passes a costume to Nadine. "I've let out the bust and hips, so you'll get another year from it," she says.

"Thanks so much," Nadine says, then she stands up and slips it on. She steps closer and turns her back to me. "Zip me up."

My hands feel rubbery. I fumble with the zipper for what feels like forever, then finally get it up and clasped.

When she turns back around, my breath catches. The cherry red of her costume perfectly matches her lips, and the gold bodice and coins at her waist catch the warm tones in her hair.

Mrs. Haddad's assistant looks over from measuring Sylvie and says, "Still a little snug, but it's one of my favorites. It's gorgeous on you!"

"Thanks. It's my favorite, too," Nadine says with a smile. Then she tosses her hair and slips out of the room.

The quiet in the kitchen immediately erupts with clucks and whistles when Nadine appears. My heartbeat quickens as I peek through a crack in the door.

She smiles, twirls around, and everyone starts clapping. The kitchen turns into the ladies-only party Mrs. Haddad says it is.

I hold my breath and watch.

Finally, Mrs. Haddad pinches Nadine's cheek, then

Nadine hurries into the laundry room. She turns her back to me again. "Undo me."

I work the zipper in slow motion. Mrs. Haddad's assistant says, "Next, Yasmeen." I look up, and Sylvie's already dressed and walking to the door.

"What are you waiting for?" Nadine says, slipping her blouse on. "Get undressed."

I try not to think about my little girl chest and my narrow hips. I try not to think about my short, compact figure that doesn't seem like Nadine's or Sylvie's—like a dancer's figure. I try to imagine what I'll look like in my Magic Is the Night costume.

I don't think I'll look anything like them.

I take a deep breath and drop my dress to the floor and my new bangles jingle. Then I turn my back to the three-way mirror while I'm being measured for my costume.

Twenty-Two

I'm still in bed Sunday morning when it's time to leave for St. Anthony's.

My mother barges into my room and flips on the lights. "Yasmeen! Get dressed! Today is your first Magic Is the Night dance practice after church," she says, as if I didn't already know. As if I could somehow forget that I'm signed up for the dance troupe after last week's fitting.

With my two left feet, I'm almost as worried about Magic Is the Night as I am about the Sapphires, and that's saying a lot.

All last week, new whispers floated down the hall at school. Rumor has it that Hallie's been absolutely furious about serving her after-school detention and she's out to get me—again.

"Mama, I think I have the flu," I whimper.

But this time, she's not buying it. She walks to my bedside and holds the back of her hand against my forehead and tsk-tsks. She says, "No fever. Come downstairs in ten minutes," then she breezes out of my room.

All during services, I shift in my seat and can't get comfortable. The knots in my stomach twist tighter and tighter.

"What is wrong with you?" my mother says. "You have so many ants in your pants!"

I guess that's one way to describe it, but whatever it is—knots or ants—I've got it bad.

I close my eyes and pray, since church is the perfect place to ask for something you really, really need. *Please let my mother notice how upset I am about being in Magic Is the Night. Please let her understand that I'm just not a dancer. Please let me skip my first practice today.*

But my prayers aren't answered.

After services, I slide out of the pew and follow Sylvie and a stream of other girls to the bathroom to change for practice. Right away, I see I'm not dressed for the part. I brought a baggy T-shirt, sweatpants, and sneakers; they brought tight black leggings, cute blousy tops, and ballet slippers.

The girls pull their hair away from their faces into high ponytails and buns. I try to push my unruly hair behind my ears since I didn't bring anything to tie it back, but it just springs into my eyes again.

We line up in the community hall in front of a dance area that's been cleared of tables. "She was a lead ballerina for the San Antonio Ballet." Sylvie nods toward Nadine, who sits by herself at a table in the corner of the hall flipping through a magazine. "Clara in *The Nutcracker* for two whole years!"

The girls around me put their hands to their mouths and *ooh* and *ahh*.

A tall, slender woman glides into the room and introduces herself as Ms. Mansour, our dance instructor. She tells us she was a dancer with the troupe when she was a young girl, which from the looks of it was ages ago. Apparently, Magic Is the Night has been an important part of St. Anthony's for forever.

"Girls! I have a big announcement!" She walks back and forth in front of the line, making eye contact with each one of us. "This year we are so lucky. Our lead dancer Nadine has time to help choreograph for Magic Is the Night!"

Excited whispers pass down the line and the girls clap, so I do, too. Nadine stands up and waves like she's the winning contestant in the Miss America pageant.

Ms. Mansour continues. "Next June, our dance troupe is going to be featured at the annual Texas Folklife Festival on the main stage, for the first time ever! Hundreds of people will be there to watch!"

All the girls start clapping again.

What? I knew we would be dancing at the festival this spring, but I kind of thought that we'd be in the background, and maybe adults would be the feature entertainment, not a bunch of middle- and high-school-aged girls in sequined tops and chiffon skirts.

But we're not just a part of the show next year, we *are* the show. My stomach knots tighter; now, I really do feel sick.

Ms. Mansour divides us into groups by age and I spend the next painful hour learning basic dance techniques, which of course I'm horrible at. Then she passes out finger cymbals and tries to teach us to produce a pleasing sound. But some of us make noises like kindergartners smacking tambourines—me especially.

The new steps and dance routines are confusing, and I can't keep time. I listen and watch and try to mimic the other girls but somehow, it only gets worse.

I crash right into Sylvie and my finger cymbals fall to the floor with a *clang!*

"Ow!" she cries, rubbing her arm.

I say, "Oh my gosh, I'm so sorry!"

"That's okay, Yasmeen," she says. "But can you please watch where you're going?"

I nod, then notice she puts some extra space between us before she resumes her routine.

Nadine takes notes the whole time we're practicing, then she assigns us our positions. I'm placed in the front row next to Sylvie.

This must be some terrible mistake!

It means I'll be in the row closest to the crowd next June at our festival performance, and then everyone—my parents and the whole congregation—will be right there to watch me mess up.

I start to raise my hand, to ask Nadine if maybe I should be in the back row since I'm new and, well, I'm obviously a horrible dancer, but the look she gives me keeps me quiet and makes me put my hand down.

The look says, "Practice makes perfect, Yasmeen, and I expect nothing less. And next time . . . lose those sweatpants."

Most of the girls have danced in the troupe before, and some of them even talk about being on school teams like the Sapphires. They're dancers and I'm not. Just like at school—I don't belong here, either.

My mother was wrong. Dancing with Magic Is the Night is anything but fun.

Finally, Ms. Mansour motions for us to clear the dance area. "Girls, good work for today. Take a seat and rest your feet, and our lead dancer will show you how it's done!"

I find a spot at a table and massage my sore feet while

Nadine glides to the middle of the floor.

She stands perfectly still, her head held high like the ballerina she is, her arms stretched long at her sides, her finger cymbals open and ready. A sheer scarf drapes her long, shiny hair and covers the lower half of her face. Her eyes half close and focus on the distance.

She extends one long leg and points her toes, then hovers her leg over the dance area, ready.

The music begins on the overhead speaker system, a song I recognize from my mother's playlist. It's about a girl who drinks from a magic well in her village and transforms into a phoenix—free—flying high in the sky.

Nadine's hips sway side to side. The veil falls to her shoulders, exposing her beautiful face, wistful and full of emotion.

The song builds, and she moves faster and faster, each step timed perfectly to the beat. Her hands flutter like hummingbirds' wings and the sound from her cymbals fills the air. She flies her scarf overhead and twirls round and round. It's almost like Nadine becomes the phoenix in the song.

It's almost like she's flying.

Everyone watches, silent: there is only the music and Nadine's dance.

I can hardly breathe. I've never seen anyone dance like this. It's like her body tells the song's story and there are no What Ifs, there's no pretending. Nadine tells the story like it's her story.

And I wonder for the first time—is it my story, too?

Unfamiliar emotions well up and I fight back tears. I've been listening to this kind of music—Arabic music—my whole life. But I never felt anything, until now.

Twenty-Three

The next few weeks at school, I'm not sure where I belong. I'm not sure I intersect with anyone.

I clearly don't belong with Waverly and the Sapphires—with each passing day of Hallie's after-school detention, she seems to get madder and madder. I'm not sure I belong with Esme and Carlos, even though I'm sitting with them most days at lunch, since Esme is still really competitive with me in Math Lab. And Ayelet Cohen—she's Jewish and Israeli, and I'm Arab—so how could we ever be friends?

I stick to myself while I try to figure things out, but it becomes hard since someone else starts sticking to me, too.

Hallie bumps into me in the hall one morning after first period math. She slams her shoulder into mine and I teeter off-balance. "Oops! Sorry," she says, in a way that doesn't sound sorry at all.

The next day, she's waiting in front of my locker between classes. "I need to get some books," I say.

She leans her back against the metal door and smirks, and my eyes dart from side to side. I catch Waverly standing in the doorway to her class, eyes big, mouth turned down. But she turns away.

Hallie cackles. "No one's going to rescue you this time, snitch!" Then she blocks my locker until the bell rings before skipping off to class.

My hands get rubbery again. It takes me three whole tries to get my combination right and I'm five minutes late to class.

A few days later, I go to the bathroom at lunch and Hallie corners me with Chloe and Kayla. She stands inches from my face, clenches her teeth, and says, "We don't want you here. Why are you still at this school?" and waits for my answer.

I open my mouth, but no sound comes out. My eyes well up.

Because my parents left our home forever. Because I didn't have a choice. Because if I had a choice, I would've gladly been left behind in Detroit.

Hallie laughs at my tears and the other girls join in. She says, "Maybe it's best you leave."

My body starts to shake. I've heard that line before—from that terrible racist man at the fast-food restaurant. Now I understand what Baba meant about not being welcome someplace, not being wanted.

I'm not welcome or wanted at Forest Hills Middle School.

They leave me crying in the bathroom, and I remember the Sapphire that Waverly told me about who messed up in last year's Elite Showcase and cost them the win, whose transfer was "for the best."

Maybe Hallie's going to bully me until I transfer schools like that girl did.

So while the Sapphires serve after-school detention, I hug the corners at school and keep my head down. I'm still a fly-on-the-wall, I'm just one that gets swatted over and over.

The last Friday before winter break, I walk around the track by myself again during gym class. I'm about to round the bend where the Sapphires practice, and they notice me.

I'm torn between turning around and walking against the flow of students and trying to sprint past them. But I know I'd never outrun them, since I'm way too slow.

Maybe I really should transfer schools.

The Sapphires cup their hands to their mouths and start to whisper, and someone runs up alongside me. It's Ayelet.

"Hi," she says.

"Hi," I mumble.

"Rough week?" she asks.

"Rough *weeks*," I say. "Really rough."

"I'm so sorry, Yasmeen. Those girls are such jerks!"

We walk in silence for a few minutes, and I'm grateful to have some company during gym for a change—even if it's a little awkward again and I still don't know what to say to her. I've been at this school for months now, and the whole time, I've been walking by myself.

The Sapphires stop whispering and back off. They look disappointed, like Ayelet has just ruined their fun. Maybe bullying one person is easy, but two people, well—two people might just fight back.

The look on Ayelet's face as we pass them doesn't hurt, either: her green eyes flash hard.

Right then, Esme whizzes by us on the inside lane of the track, her thick ponytail trailing behind her. The force of the wind she creates practically knocks us over. "Hey, slowpokes!" she calls over her shoulder, laughing.

"Hey!" we call back in unison.

"Whoa," Ayelet says.

"Whoa is right. She's super fast." I may be able to beat her in Math Lab, but on the track—no way.

Esme pauses for a second and talks to Carlos, who's practicing with his soccer team at the other end of the field near the gym. He sees me and yells, "Hey, Yasmeen!" and I can't help it, my face heats up red-hot again.

I raise my hand and give him a little wave, then I put my hand down, quick. He waves back and runs after his soccer ball.

"Who's that?" Ayelet raises an eyebrow.

"Oh, that's just Esme's cousin Carlos . . . he's really nice." My voice catches a little.

Ayelet smiles like she knows something.

"What?" I say.

She smiles bigger and says, "Oh, nothing!" and glances at my baggy gym uniform.

My sweats slouch around my ankles and my shirt billows out like a camping tent. Her gym uniform must be at least two sizes smaller than mine. It hugs the curves of her body in a way that I'm sure would seriously alarm my mother.

She notices me gaping at her. "My mom thinks my uniform's a little *showy*, but whatever."

I crack up. Where our mothers are concerned, we're not so different after all. "My mom uses words like *showy*, too!" I look down at my uniform and laugh. "I don't have much to show yet so no chance of that for me!"

Esme laps us a second time and calls, "Hey! Are you two standing still or what?"

Now we're all cracking up, and I can tell for sure—my

Math Lab competition with Esme's going to be a friendly one.

Ayelet's eyes follow mine back across the field to Carlos. His face breaks into a goofy smile each time he looks my way.

She looks at me and wiggles her eyebrows. I cover my laugh with my hand and shake my head. Then we walk together for the rest of gym class.

That afternoon when I hop on the bus, Ayelet's backpack isn't on the bench next to her like it usually is—it's stowed underneath. So, I slide in next to her and we talk the whole way home.

Twenty-Four

Saturday morning, furious chopping noises echo up the staircase from the kitchen.

I stumble down in my pajamas to a near-restaurant-style assembly line. There's a big platter covered in layers of aluminum foil along with several smaller ones, and nearly all our recycled yogurt containers sit waiting to be filled.

"What's all this for?" I ask.

My mother grins at Sitti and gestures to an invitation on the refrigerator, a small card I've somehow missed amid all her sticky notes. "We are preparing for tonight's neighborhood holiday party! It is another potluck!" she says.

The good feelings I've had since yesterday on the bus instantly evaporate.

A neighborhood party? Will the Joneses be there?

I walk to the refrigerator to read the invitation. It's even worse—tonight's holiday party is being held right in their cul-de-sac.

Ever since Waverly walked away from me that day on the school steps and broke my heart into a thousand pieces, I've been avoiding her, and she's been avoiding me.

On the bus, I sit in the front and she sits in the back; at lunch, I eat with Esme and Carlos as far away from the Sapphires' table as I can; and during seventh period advisory, she sits behind me and I never turn around.

My mother doesn't know that we haven't said a word to each other in over a month. She thinks we're still friends, since Waverly never responded to the Sapphires' racist texts and she didn't get detention like the other girls.

She doesn't know that Waverly chose her mean friends over me. She doesn't know that Waverly's best friend, Hallie, still torments me at school while Waverly looks the other way.

My mother doesn't know because I haven't told her. If I did, just like at school, she'd only make everything worse. She'd probably call Mrs. Jones!

Then I have a horrible thought. *What about the Cohens? Will they be at the potluck, too?* Mr. Cohen doesn't know that I never told my parents that he coaches Math Lab.

And neither does Ayelet.

I feel dizzy. I stagger over to the kitchen table to sit

down. If everyone finds out that I lied, I don't know what they'll think of me. I have to tell my parents about Mr. Cohen, but I don't know how.

So, I squeak in my smallest voice, "Do we have to go?"

My mother looks at me, perplexed. "Yasmeen, what are you saying? Of course, we are going to the party! Of course, we would like to meet more neighbors!"

It's pointless—there is no talking my mother, Mrs. Myriam Khoury, out of anything at all.

That afternoon, I drag myself downstairs behind my skipping little sister when we're called. Sara's super excited about the holiday party, unlike me.

She doesn't have any little white lies to worry about.

Despite my family's obvious attempts at blending into tonight's holiday scene, I'm sure we won't: my mother's wearing a velvety forest-green dress, her high heels, and all her gold jewelry; my father's in slacks and a festive red button-down shirt; Sara's wearing a skirt and a much-too-hot Frosty the Snowman sweater with tiny pom-poms for buttons, and Sitti's wearing what she always does—a long Palestinian thobe.

I'm wearing another church dress.

Little Salim tugs at his itchy holiday sweater, until Baba shows him that the nose on the reindeer lights up. He's excited for a minute, but then he frowns at his little red wagon outside on the front porch—it's loaded with the food platters and all the yogurt containers for the potluck.

Baba pats his head and says, "Big boys can walk a little way!"

But Salim whines and shakes his head.

I stick up for him. "Mama, I'm no expert but I think you're only supposed to bring one thing to a potluck," I grumble, but she ignores me.

We head up the hill to Waverly's cul-de-sac, each taking turns carrying Salim. When we get to the party, we wheel our wagon straight to the long buffet tables to unload it.

I scan one of the tables—the buffet doesn't look anything like the ones at our after-church luncheons. We usually have rice with chicken or lamb, chopped salads with tahini dressing, sides like hummus and baba ganoush, and big trays of baklawa dripping with sticky sweet syrup.

This buffet consists of carved turkey and roast beef platters, trays of mini sausages, and saucy meatballs on colored toothpicks. There are bowls of creamy macaroni, jiggly green Jell-O molds, and salads with chunks of ham, red peppers, and peas.

Salim makes a break for the table where the desserts are located, and my mother rushes after him. Just as he reaches for a sugary cookie, she grabs his hand and shakes her head. "Let us mingle before eating!" she says, and click-clacks off with him on her hip to meet some new neighbors. We all file in behind her, even me.

Within minutes, I see everyone I'm worried about—the

Cohens, the Joneses, and even Chloe and Kayla with their families.

And they see us.

Ayelet smiles at me from her family's table, and I muster a half smile back. I close my eyes for a second and try to feel brave. Maybe it's time for me to face my little white lies because now, they don't feel so little anymore.

But when I open them, my parents and Sitti have already turned away. They're whispering and hustling over to the Joneses. Ayelet's parents are whispering, too. Her face has clouded over and she's hugging her arms across her chest.

And it's just like Baba says it is in Jerusalem. Palestinians and Israelis may live side by side—they're neighbors—but they don't ever want to be friends.

Not even in America.

But I know Ayelet likes me, and I like her, too. I hope that somehow, I'll have a chance to explain what just happened. I hope that somehow, we can still be friends even if our families can't.

She looks at me for a second, and there's no more smile. I give her a small, sad wave, then I turn and follow my family.

"Myriam! How nice to see y'all again!" Mrs. Jones is saying when I walk up. She air kisses my mother, who laughs and air kisses her back.

Mr. Jones pumps Baba's hand up and down. "Elias! It's

great to meet the whole Khoury clan!"

Waverly hides behind her parents. It's obvious from her face she hasn't told them we're not friends anymore. I guess I'm not the only one who's been pretending and holding on to lies.

Mrs. Jones turns to me. "Sugar, we've missed having you over! It's been way too long, right, Waverly?"

Waverly nods a little too slowly.

My mother catches my eyes and her smile wavers. I must look how I feel: upset about what just happened with the Cohens, upset about seeing Waverly.

Then she puts her smile back on and tells Mrs. Jones, "Of course we miss our Waverly, too!"

The whole time our parents talk, Waverly looks anywhere but at me. Her eyes shift around the crowd for an escape plan, but there's nowhere to go.

If there were, I'd be there, too.

I'm sad, just being around her, even though I don't want to be. The hurt's still there, right below the surface, even though I want to push it out. Maybe just like Sitti beginning again after her house was torn down, beginning again after what the Sapphires did to me will take some time.

I think of how Hallie treats me at school, and shudder. *How can you begin again when someone's still hurting you?*

When Chloe and Kayla call, "Waverly!" she gets her escape plan.

"Merry Christmas, everyone! Bye, Yasmeen!" she says

and runs off to join them.

My parents talk with the Joneses for a few more minutes, then we mingle and meet more neighbors.

I watch them work the party. They call *Merry Christmas!* and *Happy holidays!* They laugh at everyone's jokes.

When our neighbors ask them where we're from, they say we're from Michigan. If they ask where we're from before that, my parents don't say we're Palestinian or Lebanese and certainly not Israeli. They don't say we're from places where there's unrest and war.

They say we're from the Middle East—like it's a country you could be from. Like it's a place that smooths over the details that might make someone uncomfortable about exactly who we are.

And it works. Our neighbors ask my parents about their college days at the University of Michigan and about my father's new job. They talk about our schools, the traffic, and the weather—like we're Americans, all the same.

Finally, Salim starts whining that he's hungry and we walk back to the buffet tables. We move through the line piling unusual foods on our plates, and when we get to our platter, my mother announces loud enough for everyone to hear, "I made these delicious American hamburgers for our potluck!"

Then it dawns on me: at least on the outside, my parents want to blend in here, too.

Twenty-Five

Sunday after church, I mope around the house. Every time I look through our big picture window hoping to catch a glimpse of Ayelet, she's not there. Her house looks dark, empty. Maybe her family went out of town.

I'll have to wait for school to start back up to try to talk with her.

My father notices my sad face and takes me with him to a grocery store parking lot to pick out our Christmas tree. Only a few trees are left, their pine needles browning and dropping in the warm Texas weather, collecting in little piles on the pavement around their trunks.

I can't help thinking that just like me, they'd rather be up north.

We choose the best one and bring it home and stand it

up in the corner of the living room, then I help my mother unpack the very last boxes from our move down to Texas.

Each ornament revealed from crumpled paper and hung on the tree makes me feel a little bit brighter. There's the little gold North Star that I got on my first birthday, that started all my starry wishes; there's the Santa with his fuzzy white beard and jolly red cheeks; there are real crystal icicles that catch the multicolored Christmas light strands, one for each member of my family.

My mother runs to the kitchen and brings back a little box and presents it to my grandmother. Sitti opens it, and a tear slides down her cheek. Now, there's an icicle on our tree for her, too.

Last, we carefully unwrap the olive wood nativity set that Baba brought with him from Jerusalem when he came to college in Michigan, and arrange each piece on one of the brass tray tables in our living room.

"Where is baby Jesus?" My mother sifts through the box of crumpled paper, alarmed.

I unfold my hand. I've been clutching him tight, just like I've done so many times before. He's way shinier than all the other pieces in the set from how often I've held him this way.

My mother places him in the manger and pushes the hair away from my face. She's been watching me since yesterday at the potluck. She holds my eyes with hers and says, "Now, it is home sweet home, yes?"

I nod. *Maybe it is, just a little.*

Later, I video chat with Dina in my father's office. I enter her mother's address and her face fills the screen. "Hi, Yasmeen!" she says. "Merry Christmas! Happy early birthday! Did you get my card?"

Seeing her makes my heart squeeze tight, but I try to sound chipper. "Hi, Dina! I did. Thanks so much!"

She picks up her mother's laptop and goes to the window. The snow outside her house is falling in huge, soft flakes. "Look, Yasmeen!" she says. "We're going to have a white Christmas in Detroit this year! Isn't that amazing?"

"How great!" I say, but it doesn't feel great. The grass outside Baba's office window still grows green in the warm Texas sun. The temperature in San Antonio hasn't even fallen below fifty degrees.

Dina takes her mother's laptop around her house and shows me different snow views, and we talk a while longer. Then my old best friend and her white Christmas fade from the laptop with a *pop*!

I convince myself that if it would just snow—things would be better. That a white Christmas might make San Antonio feel enough like home, for now.

All December, I prayed in church for it to snow this winter in Texas, but it hasn't. Our puffy Michigan jackets hang untouched in the hall closet by the living room.

I head into the kitchen where my mother is chopping away. "Will we ever need our winter jackets here?" I ask her.

She looks outside and shakes her head.

My throat tightens. "Never?"

Sara pipes up from the table. "Yasmeen, Texas is a lot more *temperate* than Michigan. Actually, the climate here is *subtropical*, with hot summers, mild winters, and occasional flash floods during the spring. Didn't you know that?"

I go back to Baba's office and type "San Antonio annual snowfall" on his laptop to double-check my know-it-all little sister. Sara's right. According to the National Weather Service, it rarely snows here.

But rarely doesn't mean never.

There have been a few real snowstorms in San Antonio's history, but usually, the city barely gets enough to scrape a snowball together.

But even a little snow would be a white Christmas, right?

That afternoon, my family assembles in the living room: Baba helps Sara memorize her flash cards for the regional spelling bee in February; my mother flits between baking Christmas cookies in the kitchen and checking the big picture window for neighbors she might talk to; and my grandmother sits in a rocking chair, knitting what looks like a winter cap.

What if it's a sign?

Outside our window, sure enough—the sunny Texas sky has turned cool gray, like right before it snows.

I get up from sulking on the sofa and go to the hall closet, and even though it's balmy and warm, I put on my puffy jacket and walk back through the kitchen and out the patio door into the backyard.

I open the narrow little door on the far side of the fence and step into the wide-open space, then I sit on the bank of the little creek and pray for snow again.

I hope someone is listening.

After a while, Sara walks outside with Salim and they sit on either side of me. "What are you doing out here, Yasmeen?" she asks.

"It's none of your business!" I snap. She looks away, hurt, and I soften. "I'm waiting for snow."

She nods. "I miss it, too. Having a polar bear poster in my room feels a little silly now."

Salim holds his little hand to the gray sky. "Snowballs, Meenie?"

I shake my head. "I don't think so."

"I'll be right back!" Sara runs inside and comes back with winter jackets for her and Salim, and she helps him put his on. She's put crushed ice into little plastic baggies for us to mush into balls. "Maybe these will help," she says.

After we make our snowballs, I put my arms around

my siblings. Then we sit in the wide-open space and wait together.

On a bright and sunny sixty-degree Christmas morning, we unwrap all our presents. My mother surprises me with a few pairs of leggings and some cute blousy tops that I can wear to my Magic Is the Night practices. Santa gives me a *Just Dance* video game, and she winks.

Salim gets another ride-on vehicle—a little race car— and he zooms around the house on it making *vroom, vroom!* noises until he falls asleep under the Christmas tree. He doesn't get his speed from Baba, that's for sure.

Sara gets more sparkle pens for her spelling bee flash cards, and some bright-colored boxes to organize them in. She also gets a pink cowboy hat studded with little rhinestones to match her pink cowboy boots.

But her favorite gift is a Spanish dictionary. She hugs each of our parents. "I wanted this so, so much!"

My father gives my mother a bright red apron that says: Kiss the Cook. She blushes almost the same color as the apron. She gives him a pair of white sneakers for the long neighborhood walks he likes to take.

My parents give Sitti a little silver-colored spade and some vegetable seed packets, and she says, "Shukran, shukran," and tears up.

"What are those for?" I ask, and Baba's eyes twinkle.

He says, "This spring, we will help your grandmother plant a new garden."

The Saturday before school starts back up is my thirteenth birthday.

"We have a little surprise for you!" my father announces. "We are going on a family outing to a fancy restaurant your mother selected, followed by a trip to the San Antonio River Walk to see the Christmas lights!"

"Finally, a real restaurant! How *extravagant*!" Sara cheers.

I have to admit—I'm excited, too. Dinner at a real restaurant sounds like a birthday treat, and ever since Baba told us about the candlelit Fiesta de las Luminarias along the River Walk at Christmastime, I've wanted to see it. He says that over two thousand candles will glow inside sand-filled paper bags along the river's banks.

The fancy restaurant turns out to be a new Lebanese restaurant on the other side of town near St. Anthony's: the Phoenician Palace. My mother orders for us all, then spends the next hour and a half gleefully critiquing each dish.

When we stand up to leave, she turns to me and says loudly, "I know! I know! Next year, I will cook for your birthday, habibti. These restaurants are no match for meals at home!"

But the River Walk turns out to be my real birthday gift.

I've never seen so many festive Christmas lights all in one place; the entire tree canopy has been draped in them. If it weren't for the luminarias, I'd hardly be able to tell where the river starts and ends with all the colors bouncing along the shimmering water.

As my family joins the tight stream of people making their way around the river, the holiday cheer is contagious. Before long, we're smiling and laughing, pointing out items we like in the shop windows, tipping our faces to the sparkling lights.

For a while, all our worries fade away.

It doesn't matter that my grandmother is still having a hard time adjusting to her new life here, and it doesn't matter that Baba still watches the evening news reports with faraway eyes. It doesn't matter that Hallie's still so mean to me at school, or that I'm worried that Ayelet and I might not be able to be friends.

It doesn't matter that our Christmases in Texas might not ever be white Christmases.

My sister sees a group of mariachis singing with the crowd and yells, "I know what they're saying! Feliz Navidad means 'Merry Christmas' in Spanish! I looked it up in my new dictionary!" Baba smiles and pats her head.

Sara and I belt out the song with the crowd, and for just

the hint of a moment, I'm really a part of things in San Antonio.

My parents stop in a small open square with less of a crowd to rest on a bench, and I grab Sara and Salim by their hands. We spin around and around in the clearing, laughing until our sides hurt.

And soon enough—everything seems like it's spinning: the candles on the banks, the kaleidoscope of lights in the tall trees, the twinkling stars high above in the big Texas sky, and my parents and my grandmother, smiling from the bench.

The whole world spins, and we spin with it—all the new people we've met in San Antonio, all the old friends we left behind in Detroit, and the people in the West Bank, Gaza, and Israel far across the ocean.

I close my eyes and make a birthday wish—when the whole world stops spinning, when I land where I'm meant to be—that I'll finally feel at home again.

Twenty-Six

The first morning after winter break, Ayelet and I rush up to each other at the bus stop and both start talking at once.

"I have to explain about the holiday party, why my parents . . . ," I say.

"Me too! I was so mad! I worried about what happened the whole time I was visiting my cousins! My parents didn't want to talk to yours . . . ," she says.

"Really? I thought that it was just my family . . ."

"No! Are you kidding? There've been *lots* of tense discussions about having Palestinian and Lebanese neighbors at my house! Don't *even* get me started!"

"Us too! We've never had Israeli neighbors! At least, my father says he hasn't in America!"

"My dad says there were Palestinians in our neighborhood in Israel when I was little, but we never even talked to them!"

I stop and take a breath and smile at Ayelet. "Well, you're talking to one now."

She smiles back. "Yup, I sure am!" Then we pick up right where we left off before winter break.

The whole time, Sara looks from me to Ayelet and back again. Her eyes practically pop out of her head. As the elementary school bus pulls up, she turns to Ayelet's little brother and holds out her hand to shake. "Hi, I'm Sara."

"Shalom," he says. "I'm Tal."

"I know," she says. "Is that Hebrew?"

Tal nods. "We say it for *hello*, but it really means *peace*."

Sara lights up. "Just like salaam! Shalom! I think I'll add Hebrew to the list of languages I want to learn. I already speak some Arabic and I just got a Spanish dictionary for Christmas."

Tal smiles and pumps Sara's hand up and down, then they hop on the bus and sit together in the very first row.

On the ride to school, Ayelet and I are so deep in conversation that I don't even notice that Waverly's gotten on the bus, but Ayelet does. Her eyes narrow, and she turns around to glare at her. But not me—I'm not thinking about the Sapphires at all.

When we get to school, my day only gets better and better. I actually pinch myself to make sure it's all real, that I'm not caught up in another silly daydream, that I'm not just playing What If.

During Mrs. Shelby's math class, Hallie doesn't glance my way. And at lunch when I eat with Esme and Carlos, it feels like we've been sharing a table all year long.

No one at school looks at me funny like I don't belong. No one calls me a name that's not mine.

I float down the halls between classes and think— maybe everything that happened with Waverly and the Sapphires has finally blown over. Maybe it's finally been enough time, and everyone's used to me. Maybe I finally blend in.

Mrs. Shelby catches me as I walk out the door after advisory. "Yasmeen, you must have had a wonderful winter break!" she says. "I'm so happy to see your smile again."

I nod and say, "Thanks, Mrs. Shelby." Then I hustle to gym class.

She's right—I did have a wonderful break. I made a birthday wish, and it's starting to come true.

Later that afternoon in Math Lab, Mr. Cohen glances at the timer on his phone. "Whoops! Pencils down, wizards . . . we've run a little over. I'm sure your folks are waiting for you outside."

"I got it!" Esme says, and flies up to his desk so he can check her work.

"A magician you are, indeed, Miss Gutierrez!" he says, looking at her answer.

She grins at me and skips back to her desk.

We're working mini challenge problems today and Esme's managed to finish two of them correctly before I have. Usually, we're tied neck and neck, but who's keeping score? Especially now that I know our competition is a friendly one.

I glance at the clock on the wall. We're more than a little over—our session has run an hour and fifteen minutes!

I hurry up and pack my things, and grin back at Esme. "You got me today, but I'll catch up on Thursday! You're not the only wizard in this room with a stellar wand!"

Ayelet groans from the desk behind me. "Why are you two playing into my dad's magic obsession? I thought you guys were my friends!"

Esme and I laugh. "We *are* your friends," I say, turning around and smiling at her.

She smiles back, and I giggle. "It's just that Math Lab is so magical, Ayelet. We're caught in its spell!"

She rolls her eyes and starts throwing her things into her backpack, just as my father's voice booms from the front of the room. "Yasmeen, yallah! Let's go. NOW!"

It's so out of place. My parents never come to the

classroom to get me after Math Lab. I always meet them in the parent visitor spots of the parking lot. I guess they've never had to, since we've never run late—until now.

I slowly turn back around. Baba stands in the doorway, and he doesn't look happy. His face is cut in hard lines and angles again. His nostrils flare as he tries to control his breathing, but it's barely working—he's fuming.

He's glaring at Mr. Cohen, whose eyes shift from my father to me and back again.

My face burns. My not-so-little white lie has finally caught up to me.

Mr. Cohen clears his throat, walks to the doorway, and holds his hand out for my father to shake. "Hello, Mr. Khoury! We finally meet . . ." His voice trails off when Baba refuses to shake his hand. He steps backward into the room.

I stare at my desk. I can't look at Baba's angry face or Mr. Cohen's confused one.

Ayelet taps my shoulder. Her voice shakes. "Yasmeen, what . . . what's going on?"

And I wish I had told her about my white lie to my parents. I know now, my lie wasn't just to them—it was to Ayelet and her father, too.

Esme echoes Ayelet. "Yasmeen? Why is your father so . . . so mad?"

I can't look at them—the shake in their voices is too

much. I can't see what might be in their eyes, too.

I keep my face down as my eyes fill with hot tears. I follow my father out of the room and into the hall without saying goodbye to anyone.

Left, right, left. We retrace my now familiar pattern through the long hallways of Forest Hills. Baba doesn't turn around to look at me, and he doesn't say anything more. I shuffle behind him, sniffling and wiping my runny nose on my sleeve.

We push through my school's front doors into the bright afternoon and there's a shiny new truck loaded with gardening equipment parked next to Baba's car. Bold forest-green letters read: Gutierrez Landscapes. A man who looks just like Esme smiles and waves as we approach, but when he sees my teary face, he glances away.

My father turns to me in the passenger seat and hurls questions without waiting for answers in between. "So, Math Lab is coached by Mr. Cohen from across our cul-de-sac? You have not been spending your afternoons with Mrs. Shelby, your favorite teacher? You've been lying to us, all this time?"

"Yes, Baba. Yes, Baba. Yes, Baba." I feel smaller and smaller as I answer each question. "I'm so sorry, but I didn't think you would—"

"Would what?" His eyes flash dark and hard. "Want my daughter to be around an Israeli, who thinks what happens to Palestinians is all right? Who thinks demolishing peo-ple's homes, like your grandmother's home, is all right?"

"But Baba, Mr. Cohen wouldn't hurt anyone! He isn't like those people. He's different."

My father doesn't answer, so I keep going. Maybe he'll hear me. Maybe he'll understand.

"Mr. Cohen is funny and he's a really good math coach. His daughter, Ayelet, says her dad's family moved to Israel when he was in high school, but he wanted to raise his kids here in Texas. He's American, too . . . just like us."

Baba starts the car. He grips the steering wheel with stiff arms and tight knuckles just like he did at the fast-food restaurant. He turns to me one last time. "I thought a daughter of mine would never lie, Yasmeen. I am very disappointed in you."

His words feel like a slap, even though my father would never raise a hand to me. And I know—our conversation is over.

He turns the radio on, and faraway voices fill the empty space in our car. Then he backs out of the parent visitor spots and drives silent the whole way home.

When we pull into our driveway, I bolt from the car and run inside. The rest of my family is nowhere in sight. I rush upstairs and slam my bedroom door shut.

A few seconds later, Baba's office door on our first floor slams, too.

I collapse on my bed, and tears come harder and faster, like a raging river that might carry me away.

I knew lying to my parents was wrong, but I told myself that if they ever found out, they'd see what I see—that Mr. Cohen and Ayelet are nice.

But Baba didn't see that at all.

I'm so confused. *The Cohens are nice, aren't they? They're Israelis, but they're not like the people who demolished Sitti's house, are they?*

They can't be—they're our neighbors—and Ayelet's my friend.

My stomach twists into worry knots. *What if I can't go to Math Lab anymore? What if my new friendship with Ayelet is over just as fast as it started?*

I'm getting so tired of all my useless What Ifs.

Twenty-Seven

By the time I calm myself down, it's almost dark; the winter sun fades outside my window. I listen for the rest of my family, but our house is still quiet. They must not be back from Sara's after-school activities.

I tiptoe downstairs through the kitchen to the living room, and that's when I hear it: my father's voice in front of our house—even angrier—along with Mr. Cohen's.

Baba yells, "I don't need *you* to tell *me* about my daughter!"

Mr. Cohen yells back, "She's gifted, and she needs to continue with Math Lab!"

My head spins. My father and Mr. Cohen are arguing. About me.

I storm out the front door onto the porch. Ayelet stands in the big picture window of her house. Her scared eyes hold mine.

We watch our fathers stand face-to-face in the cul-de-sac, flinging words at each other.

I hear a series of *I*s and *you*s and *did you ever*s and *you have no right*s, but within minutes, their argument is no longer about me, the Math Lab, or Mr. Cohen being my coach. It becomes the age-old fight between Palestinians and Jews: whose country is the land of Israel, anyway?

"I know why *we* are here in America!" my father says. "But why are *you* here? You still have a home! You still have a country!"

"I don't want my children to have to fight like I did. I don't want my children to know war. It's no childhood. We're here because we want the same as you . . . to raise them in peace!"

My father laughs bitterly. "You could have had peace long ago, if only you shared! But you won't!"

Suddenly, my father's anger becomes my own. I confront him with it—head-on.

I scream from the porch, "Stop it, Baba! Stop it! You're wrong about the Cohens! I know that Sitti was really hurt, I know her house was destroyed, but it isn't their fault! The Cohens aren't our enemies! They're good people! Ayelet is even my friend! WHY CAN'T YOU GIVE THEM A CHANCE? WHY CAN'T YOU MAKE AN EXCEPTION?"

Baba leaves Mr. Cohen in the middle of the cul-de-sac

and comes to our porch. He holds up his hand for me to stop, but angry words keep flooding out of me. I yell louder and louder. "Why does everything have to be about the Palestinians? Why does everything have to be about Israel? You live here now, in San Antonio, with us . . . with me! WHY CAN'T YOU JUST BE AMERICAN? WHY CAN'T WE ALL GET ALONG?"

The more I yell, the more my father's shoulders slump, but I don't care.

Mr. Cohen and Ayelet look on, sad and quiet, not knowing what to do, until finally—I'm all yelled out. I crumple, my anger giving way to more hot tears. My head hurts and my throat hurts, but my heart hurts most of all. It squeezes and throbs like it might burst.

My father moves toward me with outstretched arms to comfort me, unlike ever before. I've been waiting for his pats on the head to turn into hugs for so long, but right now—I don't want anything from him.

I run inside to my room, slam my door, and collapse on my bed again.

I finally told my father how I feel, but it won't change anything. Baba will never leave his sad past behind. He'll never feel at home here in Texas, or anywhere.

And neither will I.

An hour later, there's urgent knocking at my door. "Habibti, I have brought you some dinner!"

"Myriam, hand me the plate and go back downstairs, please," my father says. "I will handle this. It is a matter between Yasmeen and me."

I hold my breath while my mother click-clacks downstairs and hope that somehow, my father will go with her. I'm not ready to talk to him. I'm not hungry, either.

But Baba clears his throat. "Yasmeen, can I please come in so we can talk calmly?"

I squeak, "Yes," then I pull my comforter up over my head. I can't look at him—not after I yelled at him and said what I said, not after what he said to Mr. Cohen.

I hear him set the plate on my dresser, then feel his weight on the edge of my bed. He hardly ever comes up to my room but now, he's sitting right next to me.

"Masalkher, Yasmeen," he says, tugging at my comforter. "Can I please see your face?"

I hold my comforter up tight. "Hi, Baba," I say with a muffled voice, answering his greeting in English instead of the Arabic "masalnoor" on purpose. Then I listen to his long, sad exhale.

"I am very sorry about what happened this afternoon, Yasmeen," he says. "But you should have told me the truth from the beginning. You should have told us that Mr. Cohen would be your math coach, and not Mrs. Shelby."

I flip my comforter down. "I was afraid to tell you, Baba! You hate Israelis! You would have never let me sign up for Math Lab!"

My father looks tired, and older. He shakes his head. "I don't hate anyone, Yasmeen, but I do hate what Israel has done to our people since the Nakba. You know the Nakba, Yasmeen?"

Right away, my anger bubbles up again, but my father's sad face pushes it back down.

Of course, I know the Nakba—since it chases us everywhere.

The Nakba was in our house in Detroit, it moved with us to San Antonio, and it's in the news reports almost every night. Baba has talked about the Nakba for as long as I can remember.

Will anything ever matter to my father as much as the Nakba? Will I ever matter as much? Will he ever let go of the Nakba and be happy in San Antonio, with us? Will the Nakba ever become just . . . history?

The questions in my heart don't rise to my lips. They seem too hard to ask, and I'm worried that the answers my father will give me are not the ones I want to hear. So instead, I ask in a small voice, "Baba, do I have to quit Math Lab now?"

"No, Yasmeen, you can go. I am sure that our neighbor Mr. Cohen is a good math coach."

It's not the only answer I want, but at least it's something.

My father looks out my window at the dark, starry sky, and the faraway look that means he is here, but not really here, returns to his eyes. "It is just not easy between us,

Arabs and Jews. Perhaps we are not meant to be friends."

I don't understand. *We're not meant to be friends . . . ever?* I squeak, "Why can't we be friends as Americans?"

"Yasmeen, it is complicated. You are American, but you are also Palestinian and Lebanese. One day you will understand everything you are."

I nod like I understand him, but I don't.

He reaches over and pats my head. "Rest now, habibti. Tomorrow is a new day for a new dream."

I turn away from him and pull my comforter back up tight, then I wait for him to shuffle out of my room.

I'm not sure what my father's dream will be, but I know this: he may dream in Arabic, the language of his birth, but I dream in English, the language of mine. And I want my dream to include all our neighbors.

Right before sunrise, I dream a new dream, just like Baba said I would.

Ayelet and I are at the bus stop, smiling at each other. The sun's shining, and I finally feel happy in San Antonio. The yellow school bus comes, and we sit together in the very first row like it's something we always do. Like we're best friends.

But when we try to talk to each other, her words come out in Hebrew and mine come out in Arabic.

Twenty-Eight

The next morning, I stay in my room until I hear my father's car pull out of the garage, then I creep downstairs.

Through the kitchen window, I notice Sitti pushing Salim on his backyard swings. Sara's eating breakfast at the kitchen table, leafing through her Spanish dictionary. "Could you please pass the mantequilla, Yasmeen?" she says when I sit down. Then she points to the butter and smiles.

I slide it over and glance at my mother. She's still in her robe and she hasn't done her makeup routine yet. Her eyes are puffy and her hair's an uncombed mess. She sips her morning tea.

"Sabahelkher," I say, and wait for her rapid-fire questions

about my not-so-little white lies. I know I deserve them.

"Sabahelnoor," she says back. "What would you like for breakfast, habibti?"

I shake my head. "I'm not very hungry, Mama."

She says, "Oh?" and leans over to feel my forehead. "You are fine," she says, but it sounds more like a question.

So I give my mother a quick nod, but really—nothing's fine.

She gets up, opens the refrigerator, and puts an orange and a hard-boiled egg in a brown sack. "In case your appetite returns before lunch."

We talk for a few more minutes while Sara finishes eating, not mentioning Baba at my door last night, or the matter between us. The hard questions I've braced myself for don't come, but I'm not sure why.

My father must not have told her what happened yet.

She doesn't know that I lied about Mr. Cohen being my math coach; she doesn't know what happened when Baba picked me up yesterday from school; and she definitely doesn't know that he and Mr. Cohen were flinging words like stones.

I'm sure my father will tell her everything soon, and we'll have a big family conversation about the Cohens and Math Lab and all of my lies.

"Thank you, Mama," I say, slipping the sack into my backpack. Then Sara and I get up from the table and my mother waves us out the front door.

But when we get to the bus stop, Ayelet and I take our old places sitting on opposite sides of the mailboxes, completely quiet again. We're right back where we started.

Our younger siblings start chatting away.

Tal points to the apple in his lunch box and says, "Tapuach."

Sara repeats the word, then she opens a recycled container and says, "Falafel."

"Sara, I'm from Israel." Tal laughs. "I already know that one!"

Ayelet and I watch them talk, but we don't know what to say to each other after the fight between our fathers yesterday. Maybe there's nothing to say. When the bus comes, we sit in separate rows like before.

At lunch, I'm still not hungry. I go through the line with my tray and hardly take anything. One of the nice ladies says, "Hola, niña," and puts a dessert on my tray anyway.

I manage a small smile for her. "Hola," I say back.

I scan the cafeteria for a place to sit. I'm sure by now Esme's told Carlos what happened in Math Lab; how angry my father was and how he wouldn't shake Mr. Cohen's hand. I guess I could try to explain to them why my father doesn't like Ayelet's father—but I'm not sure even I understand anymore.

Things could be different for Ayelet's family and mine in America, right?

I make a beeline for my old corner to sit by myself again,

but Carlos darts in front of me. "Come sit with us," he says, taking my tray. Then he leads me over to his cousin's table.

Esme flips her ponytail, raises her eyebrows, and pats the seat next to her. "Sit down and spill it, Yasmeen."

So I do. Even though I don't really know Esme and Carlos that well, yet—I tell them everything. I tell them all about Palestinians and Israelis, and all about my little white lie that turned big. I tell them all about what happened last night after I got caught.

When I'm done, I sit back and realize I'm hungry all of a sudden, so I eat my dessert. It feels pretty good talking about everything with friends and not holding it all in. I can breathe a little easier for the first time in a long time.

"Man. That sure sounds rough," Carlos says.

I nod. "And now I'm worried that Ayelet and I won't ever be friends again."

Esme takes a bite of another delicious-looking pastry and sees me eyeing it. It's seashell-shaped this time. She rips it in half and slides some over, so now I have double dessert. "My dad makes the best conchas," she says, taking another bite. "Know what I'd do, Yasmeen?" she says while she chews. "I'd just talk to Ayelet. What's the worst that could happen?"

I frown at her, and I'm about to explain, but the bell rings. Lunch is over and we've run out of time.

What's the worst that could happen?

Exactly what's been happening all the way across the Atlantic Ocean, across Portugal and Spain, across the Mediterranean Sea and the southern tip of Italy, in a place I've never been. The worst has been happening for more than seventy years in Israel and Gaza and the West Bank.

And I don't want anything like it to happen in San Antonio, too. I want things to be different. I want things to be better for all of us, here in America.

The rest of the week, each day is about the same: I wait for Baba to leave for work before I come downstairs each morning, I avoid talking in Math Lab, and I walk the track by myself during gym class. What Ifs fill my brain and squeeze everything else out.

One thought plays over and over in my mind—I have to find out who's right about Ayelet and Mr. Cohen once and for all—Baba or me.

Friday afternoon, I finish my homework at my desk, then carry my backpack downstairs. I find my mother in the kitchen chopping a big pile of parsley and onions for dinner as usual, while my grandmother scoops rich, dark soil into the pockets of empty egg cartons and pushes tiny seeds inside.

I'm momentarily distracted, watching Sitti whisper to each finished carton in Arabic as she places it along a windowsill. "What's she doing?" I ask my mother.

She smiles. "Your grandmother is growing little seed-lings for her vegetable garden."

I take a deep breath and clutch my backpack. I know what I'm about to do. I know I have to.

"Mama, is it okay if I go over to Waverly's for a while? She needs help with math again, and I'm still her study buddy and all."

The lie rolls off my tongue like another runaway train. Now that I'm on it, it's almost impossible to get off. Especially since my heart is filled up with all the questions about Palestinians and Israelis that Baba can't answer.

My mother looks at me closely; it's been months since I last studied at Waverly's house.

She glances at the clock, wipes one hand on her apron, and smooths the hair away from my face. "Of course, habibti," she says with a tired smile. "Be back in time for dinner, and please tell our Waverly hello."

Twenty-Nine

I start up the hill toward Waverly's house. I pass five cream-colored homes that look about the same, and when I'm sure my mother isn't watching out our big window, I sneak back down through the yards to Ayelet's.

I raise my hand to knock on her front door, then I put it back down. It's shaking, and I'm breaking into a sweat in the middle of winter. Maybe Baba's right—maybe Arabs and Jews aren't meant to be friends—in Israel or anywhere.

I push the thought away. Ayelet and I were starting to be friends. We both thought so.

Then I suck as much air as I can into my lungs, and knock.

Ayelet opens the door a few seconds later and throws her arms around me, knocking the air back out of my chest. I cough a little as we hug, then we both step back, embarrassed.

"Yasmeen! I'm so glad you came over!" she says. "After what happened in Math Lab . . . and when things were so weird on the bus and at school after that . . . I was so worried you wouldn't want . . ."

A car pulls up to the curb in front of her house and her front door opens wider. The girl Ayelet eats lunch with at school appears with her backpack.

"Bye, Lauren," Ayelet says, "I'll see you at shul tomorrow!"

Lauren waves to both of us and gets in the car and rides away, and I wonder if she's Ayelet's best friend, or if Ayelet's like me—still looking.

Ayelet's mother walks up, wiping her floury hands on her apron. She seems surprised to see me, too. Then Ayelet introduces me to the woman whose flower garden my parents admired on our very first walk around the neighborhood.

Up close, Mrs. Cohen's dark skin and eyes seem distinctly Middle Eastern. No wonder my mother was so confused. She looks more like me than she does her own daughter.

How could that be?

They invite me in. "Welcome to our home, Yasmeen," Mrs. Cohen says in a thick accent that sounds just like my family.

I'm even more confused.

"Thanks," I say, gathering my nerve. I've risked so much, coming here for answers. If I'm going to get them, I need to be brave enough to ask. "Mrs. Cohen, how . . . why do you look and sound so much, umm . . . like my family?"

She throws her head back with a deep, throaty laugh. "Yasmeen, I am Jewish, but all of my grandparents are from the same village in Iraq, an Arab country. They brought my parents to Israel when they were children. Their mother tongue was Arabic! So I speak a little Arabic, too, though maybe not as well as you, and of course, I speak Hebrew and English."

"Oh," I say, nodding my head up and down like I understand, even though I'm still completely confused. I didn't know that any Jewish people came from Arab countries or spoke Arabic. I don't even speak Arabic very well, but I don't tell her that.

My eyes scan the living room. Ayelet's house looks a lot like mine—not just on the outside, but on the inside, too. It's just a little more modern.

How can things be so familiar, but be so different at the very same time?

I follow Ayelet to her room. As we walk down the hall, Tal peeks his head from his bedroom and waves.

I wave back and ask Ayelet, "What smells so good?"

"That's challah," she says. "My mom's baking for

Shabbat, since it's Friday."

I nod my head again and decide that challah must be some kind of bread. But I'm not sure what Shabbat is.

Ayelet looks around her messy room and kicks some clothes aside to make a small clearing on her carpet, and we sit down face-to-face. "Sorry, Yasmeen, I haven't cleaned up in a while." We stare at each other for a few seconds, then she asks, "Do your parents know you're here?"

"No, they don't." I shift, remembering my most recent lie to my mother, feeling even more nervous than I did at Ayelet's door. "Can you keep my secret?"

She doesn't think twice. "Yes!" she blurts.

There's a thick book and a big stack of papers on her dresser, but I don't recognize the writing. I step around her clothes to examine them closer.

"That's Hebrew," she says. "It sounds a lot like Arabic, but the letters look really different. Lauren and I were doing our homework for religious school this weekend."

"Right," I say, like I know all about Hebrew, even though I don't. Maybe I'll listen closer to Sara and Tal's conversations at the bus stop next week.

"Who's this girl?" I point to a faded black-and-white photo taped to her dresser mirror. "Is she your relative?"

Ayelet gets up from the carpet and stands next to me. "That's Hannah," she says, biting her lip like she always does. "Hannah Stein, but she's not family."

I examine the photo closer. Hannah wears a formal-looking dress that's buttoned high up her neck and falls nearly to her ankles. She sits on a tall, tapestry-covered chair in a library full of books. Her dark hair is swept into a loose bun, and her light, piercing eyes smile at the camera. Her hands fold delicately on her lap and her low heels brush the floor. She looks about our age. She's beautiful.

"Who is she, then?" I ask.

Ayelet stares at the photo and bites her lip harder. "Hannah died in the Holocaust. I'm becoming a bat mitzvah in May, and I'm honoring her, since she didn't get to become a bat mitzvah. She didn't get to grow up."

I blink and fight my need to pretend like I understand what Ayelet just told me when I don't. I'm here to ask questions. I'm here to be brave. I'm here to understand what Ayelet and her family are all about.

So, I ask, "What's a bat mitzvah?"

Ayelet looks stunned for a second, like maybe she thought everyone might know what a bat mitzvah is.

"Yasmeen, when I become a bat mitzvah," she explains, "I'll lead my synagogue in prayer and read from the Torah to take my place as a full member of my community. I'll keep Jewish traditions alive for people who weren't able to. For everyone who died in the Holocaust . . . like Hannah."

Back in Detroit, my fifth-grade history teacher taught us about the Holocaust. She taught us that Hitler and the

Nazis in Germany murdered millions of Jewish people. My father explained that the Holocaust in Europe led to the creation of Israel, a new country for those who survived and didn't have homes anymore, or anywhere to make a new life.

But Baba also explained that the Holocaust and the creation of Israel in its wake led to our Nakba. I whisper, "Our Nakba came from the Holocaust, too."

Ayelet's quiet for a moment. "What's the Nakba, Yasmeen?"

Now it's my turn to feel stunned. Ayelet is from Israel—so why doesn't she know about the Nakba?

I tell her, "The Nakba is our catastrophe . . . when Israel was created. Jews who survived the Holocaust were a people without a homeland until Israel was made, but now we've taken their place, since most Palestinians weren't allowed to stay. Now we're a people without a homeland."

Ayelet and I stare at each other, then our eyes fill and spill over. Right then we both understand: for all the family discussions we've both had with our parents—about the Holocaust and the Nakba—there's still so much we don't know about each other even though our histories are forever tied.

But what if we did? What if we understood each other just a little better? And what if our families weren't just neighbors? What if, like us, they could even be friends?

We have to find out—these are the biggest What Ifs we have.

I sniffle. "Ayelet, I want to know more about your bat mitzvah, and I want to learn all about Hannah Stein."

Ayelet wipes her wet cheeks and smiles. "And I want to understand your Nakba, Yasmeen."

We sit back down facing each other on the carpet. "Yasmeen, what the Sapphires said about you . . . it was wrong. And that girl, Waverly Jones, she didn't even stand up for you." She looks over at Hannah's picture again, and says, "Real friends stand up for what's right if something bad is happening. They always have your back."

The hurt of what Waverly and the Sapphires did to me is still there, even though I'm starting to push it out. It's the hurt of being told you don't belong and being betrayed by someone you thought was your friend. But along with the hurt there's something more now—anger.

My sad's finally turning to mad.

And I have a new friend now—I have Ayelet—and I have another wish. Maybe Ayelet and I can leave the past behind. Maybe someday, for us, the Israeli-Palestinian conflict can just be history.

Thirty

The rest of January falls into a pattern: I tiptoe around Baba, but he doesn't say anything more about Math Lab or his fight with Mr. Cohen, I pretend I'm going to Waverly's house a few days a week after school even though I'm really going to Ayelet's, and I trip around the dance floor at my Magic Is the Night practices after church.

The first week in February at lunch, Ayelet sets her hot-lunch tray on the table I share with Esme and Carlos, then plops down like she's been eating with us all along.

"Where's Lauren?" I ask.

She bites her lip. "Oh, she's sitting two tables over. Don't look, she has a *boyfriend* now."

Esme and I turn around to look—we can't help it. Not

many girls have boyfriends in seventh grade. We blink
back at Ayelet.

"I *know*," she says.

In the short time Ayelet and I have been friends, we've
realized we have a lot in common.

We laugh about our mothers' funny sayings and we both
hate lentils. We agree about which boys are nice, especially
one in particular. And I showed her some of the news skits
Dina and I made, then Ayelet and I made one together.
We decided to be co-anchors, and the headlines were great
that day—all sunny skies and all happy endings.

We're also the same in a way that I hadn't even thought
about. We both feel different at school.

Ayelet swallows a bite of her sandwich and says, "There
are only like five other Jewish kids at Forest Hills. I've
counted. There's Lauren . . ." She rolls her eyes at Lauren,
who's scooted super close to her boyfriend. "There's a boy
on the school paper with me, and there's like one sixth
grader and two eighth graders. No one here understands
our holidays. When I missed school for Yom Kippur last
fall, my mother had to come up here and talk to Principal
Neeley since my Language Arts teacher wasn't going to
let me make up a test I missed. He thought Yom Kippur
wasn't a real holiday, but everyone should know it's our
most sacred holiday!"

"That isn't fair at all!" I say, remembering my mother's

visit with Principal Neeley to set things straight. "Well, I'm the only Arab student at this school. There are a couple of Indian kids in eighth grade, a boy from Pakistan in our grade, and a sixth grader from Greece, but that's not the same. We all speak different languages, and we have different religions and holidays. I guess I didn't think of you as a minority, too, Ayelet, since you know . . . you're kind of white like your dad."

"Yasmeen!" Esme says. "Didn't anyone ever tell you it's really rude to talk about someone's skin color?"

But Ayelet just laughs and throws a grape at me. "Maybe things aren't always exactly like they seem."

"I'll say," Esme pipes up, glancing at the Sapphires' table. "I don't know what you two are complaining about. Trust me, even if you're a part of a big minority, maybe even a majority in San Antonio like Latinos are, you'd still have problems with some of the people at *this* school."

Later that afternoon, all the advisories funnel back into the cafeteria for our monthly assembly. I sit with Esme and Ayelet while Principal Neeley runs through announcements and kudos.

"Listen up, students," he says. "Forest Hills Middle School extracurriculars have an exciting spring season ahead. Our soccer team is already off to a winning start. Kudos to the soccer team! Please stand up and take a bow!"

All the students in the cafeteria start cheering, and Carlos and his teammates stand up and cheer with them like they've just won the World Cup. Principal Neeley lets the ruckus go on for a few minutes, then he says, "Okay students, settle down. Soccer team, sit."

He looks down at his notes. "Next on my list, I have track and field. Please rise! I'm sure the competition season will speed past with supersonic results, no pun intended!" Esme stands up, and Ayelet and I nod to each other. Compared to Esme, we walk the track in slow motion.

"And our Sapphires drill team that took second place in last year's Elite Showcase," he continues, "will surely shine again this year!" Most of the girls in the cafeteria clap wildly when Hallie, Waverly, and their team stands up, but the boys start joking around and pushing each other off the benches.

Principal Neeley clears his throat. "Last but not least, our school's Math Lab students are busy preparing for the city-wide competition in May. We hear from our parent coach Mr. Cohen that our chances this year are, in his own words, *fantastical*! Math Lab, kudos! Please stand up and take a bow!" Esme, Ayelet, and I stand up along with the rest of the team, and a trickle of applause flows through the cafeteria, mostly from the teachers on the ends of the aisles.

Our principal has saved his biggest announcement for

last. "Students, I've been waiting to make sure that our generous parent-led fundraising came through again this year before making this important announcement, and it has! At the end of this week the whole seventh grade will experience Texas history firsthand. Instead of holding class, we're going on a field trip to the Alamo!"

Cheering erupts through the seventh-grade student body again, but Esme's face falls. She looks for Carlos down the aisle and they exchange a worried glance. I nudge her. "What's wrong?"

She says, "Nothing, Yasmeen. We've already been to the Alamo and we didn't like it very much."

"Gosh, I'm sorry. Maybe it will be more fun this time!"

Esme nods, even though I can tell she doesn't think so.

But I can't help it—I'm really excited to see the site of the battle after learning so much about it in Texas history class. Plus, Sara hasn't been yet, and she's going to be just a little bit jealous.

On the bus ride to downtown San Antonio that Friday, Esme and Carlos seem even more upset. They sit on the bench behind me completely quiet.

I turn around and ask them, "Did you go to the Alamo recently?" "No," Carlos mumbles. "We went with Esme's dad when we moved here from the Valley."

I try to sound chipper. "Well, sometimes things feel

different the second time around!"

Esme looks at Carlos. "I doubt it," she says.

All five of the buses come to a stop before I can ask her more, and the doors swing open. We file out into the wide, flagstone plaza.

The Alamo isn't at all what I pictured. The way that my teacher described it, as one of the most important sites of the Texas Revolution, I expected it would be bigger, a huge stone monument to Texas independence, but it's not. It's a small limestone building surrounded by tall office buildings.

Each bus splits into two groups of students to be paired with a docent, someone who guides visitors through the complex.

As we walk around, our docent tells us about the famous battle in dramatic, movie-script style, "The brave but tiny Texian army was no match for the larger Mexican army, and its ruthless leader, General Santa Anna. Alas, our Texians died a brutal but heroic death." Then she raises her arm to the ceiling and says, "Texans! Never surrender or retreat! Victory or death! Remember the Alamo!"

Esme's face crumples. "It's the same as last time!" she says, and bolts back through the Alamo's front doors into the plaza.

I watch her go. "Carlos, what's wrong?"

He looks down and shifts from foot to foot, digging his

hands deep into his jeans pockets and pulling them back out again. He eyes the door, too. "It's just hard for Esme and me to be here since we're Mexican."

"What do you mean, Carlos—did your ancestors fight in the battle?"

"No, Yasmeen, but didn't you read the plaque about Commander Travis's letter? The enemy he talks about, that's us. We're Mexican, Esme and me, just like General Santa Anna. It feels like we don't belong here."

"But the battle of the Alamo happened so long ago . . . it's all just history now."

Carlos's voice gets louder. "It's not just history, Yasmeen, it's happening now, too! So many people like us want to come to America, but they can't because they're not wanted! After what you told us about your family, I would've thought you of all people would understand!"

Now I'm shifting from foot to foot.

It never would have occurred to me that Carlos and Esme might feel like they don't belong, or they would feel like the word *enemy* could relate to them. Mexican culture is such a big part of Texas, and there are so many immigrants living here. But then again, I never would have thought that a word like *terrorist* could be used to describe my family or me.

"Carlos? I'm so sorry. I didn't think about it enough. I didn't understand. Can you please forgive me?"

His face softens. "I'm not mad at you, Yasmeen." He lowers his voice and looks at the floor. "I really like living in Texas with my uncle and cousin, but you know . . . sometimes I don't feel very welcome."

I understand. My family didn't feel welcome that day at the fast-food restaurant, and I don't feel welcome at school when Hallie and the Sapphires bully me.

"Really," Carlos says, "it shouldn't matter if you're white or Latino—Texas wouldn't be the same without all of us. We're just two sides of the same coin."

"Nice metaphor, Carlos! That almost sounds like one of my father's proverbs."

He flashes me his goofy smile that always makes me blush now.

"Let's go find Esme," I say, turning my flushed face toward the front doors. "I bet your cousin could use some company about now."

That night after dinner, I research the Alamo on Baba's laptop. Its history is so confusing, and the site of the battle means something different for everyone.

When we studied the Alamo in class, I saw its history through one set of eyes—but being there with Esme and Carlos today—now I'm starting to see its history through their eyes.

How can two people standing in the same place see

something so differently? How can history be different depending on who you ask?

I guess that's how the history of Israel is, too. It's a catastrophe, the Nakba, for Palestinians like my father, but for Jews who survived the Holocaust, it's a miracle.

Maybe there's more to every story, if only you look.

Thirty-One

Saturday morning during breakfast, my father makes another big announcement. "Children, the San Antonio Rodeo has finally come to town!"

My mother claps. "What a wonderful pick-me-up we will have today!"

"Yeehaw!" Sara cries, and skips toward the stairs. "I'm getting my pink cowboy boots and my new cowboy hat and Salim's little suede vest!" My parents laugh.

Everyone seems excited about partaking in another one of San Antonio's biggest cultural traditions, except for me. We've been in San Antonio for six months, and I haven't seen any signs of cowboys or horses, so what's the point now?

"Do I have to go?" I ask my mother.

She looks at me, perplexed, and tsk-tsks. "Yasmeen, what are you saying? Of course, you are going to the San Antonio Rodeo. Put on your Mexican dress—it will be perfect!"

I head up the stairs to my room and pull out my dress but decide not to wear it. I'm not sure my mother knows what she's talking about. It's obvious that a cowboy hat, boots, and a vest should be worn to a rodeo, but my Puebla dress?

My family piles into the minivan, and off we go. Baba drives across town very slowly, but finally, we pull into the rodeo parking lot with hundreds of other families.

As soon as we follow the crowd through the entrance gates, we all stop in our tracks and gape. The rodeo is amazing—we've never seen anything like it!

The grounds are packed with booths selling anything and everything Texan: little packages of bluebonnet seeds, the official state flower; cowboy boots with real metal spurs; big sombreros, the wide-brimmed hats that the River Walk mariachis wear; and long, braided lassos and spotted cowhide rugs.

People in the crowd dress every which way. Some wear ranch clothes stained with mud, and some wear their fanciest Texan digs—ten-gallon cowboy hats, gem-studded belt buckles, and shiny snakeskin boots. We even see a woman whose western shirt sparkles with rhinestones that look like diamonds.

We pass a booth selling embroidered Mexican clothes, and two girls about my age sift through the racks. They're both wearing Puebla dresses *and* cowboy boots!

My mother gives me a self-satisfied look. I have to admit—maybe my dress would have been nice to wear here, after all.

Salim sees a petting zoo and makes a run for it. He moves as fast as his little legs will carry him. "I see horsie! Giddyup!" he cries.

Baba rushes after him and hoists him onto his shoulders and laughs. "Patience, habibi! We will pet the animals in just a bit. Maybe your mother will even let you ride a pony!"

My father's nose wiggles as we walk farther into the grounds. Before we know it, he makes a beeline for the food booths.

First, he samples the winning chili from the chuck wagon cook-off and breaks into a wide smile between bites. My mother and Sitti look shocked that my father's eating the meaty concoction. They don't want to try any, but I sure do.

He offers me a big spoonful. "Wow!" I say. Just like everything else here, the chili's amazing.

Next, he comes back to our table with elotes from a Mexican food stall: corncobs on sticks slathered with mayonnaise, spicy chili powder, and crumbly white cheese. Baba bites the corn off a cob and says to my mother, "I have wanted to try this ever since we knew we were moving to San Antonio. Take a bite, Myriam!"

She nods and nibbles the corn and smiles.

We're almost stuffed from the chili and elotes, when Baba brings us dessert—fried sopaipillas covered in cinnamon sugar and gooey honey. They're a lot like the desserts Esme's dad makes. My mother bites into the corner of a pastry and nods to my grandmother, then she goes through the line to buy us several more.

We all gobble the sopaipillas and suck the honey off our fingers, laughing. We're a sticky mess.

Baba makes his way through other booths, trying as many things as his stomach can handle. Just as he shovels a last bite of saucy barbecue beef brisket into his mouth, an announcer says over the sound system, "Everyone, please make your way to the arena for our main event!"

The crowd funnels away from the food booths and we follow along. Miraculously, we find seats at the front of the arena where the performers enter and exit.

We're speechless watching the professional cowboys do an almost two-hour show. Bucking broncos kick off bareback riders, who hold on for dear life. A steer flies from a chute and a cowboy jumps right off his horse to wrestle him down. Cowboys rope cattle and race around barrels for the fastest times. And last, they ride enormous bulls as long as they can before being thrown off—the most dangerous-looking event of all.

I glance at my family's bright faces. For the first time in a while, we're all smiling, laughing, and talking. We're all happy again. At least for tonight, we're not worrying about what happens far across the ocean.

My mother is right! The rodeo is definitely a pick-me-up.

When the show's done and awards have been announced, a drumroll rings. "And now, a final victory lap for our winning charro! Please welcome Carlos Gutierrez back to the arena! Carlos, at only age thirteen, upholds this beautiful Mexican cultural tradition like his father and grandfather before him. He sure does them proud!"

Carlos Gutierrez . . . my friend from school?

Carlos sits tall and confident in a well-worn saddle astride a perky chestnut-colored horse with a moppy mane as he laps around the ring. He's dressed in an embroidered black suit with a wide sombrero tied at his neck.

His horse obeys his every command: it bows to each corner of the arena and shuffles side to side; it dances around in a circle; it remains perfectly still as Carlos stands on its back and jumps through his lasso.

My whole family sits mesmerized as the two of them perform, clapping and cheering with each new trick. I'm practically frozen to my seat.

Carlos moves with his horse like he's been riding it his

whole life, and the crowd goes wild.

He never told me he had a horse, or that he could ride it . . . like this.

I think about my friend at the Alamo with his hands deep in his pockets, when he felt like he didn't belong. Here at the rodeo, shining atop his horse to the cheering crowd, it's clear to everyone that Carlos belongs.

"What do you think about young Carlos, San Antonio Rodeo?" the announcer says, and the crowd gets even louder.

Carlos smiles wide and takes off his sombrero and waves it in circles as he gallops out of the arena. Just as he rounds the final turn at the exit gate in front of us, I stand, and our eyes meet.

At first, he looks confused and surprised, but then his face breaks into his goofy smile. He calls, "Hi, Yasmeen!" and stops right in front of us. Then he makes one final bow of his horse to me and gallops away.

I wobble and sit down, stunned. My family's eyes look like they might pop out of their sockets.

My mother turns to me and shrieks, "Who is this . . . *cowboy*? Who is this . . . *Carlos*? Is he your . . . *boyfriend*?"

I start to mumble about Esme and school, but the sticky honey from the sopaipilla seals my mouth shut. Baba tries to calm my mother down, but she'll have none of it. Her gold bangles jingle up and down her waving arms.

Sara shakes her head and coos, "Wow. Yasmeen knows a real cowboy."

My mother grabs her purse off the bench and keeps shrieking. "These American children!" she says with a huff, then she weaves back through the crowd to our car.

We all fall in behind her—even me.

That night, I dream rodeo dreams about wild, bucking horses and swirling, braided lassos. I dream about spicy chili and buzzing honeybees. And I dream about a young cowboy in an embroidered black suit, galloping in the wide-open space under the Texas stars.

The next morning, there's a new sticky note on our refrigerator. I thought my mother's note phase was over, after she proclaimed that the ones she stuck all over the house to help my grandmother learn English were a bust.

It looks like she found a new use for them.

boyfriend = no

When Carlos sits down across from me at lunch on Monday, I remember the rodeo. I remember my dream. Heat spreads up my neck to my face. I hope my blush isn't as red as it feels.

He clears his throat. "Hi, Yasmeen . . . Did you like my performance?"

I scan the cafeteria for Esme and Ayelet and wish they'd hurry up through the lunch line, so Carlos and I won't be alone. I steal a glance at him—he looks nervous, waiting for my answer.

My tongue sticks to the roof of my mouth like it's coated with honey again. I mumble, "Carlos . . . umm . . . wow. You were really amazing! Umm . . . You didn't tell me you're a charro!" My blush deepens. "I thought it was only a nickname! Where did you learn to ride a horse like that?"

A big smile spreads across his face, and he looks relieved. "Well, like the announcer said, it's a family tradition! Since my father travels all the time, being a charro falls to me. I'm next in line to, you know, uphold my culture." He starts shoveling mashed potatoes into his mouth. "It's really no big deal."

"No big deal?" I say, my tongue finally cooperating. "Didn't you hear the crowd? It's a super-big deal. I've never seen anything like it!"

Carlos's culture seems way cooler than mine. He gets to ride on a horse at the San Antonio Rodeo. All I get to do is trip over my two left feet in the community hall of our church.

He smiles bigger. "It's a lot of work with school and soccer, but I don't mind. And Esme's dad helps me take care of my horse!"

"Your horse is really pretty. Where do you keep her . . . or him? I don't know much about horses!"

He laughs. "He's a boy, Butterscotch. His stable isn't very far from here. My uncle's landscaping company keeps the grounds in exchange for a stall. Maybe you could meet Butterscotch someday." He stares into my eyes until I'm the first to look away. "I really think he'd like you . . . too."

Like me . . . too? My tongue feels sticky again, so all I can do is nod.

The instant Esme and Ayelet sit down at the table, Carlos and I go silent.

"What are we talking about?" Ayelet asks.

"Nothing!" we both say at the same time.

Then Carlos smiles at me and says, "Later, Yolanda," and gets up with his tray.

Ayelet raises an eyebrow. "What's up with *Yolanda*?"

Suddenly, she and Esme are both staring at me.

"Nothing, really!" I mumble, my face feeling hot again. "He likes to tease me by calling me Yolanda . . . It's not a big deal."

"Well, I think he likes you, Yasmeen. And he's cute."

I must be bright red by now.

Esme shakes her head and puts her fingers in her ears. "Ayelet! Gross, gross, gross! My cousin Carlos and Yasmeen? I can't even begin to handle that!"

Carlos unsuccessfully tries to juggle two oranges and an apple on the far side of the cafeteria, and I giggle. Then I think of him in the arena with Butterscotch, wearing his traditional suit and sombrero—a real charro. I think of him in my dream, galloping through the wide-open space under the stars.

Ayelet is right—Carlos is really cute.

Thirty-Two

A week and a half later, the air in my house feels charged and tense when I get home from Ayelet's. I peek into the living room—everyone's quiet.

My father flips through TV new channels without any sound on, his eyes far away again. My grandmother knits in her rocking chair, tsk-tsking at the images under her breath. Sara quietly sifts through a stack of flash cards at the big brass tray tables. Even little Salim plays with his Hot Wheels along the windowsill without making his usual *vroom, vroom!* noises.

"Masalkher," I say, but no one responds.

Bam! Bam! I blink at Sara. "What was that?"

She shudders. "Mama has been slamming cabinets for at least an hour. Good luck, Yasmeen."

In the kitchen, my mother's tapping heel says it all: the conversation I've been dreading about my lying is finally here.

"I called Mrs. Jones to invite their family to dinner!" She slams a cabinet, her hands wave, and her bangles jingle. "As a kind gesture for having you over for all of the study sessions!" There's more slamming, waving, and jingling. "You can only imagine how shocked I was that you were not studying with our Waverly! You can only imagine how worried I became!"

She stops to take a deep breath, dabs her forehead with a dish towel, and picks up her phone. "If not for a very helpful application that told me you were at the Cohens' home, I might have called the authorities!"

Baba shuffles through the kitchen doorway. She looks from him to me and points to the kitchen table. "Sit down and tell me everything."

So, we do. We tell her all about what happened in Math Lab when Baba came to pick me up after the winter break, and we tell her about Baba's big fight in our cul-de-sac with Mr. Cohen. We tell her how we both yelled and yelled until we were all yelled out.

My mother winces with each new detail and her bangles jingle louder and louder.

The whole time we're talking, Baba barely lifts his eyes to hers; he hangs his head and stares at the table just like I do. He says, "For two men whose last name means *priest*, you would think we could have behaved toward each other much better."

Then I understand why this conversation has taken so long to get here. I'm not the only one who feels bad about what happened that day in our cul-de-sac. My father does, too.

But our conversation isn't over. My mother crosses her bangled arms across her chest. The skin under her eye starts twitching wildly again and her nostrils flare. Her rapid-fire questions that aren't really questions are about to come.

And for some reason, they're all directed just at me.

"You lied about Mr. Cohen as your Math Lab coach all last fall?"

"Yes, Mama."

"You have been sneaking over to the Cohens' house to see their daughter for the last month and not studying with Waverly?"

"Yes, Mama."

"And that cowboy from the rodeo is your boyfriend?"

"N-n-no, Mama!"

"Yasmeen, put on a dress! It is time for confession! It is past time for you to receive the sacrament of Communion!"

I jump up from the table. "What? I'm not going to confession!"

Ever since I started telling not-so-little white lies, I

haven't taken Communion. During services when our priest offers cleansing wafers and wine to absolve our sins, I sit still in the pew and look straight ahead. I ignore the glances my mother gives me, and I slide my feet to the side so others can squeeze out. But I never get up.

She hasn't been happy about this—not one little bit.

I knew it was wrong to keep lying about Ayelet and Mr. Cohen. But I had to find out about them for myself. Even though my parents think that the Cohens must be like the Israelis who hurt Sitti, it doesn't mean they are.

I look at them, and my voice gets loud. "You're not giving our neighbors a chance! You're not even trying to make an exception! You're just like that man at the restaurant! You don't even know the Cohens, just like that racist man didn't know us!"

My mother dabs at her forehead again with her dish towel, and laments to no one in particular, "This teenage mouthiness! You cannot believe!" She points to the stairs. "Yasmeen, yallah! Put the dress on!"

I drag myself up the stairs. It's pointless. There's no arguing with my mother, Mrs. Myriam Khoury. I'm not in *mortal* danger, but she's decided I'm in *moral* danger. And the only thing that will save me is a visit with our priest.

But I'm not going to make the ride to St. Anthony's pleasant for her. I have some helpful observations to make of my own. "Baba doesn't take Communion, so why should

I?" I grumble in the passenger seat. I know this detail worries her greatly. "So, I guess he won't be saved!"

By now, my mother's probably praying for the silent treatment.

I can't tell her the real reason I haven't gone to confession, since I can barely admit it to myself. I can't tell her my biggest secret, a sin that makes all my white lies seem little again: that I didn't want to be an Arab girl from an Arab family anymore, that I wanted to be from a different family—a real American one.

I slump down in my seat, and my stomach twists into knots again. Maybe it is time to confess. Maybe I do need to talk with our priest. Maybe it's time for me to figure everything out.

Our sanctuary seems bigger when it's empty, when it's not full of congregants in their church clothes whispering hellos and filling the pews, when Nadine and her friends aren't parading up and down the aisles like they're on stage.

Two women kneel in the front row mumbling their prayers over and over. They look like mother and daughter. Their hairstyles are identical, and their heads are bowed at the very same angle. The older one sniffles as she prays, then stops to wipe her eyes with a tissue she pulls from the inside of her sleeve.

Someone in the back dining hall pushes a wet mop back and forth across the polished stone floor—*whoosh,*

whoosh—like rushing water. I smooth my hands over my dress, then my shoes make a hollow *tap, tap* noise on the hard aisle as I make my way to the lit wooden confessional on the far side of the room.

Our priest says, "Enter, my child," and the strong lemony furniture polish smell in the chamber instantly fills my nose.

I sit down on a small corner stool covered by a plush, velvety cushion and look around. The wood doorknob shines like the baby Jesus in our nativity set from so many hands turning it over the years.

I make the sign of the cross as our priest's gentle breath filters through the little screen we'll talk through. I say, "Bless me, Father, for I have sinned. It has been . . . too long since my last confession."

The whole ride over, I'd worked out how I was going to tell our priest everything that happened, but now—I just can't.

So, I put together a quick list of more minor sins. I'll say them to satisfy my mother. I'll sit in a pew afterward and say my penance, the prayers that will release me, then I'll take Communion this Sunday to stop her worrying.

And I'll bury my real sins deep in my heart until I feel braver.

I blurt out, "I told Mama that I would play with Salim, but I watched TV instead.

"My grandmother asked for help chopping vegetables in the kitchen yesterday, but I told her that I had to do my homework even though I'd already finished it.

"I told my sister Sara that she must be adopted, with her lighter skin and hair. She doesn't even look Arab.

"And I threw away my lentil dinner last week. I buried it in the trash can when Mama wasn't looking. I hate mjaddara, but I know it's a sin to waste food."

I listen for the priest's words about my sins, but there are none. He stays quiet and waits for me to reveal things that matter. "That's all I remember, Father. For these sins, I am truly sorry," I mumble.

I'm still on the runaway train.

He tells me to say three Hail Marys and three Our Fathers, a small penance for a good girl with a small number of sins, and for a moment—I'm relieved.

Maybe these prayers are enough.

He absolves me from my sins, then I leave him and make my way down the aisle to kneel behind the two women.

I say my penance quickly, running words into words, without thinking about anything at all.

I don't think about how Mama and Baba try to blend in here in San Antonio, just like me. I don't think about Esme and Carlos, and how they feel unwelcome sometimes. I don't think about the Holocaust or the Nakba.

But I can't help thinking about myself.

Relief gives way to a familiar feeling that stings my eyes as I look at the crucifix in front of me. I'm not the girl everyone thought I was—I'm a girl who lies and pretends.

I'm a girl who lies most to herself.

But that's not who I want to be. I want to be braver than that. I want to stand up for what's right.

The only problem is—what I think is right and what my parents think is right seem like two different things.

My mother waits for me in the minivan at the front of the church parking lot. I open the door to the passenger seat and slide inside.

Her eyes search mine. "Better, habibti?" she asks.

I whisper, "Maybe."

"Good," she says, and starts making our way home.

When we pull into our driveway, I put my hand on her arm just as she turns off the car. "Wait, Mama. There's more."

She searches my eyes again. "What is it, Yasmeen?"

I hop off the train and take a deep breath. "Ayelet is my very best friend."

My mother breathes it out for me. "I know, habibti. I know."

"What if Baba won't let me go over to the Cohens now? What if Ayelet and I can't stay friends? What if . . ."

She puts her finger to my lips. "No more worries, daughter. I will talk to your father." Then she whispers to me as much as to herself, "All new beginnings take time."

Thirty-Three

The perfect storm of activities that's been brewing all year finally arrives in late February.

For once, it seems like my mother's completely out of her league. While the rest of my family eats at the kitchen table, she bustles around packing paper sack picnics for all of us since we'll be out of the house all day.

I dare to look inside the sacks. Nothing has changed— our picnics consist of recycled yogurt containers full of last night's dinner, a layered chicken and rice dish called makloubeh, hard-boiled eggs that we seem to have an endless supply of, and mystery, foil-wrapped foods.

"Baba and I must play *team tag*!" she complains while packing.

"Mama, I think you mean *tag team*," Sara pipes up from

the table, giving me a conspiratorial look.

"Sara, perhaps Yasmeen's silent treatment was better than your preteenage mouthiness," our mother mutters, and my sister pipes down.

But it's true—our Saturday schedule is really hectic, and both of my parents will be driving us around all day.

I have a second Magic Is the Night fitting at Mrs. Haddad's house, which I'm dreading even more than the last one. Sitti has her first English class at the local community center. And my parents enrolled Salim in a gym class to wear him out since his zooming, ride-on vehicles were taking over the house.

But playing tag team isn't what my mother is really so flustered about—today is the regional spelling bee, where my sister will finally prove her spelling genius and have a chance to move on to the National Spelling Bee in May.

Here's my parents' plan: my father and I will drop my grandmother off at her English class, then we'll go to Salim's gym class while my mother signs Sara in at the Jewel of the Forest Auditorium.

When Salim is done, Baba and I will head to the auditorium to catch some of Sara's competition until it's time for my mother and me to pick Sitti up. Then we'll take my grandmother with us to Mrs. Haddad's house to double-check my measurements and pick out the perfect sequined waistband to complement the sheer peach chiffon of my Magic Is the Night costume.

Meanwhile, Sara will surely advance in round after round of the spelling bee until the winner is finally announced around 5:00 p.m.

We all have our fingers crossed for her—even me.

Practice makes perfect, and boy, has Sara practiced. She sailed through the spelling bees at her school and at the district, and now she's ready to win the region.

Our Saturday is just as exhausting as it sounds. As we rush from activity to activity, my parents get increasingly stressed. They drop off and pick up; they switch kids and cheer Sara on in between.

The time I spend with Baba alone in his car creeping from place to place feels tense and quiet. Even though we told my mother everything a few weeks ago, we barely speak.

But I know my mother talked to him about Ayelet since each afternoon when I'm finished with dance practice or Math Lab, I march right over to her house to study, and he doesn't say a word.

I suppose that's something, but it's not what I really want. I still want my father to make up with Mr. Cohen and for my family and Ayelet's to become friends someday.

I want my parents to know I'm right about them.

So we ride around in near silence, not talking about

what's probably on both of our minds. And when it's time for me to switch parents—*Tag, you're it!*—I'm actually relieved to be in the car with my mother.

Her cell phone rings on our way to pick up my grandmother. "Our little Sara has advanced, Myriam!" Baba exclaims over the car's speakers. "She is sure to make the finals!"

We practically run through my fitting at Mrs. Haddad's house. My mother whips through the sequins options, even though she could spend all day considering the choices. I drop my clothes in the dressing room and one of the seamstresses marks and pins my costume so it will fit me perfectly. Sitti gulps down a quick cup of tea. Then we hop back in the minivan to race to the Jewel of the Forest Auditorium.

My father calls us again when we're almost there. "Hurry! Sara *is* a spelling genius! She is about to win!"

Sara's prepared for sure, but win and go on to the National Bee?

We pull into the auditorium parking lot at 4:45 p.m., and my mother and I rush through the front doors with my grandmother not far behind.

Only Sara and one other boy are left on the stage. An impressive row of empty seats for competitors who've lost their rounds stretches at their sides.

My heart skips a beat—my sister has got a real chance!

She's wearing her favorite T-shirt with the polar bear that says *Chill Out*, and she looks the part. My sister's perfectly calm and confident.

Her competitor squirms and fidgets. He looks anything but chill.

My father sits with Salim in the second row of bleachers, beaming at his younger daughter. He waves us over, and we tiptoe to the front. "How I wish I could videotape our little Sara!" he says.

We've barely made it. The judge readies for the final round.

Sara's competitor will be given his word first, and if he fails, she'll be declared the winner if she can spell her word correctly.

The boy stands, shuffles to the microphone, and waits.

"Your final word is *segregation*," the judge announces.

The boy looks relieved. He says, "Segregation. S-E-G-R-I . . . G-A-T-I-O-N. Segregation."

Ding! The judge hits the bell and spells the word correctly for him. He sniffles and sits back down in his seat.

Only Sara remains. She looks stunned as she rises from her chair and heads to the microphone.

My father grabs my mother's hand. She grabs Sitti's hand, and Sitti grabs mine. I gather Salim onto my lap, and he giggles. I shush him with a peck on the cheek.

"Your final word is *apartheid*," the judge says.

Sara smiles, showing all her teeth. She looks at my father and spells the word, just for him. "Apartheid. A-P-A-R-T-H-E-I-D. Apartheid."

The judge says, "You are correct!" and the crowd cheers and gives my little sister a standing ovation.

Baba's eyes glisten and he stands a little taller.

Thirty-Four

"**Y**olanda!" Carlos calls from across the field.

I'm walking by myself around the track, which I haven't done in a while, since Ayelet got out of gym class today for an orthodontist appointment, lucky her. Esme's practicing one of her other track and field spring events, the shot put.

Carlos kicks his soccer ball to a teammate and jogs over, goofy smile wider than ever, eyes flashing mischievously. I can tell that teasing me has become really fun for him.

Normally, when Carlos ribs me with our little inside joke about my name, I kind of like it, but I don't today. I'm instantly annoyed the minute he says it.

He falls in line walking with me, and I pick up my pace. But honestly, he's not what's sending me reeling. I've been on edge since Sara won the regional spelling bee.

On the way home from her competition, it felt like an invisible hand reached out and touched me and said, "Tag, Yasmeen, you're it! Your little sister confirmed to your parents she's a genius, and now it's up to you to prove you're a genius, too!"

The Math Lab competition isn't until the first week in May, but I've already fallen behind. I didn't mean to let my challenge problem homework slide, but with everything going on, it just did.

What if I can't catch up?

"That's not my name!" I snap. "You can stop calling me that!"

"Okay, already . . . touchy. I didn't know it was such a big deal. I'm just having fun."

"Look, I told you," I say. "Esme thought I wanted to go by Yolanda when I first started school here because . . . because I turned in some homework with that name on it by accident and she heard Mrs. Shelby ask me about it. It's not funny anymore, so drop it!"

He doesn't take the hint. "But Yolanda is such a nice Mexican name. You don't want to be Mexican like Esme and me, do you? Because it seems like you might."

Suddenly, I'm furious. I lash out. "Why would I want to do that? Being Mexican in Texas seems just as hard as being Arab! Maybe it's even harder!"

There's no more goofy smile. Carlos looks hurt and confused. I feel awful for yelling at him, since what he said isn't even why I'm so upset.

My parents think if both Sara and I win our competitions, it's proof that things are working out for our family in San Antonio. It's proof that they made the right choice leaving our home in Detroit forever and moving us clear across the country.

I glance to where the Sapphires are practicing. Even if I win my competition like my sister, for me—it's not really true.

Carlos turns to walk away, and I reach out and grab his hand. We both stare at his hand in mine for a second, then I drop it. A blush spreads up my face.

"Hey, I'm so sorry," I say. "Please let me take all that back. I really don't mean it. I—I even kind of like it when you call me Yolanda."

"Really? Yolanda *is* a nice name, but I like Yasmeen much better."

Now it's my turn for a goofy smile, and I can't seem to help it: another blush follows the last.

But Carlos's question about me wanting to be Mexican instead of Arab hits home. I mumble, "Carlos, do you ever feel, you know . . . embarrassed your family is different? I mean . . . not white?"

He answers like he's already thought about it and

decided exactly how he feels. "No way! I'm so proud of my family, and how hard they work to make a life here in Texas. They'll do anything to make things better for Esme and me. Plus, it's my culture, you know? I'm Mexican—mexicano. And I'm a charro, too. Your culture makes you who you are."

Yes, I know about culture, and how important it is to families, especially mine. I want to feel good about being Arab, like Carlos feels good about being Mexican, but sometimes, I still feel embarrassed.

"But here's a not-so-funny fact," Carlos says. "I called myself Carl for a while when I started at Forest Hills. You know, so things would be easier."

"You did?" I ask, surprised. I thought I was the only one who felt that way about my name and wanted things to be easier.

"Yeah. But Carl just didn't feel right. It wasn't me. So now I'm just back to being Carlos, or Carlitos chiquito to my abuela." Carlos's face lights up when he mentions his grandmother. "I really miss her. She moved away from the Valley when we did, and now she lives in Houston with my aunt. Esme and I will get to see her over spring break and summer. My parents will be there then, too!"

I smile. *Carlitos—the boy who misses his grandmother.*

But I know how he feels about his name, as much as I wish I felt different. I guess I'm just Yasmeen, too. My name is just—me.

We notice Esme watching us, and we wave. She's standing with her feet spread apart on a concrete ring, cradling a heavy-looking metal shot in her hand. She looks from Carlos to me and back again and shakes her head. Then she bends her knees and chucks the shot as far as she can.

Carlos says, "Yes! Way to go, prima!" and starts running backward. "Later, Yasmeen!" he calls and sprints across the field to his team.

Later that week, Esme holds her head in her hands at the end of our Math Lab session while I'm packing up. "Yasmeen, I'm so frustrated!" she says. "Did you get that last challenge problem, the one where we had to figure out how many floors were in the skyscraper?"

"Yeah, I actually got that one," I say. "But some of the others . . . no way!"

Mr. Cohen waits at the door to walk out with Ayelet. He looks at Esme and blinks.

"Meet you at the car in a few, Dad?" Ayelet asks, and he nods. "You two need to chill!" she says. "You're both way too obsessed with the Math Lab competition."

Esme puts her forehead on her desk. "And that wasn't even the only problem I missed today! I'm not getting better at math, I'm getting worse! I'm going to bomb the competition this year!"

I try to make her feel better. "Esme, you're great at math. You don't need to get every single problem. You're going to do fine. You're way better than me."

"Really?" She lifts her head off the desk for a second. "You really think so, Yasmeen?"

I nod. I mean it because it's true. I'm really good at math, but Esme might be even better.

She puts her head back down and bursts into tears. "It's just . . . it's just that . . . it would mean so much to my dad if I do well, especially since I'm a Dreamer."

I look at Ayelet and shrug, and she shrugs back. Neither of us knows what Esme's talking about. "Esme?" I ask. "What's a Dreamer?"

She sniffles and wipes her nose with the back of her hand. "Yasmeen, you *still* don't watch the San Antonio news?"

"Not really," I say. "My parents are a little obsessed with what's happening in the Middle East. Actually, now more than ever, since things over there have gotten a lot . . . worse."

Ayelet nods. "My family, too. Israeli news is the hot channel at my house." She clears her throat. "The conflict between Israelis and Palestinians is really sad."

Esme nods and lowers her voice to a whisper, even though we're the only ones left in the room. "Well, the thing is, Carlos and I aren't here in Texas legally. We're undocumented, even though we've been in the United States of America almost all our lives. Someday, we hope we can become citizens."

"I don't understand," I say. "Why aren't you citizens yet? My parents came here from other countries and applied after working for a while."

Ayelet chimes in. "My dad was born in the United States, and his family moved to Israel when he was a teenager, so he's a citizen of both countries. That made my brother and me citizens of both countries, too! Then when we moved to San Antonio when I was little, my mom filled out some paperwork and became a citizen like us. Esme, why can't your family just apply like we did?"

Esme starts ripping tiny pieces off one of her Math Lab papers and putting them into a pile. "Becoming United States citizens isn't that simple for everyone. Even though my dad has a successful business, we have to lie low so we won't be deported back to Mexico. And Carlos and I can't even start the process to stay here legally until we're fifteen, and who knows what the rules will be like then . . . since everything's changing all the time."

Deported? Does that mean Esme and Carlos might not be able to finish middle school at Forest Hills and go to high school with us? Or even stay in Texas? My family might not blend in very well here, but we don't have to worry about being deported. Neither does Ayelet's.

"Yasmeen, will you go over that skyscraper problem with me? I'll feel better if I can cross it off my list."

"Of course I will, Esme," I say, pulling my desk closer to hers. I text my mother. She'll be a little annoyed when I'm late coming down, but that's okay.

Ayelet gives Esme a quick hug. "Later, wizards," she says with a wink, then she heads out the door.

Esme runs through the details of the problem. She knows them by heart like she has some kind of photographic memory. Then, she talks out the mental math. It takes her all of two minutes to find the solution, now that she's calmed down.

"See?" I say. "You didn't even need my help. You've got this, Esme."

She sniffles again and smiles, then she starts packing up.

Maybe my friend doesn't realize it, but I do. Of the two of us, she's the real math genius.

Thirty-Five

My mother starts writing sticky notes again, but now they're just for me. The first Saturday morning in March, there's a new note on the kitchen refrigerator.

> Mama = out
> Yasmeen = garden

Sticky notes actually work. I remember that today is the big day—we're planting Sitti's new vegetable garden.

I slather a half pita with some soft butter from a ceramic jar on the counter and thinly slice some sesame halawa to make a sweet sandwich for breakfast. Then I stand at the kitchen window eating and look out into our backyard.

My father and grandmother are already hard at work.

Baba has spread rich, dark soil in some of the raised planter boxes he built last weekend, and he and Sitti have laid out the rest of the garden grid with red string and wooden stakes. It looks like her new garden will eat up most of the backyard; just a sliver of grass is left around Salim's swing set.

All the vegetable seedlings my grandmother grew in egg cartons on our windowsills are gathered on the back porch. There are so many little plants!

My father stops spreading dirt and wipes sweat from his brow, then he peeks his head through our back patio door. "Yasmeen, you are awake! Your grandmother has been waiting for you."

I nod and stare at the floor.

I want things to be the way they used to be between us, before everything changed. I want to feel good about being a part of my family, like Esme and Carlos feel about theirs. I want to feel like my family is exactly where I belong.

But I don't know how.

Baba steps inside and shuts the door. He lifts my chin and looks into my eyes, like he knows exactly what I've been thinking. "Yasmeen, habibti, I know our move to San Antonio has not been easy for you, but you must learn to extend your feet as long as your mattress."

I blink at him, confused. *What does he mean, extend my feet as long as my mattress? I'm standing up in the kitchen, not lying down.* It's just another one of his cryptic Palestinian proverbs. My father's talking in riddles again—ones I can't solve.

I slip my sneakers on and follow him outside into the bright March sun. Up in Detroit, there would still be snow on the ground, but here in Texas, it's warm and humid though summer is months away.

My grandmother waits patiently on a low stool in the middle of the backyard with her housedress hiked up to her knees. She smiles at me and resumes directing my father.

He pounds long wood planks together to make more low planter boxes and sets them next to the others. Then he hauls wheelbarrow after wheelbarrow of musty-smelling soil from a big pile he had delivered to our driveway. He dumps the soil into the boxes, and I take a shovel and smooth it out.

Baba explains that we need the raised boxes since it's too rocky in San Antonio to plant vegetables right in the ground. The boxes will give the plants plenty of soft soil to spread their roots and grow tall.

When he carries some little tomato plants and places them near one of the boxes, my grandmother jumps up from her stool faster than I think she's able and carries them to a different box. She wags her finger and gives him a stern look. Then she examines a folded piece of paper from the pocket of her dress and surveys the garden.

Baba shakes his head and smiles. "Your grandmother knows exactly what she wants!"

"She's really serious about this garden," I say.

He's quiet for a moment, then he explains, "She is remaking her garden from Jerusalem, Yasmeen. At least, as clearly as she can remember. Inshallah, maybe it will help her feel more at home here with us in America."

I walk over to look at Sitti's paper. She's drawn a detailed map of all the raised boxes with what must be a list of plants. I can't read her Arabic writing.

She leads me to one of the boxes and places her spade in one of my hands and a tomato seedling in the other. She shows me how to plant the tomatoes deep, with most of their stem underground so they'll grow strong roots to support their fruit. Then she shows me how to plant some of the vegetables in mounds of dirt so that the water will drain away from their roots.

My grandmother has grown seedlings for peppers, cucumbers, eggplants, lettuces, and summer squash. She even has tiny watermelon plants! She's also grown herbs like sage, oregano, and thyme. Not everything in the new garden had to be started indoors: she has seed packets for green beans, okra, turnips, radishes, beets, and of course parsley and mint. We'll put the seeds right in the ground and the plants will sprout in no time.

Baba walks around the side of the house and comes back with a surprise. He's found grape vine transplants with red stems and bright green leathery leaves like the ones that grow in Jerusalem to plant along a wood trellis he designed for her.

My grandmother kisses both sides of his face. She and my mother will roll the grape leaves into tight cigars with meat, rice, and spices, then boil them with tomatoes and fresh squeezed lemon.

The warm sun feels good on my back, and a gentle breeze carries the whisper of rustling trees. Before long, I'm immersed in the rhythm of digging and planting, digging and planting. Sitti even trusts me to lay out a whole planter box on my own.

For a few hours, we work in near silence, but it's the good kind. Then Baba and I pick up talking, just like we used to.

I watch my grandmother, who looks so much like me, as we work. She seems happy, re-creating her garden on this small patch of land so far from home. Everything changed for her, but she's beginning again.

A strong flowery scent fills my nose. I stop planting and follow it to the vine in the back corner of our yard that's filled out even more in springtime. Now it doesn't just cover the old rock wall and the narrow door to the wide-open space, it even trails up a giant oak tree.

It's covered with hundreds and hundreds of star-shaped white flowers, and up close, the scent's so powerful it's almost overwhelming.

The smallest bird I've ever seen, a hummingbird, swoops and flits from flower to flower, hovering a second at each one. Its body and head remain motionless while its tiny wings beat almost faster than I can see.

I hold my breath—it's almost like magic—then the bird is gone just as fast as it came.

I turn around to call for my father, but he's right there. "What's this beautiful vine?"

Baba's eyes twinkle. "This rock wall and vine are all that is left of the ranch that was here before our neighborhood was built. It is the same vine that grew wild in our garden in Jerusalem. I knew when I saw it that this would be our new home."

He tips my face to look into his eyes again. "The vine is jasmine, just like your name, Yasmeen. It thrives in San Antonio, and one day, so will you."

My eyes flood with tears. Moving to Texas has been even harder than I imagined. So much changed, and I didn't want it to.

But maybe, if my grandmother can begin again after her whole life changed, so can I.

I sniffle. "What does it mean Baba, your riddle—extend your feet as long as your mattress?"

He pats my head the way he always does. "Stretch long, Yasmeen. Grow tall like this vine. Be proud of who you are."

Thirty-Six

The next morning at St. Anthony's, I breathe in strong, sweet incense as our priest swings its jingly brass container around the sanctuary. I say the prayers I know by heart, without even thinking about them. I follow my mother into the line for Communion.

And I think about Baba's proverb over and over.

I imagine stretching tall like the jasmine in our yard—to the top of the stone wall, to the top of the oak tree. I imagine stretching even higher than the clouds, to the stars.

Maybe someday, just like the jasmine, I'll thrive in San Antonio, too.

As our service comes to an end, I look around at my family. My mother and Sitti stand in the aisle talking to a group of friends in Arabic. Sara sits in a pew with her head bent toward a girl her age, whispering. Salim races up the center aisle to the stone altar and back, giggling as he jumps into Baba's outstretched arms.

And I realize—at church and at home—I'm just Yasmeen Khoury.

I'm the daughter of Elias and Myriam Khoury, who moved here from Detroit. I'm the granddaughter of Sitti Khoury, who arrived from Jerusalem. I'm the sister of Sara and Salim.

I'm not the girl with the olive complexion who's not Mexican. I'm not the girl with the family from someplace far away. I'm not the girl who was bullied at school. I'm an Arab girl from an Arab family—my family.

And for the first time in a long time, I think maybe that's okay.

After services, Ms. Mansour announces that she's adding Fridays to our Magic Is the Night schedule after spring break so we'll be ready for the Folklife Festival at the beginning of the summer.

That means that instead of just stumbling around on Sundays, I'll stumble around another day of the week now, too.

Dance steps aren't at all like steps in a math problem, I've discovered. With math, I'm on autopilot: I just know what the next steps should be. But with dancing, there aren't any neat lines drawn on the floor like the lines on my notebook paper for me to stay within. There's nothing to prevent me from bumping into someone else.

So, I do that—a lot. I literally flail all over the place, and Sylvie inches farther and farther away.

Sara's started coming to all my practices since she can't wait to be a dancer in the troupe next fall in middle school. She sits at a table and studies her spelling bee flash cards for the National Bee while making helpful observations. She takes notes about the routines so I can practice them at home. We've been playing the *Just Dance* video game I got for Christmas a lot, so maybe that will help me, too.

I have to admit—it's been kind of nice having her in my corner. Having a sister means there's always someone around to stick up for you. Sara's got my back.

She watches me for a while, twirling her side ponytail, then she shakes her head. "Yasmeen, I think the main problem you're having is that you lack *spatial awareness*. Without getting some, you might be doomed."

Leave it to my little sister to point out the obvious.

There are so many steps to remember for each of our numbers, and I'm trying my best to keep time to the music and notice what's going on around me. I'm trying to figure out how to acquire some spatial awareness.

I've never had to work so hard at anything.

I'm just one part of a routine that the entire dance troupe

does together in unison. We're supposed to move together like a sweeping current, a brightly colored magical wave.

I'm not even sure why it matters to me so much, but it does.

Since Nadine placed me in the front row, if I mess up, it will throw everyone off behind me. The wave will break, and the magic will end. And after everything that's happened since we moved to San Antonio—I could use a little magic.

Nadine runs most of our practices now. She claps her hands and pushes a remote to start the songs over from the beginning if just one of us misses a beat. She orders, "Girls, again!"

It's usually me. No matter how hard I try, I stumble over the steps, I lose time, or I somehow forget what's next.

It's anything but magic, and I'm worried that I'll let everyone down at our big performance. I'm especially worried I'll let Nadine down.

"Yasmeen!" She calls me from across the room as practice ends. I slide my finger cymbals off my hands, loop my scarf around my neck, and shuffle over to her.

She's sitting at a table next to dreamy-looking Khalil, who must be her boyfriend. He's the leader of the boys' dabke troupe that performs at the Texas Folklife Festival, too. From the looks of it, dancing the dabke seems way easier than our troupe's complicated routines, since the boys mostly stay in a line.

He sits as close to Nadine as she allows as she winds and unwinds her long, shiny hair in her fingers. He glances underneath the table at her toned dancer's legs. She pretends that she doesn't notice.

"You know, Yasmeen, you're not half-bad . . . sometimes. You need to try harder. Practice makes perfect."

I stammer, "I—I really want to Nadine, but I—I can't figure out my spatial . . ."

She gets up from the table. "Look. I can tell you care. I can tell you want this."

She can? I'm not sure how she knows this, since I've only just figured it out myself. But it's true: I want to be a part of this; I want the magic. Here at St. Anthony's—I belong.

Nadine leads me back out to the dance area and starts the music again.

I look around, and suddenly we're all alone. Sara packed up her flash cards and went out to our mother's car, and the other girls left, too. Even Khalil slinked off after Nadine turned her attention to me.

"Clear your mind of everything but your routine, Yasmeen," she says. "Stand behind me and do exactly as I do. Listen to my finger cymbals and the beat. I want you to stop thinking. I want you to feel the music."

So, I do. I follow Nadine's every move without thinking about it. I feel the music, and my body responds. My cymbals move fast—just like hers—like hummingbirds' wings.

Soon, we're gliding around, keeping perfect time together. We're riding the wave like magic.

And for once, I'm not worrying about what comes next—there are no What Ifs.

We finally stop and Nadine gushes, "Better, Yasmeen!" She's smiling ear to ear like she's surprised.

So am I. I'm smiling, too.

"Look. I'll work with you," she says. "Thirty minutes extra after each practice."

I stare at her. *Work with just me? Why would she do that?* I'm trying to work up the nerve to ask but she gathers her things and heads for the door.

"Tell your mother you're staying late from now on," she says, flipping the lights off in the community hall.

I stand in the dark for a moment, then I practically skip outside to where my mother and Sara wait in the car.

That night before bed, I make a new sticky note for my mother.

Maybe I realize now that she stood up for me with the Sapphires in a way she couldn't at the fast-food restaurant. Maybe I still feel bad for lying to her about the Cohens for so many months. Maybe I feel like it's time for us to begin again, just like Sitti.

So I write my mother a little pick-me-up note, then I stick it on the refrigerator.

dancing = fun

Thirty-Seven

The very next week, the magic that started suddenly stops. Our world cracks open when another war breaks out between Israel and the Palestinians in the Gaza Strip.

This isn't the first war, and Baba says it won't be the last. "The Gazans live in a big prison," he tells me. "And they will do almost anything to get out."

And they do. A group of Gazans rains rockets on Israel, and Israel launches airstrikes back. The result is terrible—people are dying.

Baba's face returns to hard lines and angles again, his body stiff and tense. He watches the news coverage hour after hour, looking for signs that things will get better, but they don't. He becomes the old Baba again, the one whose mind and heart fly far away.

My mother wakes up every morning with puffy, red-rimmed eyes, and Sitti stands at the windows each morning like Baba does, raising her hands to the sky.

I worry—is anyone listening?

Every wave of violence closes my family's hearts tighter and tighter. "Will there ever be peace there, Baba?" I ask.

My father watches the TV coverage and shakes his head—no.

At school, no one talks about the war in Israel and Gaza. No one knows that far across the ocean, people are dying. The war doesn't even exist in San Antonio, Texas. While my family is glued to the television, hanging on every new development, American families live life as usual.

So, I try, too—but I'm just back to pretending.

I go through the school day with my friends, and wear a fake smile; I try my best to pay attention in class; and I try to push my scariest worry out of my mind: what if the war lasts forever?

The only person who understands what I'm feeling is Ayelet. Her family sits in front of the television, just like mine. But it's obvious to both of us—our families aren't just on different sides of our cul-de-sac—we're on different sides of a war.

"Nothing can change our friendship," we tell each other. But as the violence grows each day, we're not so sure.

★ ★ ★

It doesn't take long until we have our first real fight. We sit face-to-face on the rug in Ayelet's room the first day of spring break, and our words sail through the air like stones.

"Lots of Palestinians were kicked out of their homes just like Sitti! They just want to go back!"

"But if they come back, where will Israelis go, Yasmeen?"

"I don't know! Palestinians are all scattered! Where are they supposed to go?"

"But Israel is *our* homeland, where we can finally be safe!"

"That land is *our* homeland, too, where we can be safe! HE WHO HAS NO LAND HAS NO HONOR!"

We're both sobbing, our hearts closing like fists.

"Maybe I should go home!"

"Absolutely! Go home!"

I race through Ayelet's house and out her front door. I ignore Mrs. Cohen as she calls goodbye. I run home like I'm fleeing a battle I can't win.

My mother hears my stifled sobs as I run upstairs. "Yasmeen, what is wrong?" she cries.

I choke out, "I . . . can't . . . talk about it! I have . . . to be . . . alone!" Then I slam my door and collapse on my bed in tears.

I can't stand that Ayelet and I are fighting, just like our

fathers. I can't stand that we're flinging words like stones. I can't stand that I'm losing my new best friend, just when I've finally found her.

Four whole days go by without Ayelet.

I sit in our pew in St. Anthony's and try not to cry. I run through my Magic Is the Night routine and try not to cry. I help my grandmother water her garden and try not to cry. I push Salim on his swings and try not to cry. I chop onions for my mother and try not to cry.

But I don't do a very good job of not crying.

Mostly, I stay in my room for hours and hours replaying our fight. What I said and what Ayelet said, how our words hurt each other. I didn't think that what happened far across the ocean mattered to me as much as it does to my family, but I was wrong.

What happens there is my story, too—and it's Ayelet's.

I text Esme in Houston where she and Carlos are visiting their family for the break.

> **Me:** Ayelet and I had a terrible fight.
> **Esme:** I'm so sorry! About what?
> **Me:** Palestinians and Israelis.
> **Esme:** Oof.
> **Me:** Yeah, what should I do?
> **Esme:** Make up with her.

Me: It's not that easy.

Esme: Maybe not, but you have to try.

Wednesday night at dinner, I push my food around on my plate and think about what Esme said. I really want to make up with Ayelet, but it's so, so hard.

My eyes well up again. I can't help it. My tears fall right into my makloubeh.

Sitti reaches over and squeezes my hand. My mother exchanges a worried look with my father. She dabs my face with a napkin and shushes me. "Yasmeen, it will be all right," she says. "Whatever has happened, it will be all right."

No, it won't. It hasn't been all right for such a long time. I don't know why I thought that could change now . . . that things could be different for me and Ayelet.

I mumble, "Israelis and Palestinians want peace, don't they? They want to be friends, right?"

My mother looks at my father again. They both nod.

"Then why aren't they trying harder?" I squeak.

They don't answer.

"Can I please be excused?" I ask.

"Of course, habibti," my mother says.

That night, I can't sleep. I lie on my stiff mattress and stare out my window—but it's cloudy and I can't see the North Star.

I think about the war in Israel and Gaza, so very far away. I think about how my story and Ayelet's story are forever tied. I think about how much I want to change our story, but I don't know if we can.

When I finally fall asleep, I toss and turn all night. And for the first time I can remember, I have no dreams.

For a minute when I wake up the next morning, I forget about our fight, but then it all comes flooding back. But so do Esme's words. Maybe making up isn't easy, but I have to try. I pick up my phone and text Ayelet.

> **Me:** R u up?
> **Ayelet:** Haven't slept much.
> **Me:** Me neither. I'm so sad. I'm so sorry.
> **Ayelet:** Me too. Both!
> **Me:** Can we meet up?
> **Me:** Ayelet?

My phone stays silent. My worries race out of control. My What Ifs aren't just silly pretending now, they're scary and real.

What if I should have waited longer before trying to make up? What if Ayelet doesn't want to be my friend anymore? What if enemies can never be friends? What if . . .

Then my phone dings.

Ayelet: I'm here.

Me: Where?

Ayelet: Ur front door, silly.

I fly down the stairs and fling the door open. We see each other and we both start crying at once. Then we hug in the doorway, not embarrassed at all.

When Baba clears his throat behind us, we pull apart and wipe at our tears. He shakes his head in wonder as he walks away with his morning cup of tea. "Perhaps the pan has finally found its lid."

Ayelet raises an eyebrow. "What does your dad mean by a pan and lid, Yasmeen?"

I laugh. For once, I actually understand his riddle. "It's a Palestinian proverb that means I've finally found my missing piece, and so have you."

Ayelet Cohen is the best friend I was never supposed to have, and I am hers.

It's kismet. We are two sides of the same coin.

I invite her inside my house for the very first time, a house that is a lot like hers on the inside, and a little different on the outside, but not too much.

I formally introduce her to my family, and I show her my room. I show her my father's nargila and our big brass tray tables and the comfy stools tucked under them. I show her the lantern above our kitchen table with the little star cutouts. I show her my grandmother's new garden.

Ayelet and I help Sitti tend her planter boxes all morning, then at lunchtime we make sandwiches and I show Ayelet our secret—the wide-open space.

My breath catches when I open the narrow little door beyond the jasmine rock wall. A rainbow blanket of Texas wildflowers stretches in every direction.

We sit on the rocky bank of the little creek eating our picnic lunch and try to solve our biggest What Ifs. *What if our families understood each other just a little better? What if our families weren't just neighbors? What if, like us, they could even be friends?*

They're no longer just a game. They're no longer daydreaming or pretending. They're no longer worries that bubble up and spin. These What Ifs seem more like wishes now—our most important ones.

When the sunlight dims and the first stars shine bright, we finally come inside. My mother pulls me into the hall where no one will hear. She pushes the hair away from my face and whispers, "Would our Ayelet like to stay for dinner?"

I throw my arms around her. "Shukran, Mama, for making an exception for my friend."

She holds me at arm's length and looks into my eyes. "Perhaps if we make exceptions for each other more often, one day friendships like yours will not seem so exceptional. Perhaps they will just seem . . . usual."

Nothing gets past my mother, Mrs. Myriam Khoury. Maybe she sees a lot more than I thought.

Thirty-Eight

The last Saturday of spring break, the Texas sky opens up.

I wake up right before midnight to a loud crash of thunder, unlike anything I've ever heard. A torrent of rain pelts our roof and wind thrashes tree branches hard against our house. My bedroom window flashes over and over with lightning strikes close by.

Salim whimpers in his room and not a minute later, my mother's bare feet patter up the stairs and down the hall. She tells him, "Shh . . . habibi. It is all right. It is just a little rain. Everything will be fine."

He sniffles as she carries him back down the stairs to sleep with her and Baba.

Before I know it, Sara's in my bed clinging to me under

the covers. I'm a little annoyed, but also relieved that I won't be alone.

Bam! Bam! Lightning strikes even closer. Sara screams and starts crying. I wrap my arms around her and mimic our mother. "It's all right," I say over and over. "It's just a little rain. Everything will be fine." But as the storm becomes more violent, I'm not so sure.

We watch the light show for as long as we can stay awake. Our house shakes like the big Texas storm might carry it away and turn our neighborhood back to wide-open space. I'm not sure when we fall asleep.

When I wake up, everything's eerily calm. Bright sun streams through my window and raindrops dry on my sill. Sara lies curled up next to me, drool dribbling down her chin onto my pillow.

I sit up and shake my head: it feels foggy like I've either slept way too little or way too much; familiar kitchen noises downstairs sound far away, like my ears are clogged with water.

I leave my sister asleep in my bed and head downstairs in my pajamas. Then I sit with the rest of my family at the kitchen table staring out the backyard window at the brilliant blue sky.

It's almost like the big Texas storm last night never happened, like it was just a bad dream.

Sara appears in the kitchen a few minutes after me, her hair glued to the saliva on her cheek. She's carrying her big dictionary with her. "Did you know that lightning is an *electrostatic discharge*?" she says. "The Texas Hill Country is prone to violent storms just like the one last night!"

When my father opens the back patio door, we all hear it—a roar beyond the fence in the wide-open space. It's the sound that's making my ears feel clogged with water.

Baba holds up his hand. "Wait here," he commands. He puts his sneakers on and tramples through our soggy yard to the narrow little door at the far side of the fence and disappears. A few minutes later he comes back, and his face looks ghost white.

He tells us that the trickling little creek has become a raging river—a flash flood. Muddy water filled with debris churns and rushes over the rocky soil, carrying everything in its path to the big reservoir behind our neighborhood.

All the little trees growing along the creek's banks and the tall grasses are gone. But even more than that, he says, my grandmother's new vegetable garden is destroyed.

I run out the door past my father in my bare feet.

Sitti's plants lie on their sides from being pelted over and over by hard rain all night, and some of the stems have snapped in two. The dirt mounds we made in the rows for their roots have washed away, and the trellises that Baba made for the grape vines are scattered across the yard.

Puddles of standing water pool everywhere.

I sink down in the mud in my pajamas. I lift the little plants one by one to make them stand up, but they won't. They just flop back over on their sides.

My whole family walks outside. Sitti kneels next to me and starts to cry.

I take her hand and whimper, "Baba, will the plants ever stand up again, will they ever grow tall?"

My father shrugs and shakes his head.

We lead my sniffling grandmother back inside the house, and my mother brews a fresh pot of mint tea for her.

Sara says, "Should I get dressed for church, Mama?"

My mother hands Sitti a tissue and looks out the window. She shakes her head and says, "Our prayers are needed here today, habibti."

I stumble up to my room to change into dry clothes. *I want to do something to help Sitti, but what?*

My heart squeezes tight. Without her garden, how can she begin again in Texas, how can she make a new home? How can any of us? How can I?

We have to save my grandmother's garden, but we're going to need help. I text Ayelet, and just fifteen minutes later, there's a knock at our door.

The entire Cohen family stands on our front porch, ready to garden.

Mrs. Cohen wears a wide-brimmed sun hat and has

brought over a wheelbarrow loaded with tools. Mr. Cohen's nose is covered in thick white sunscreen. Ayelet wears an old T-shirt and green gardening gloves up to her elbows. Tal carries a kid-sized shovel and rake.

We face each other in awkward silence while Baba shifts from foot to foot. I hold my breath and wait.

Did I do the right thing, reaching out to the Cohens for help?

My mother's bracelets jingle behind my father. She steps beside him and turns his face toward hers and looks deep into his eyes. She whispers, "Khalas, Elias. It is time. Our girls are best friends. I will let you read their texts!"

She shakes Mrs. Cohen's hand and says, "Thank you so very much for helping us." Then she winks at Ayelet and me.

Who would have thought? My mother the expert spy has turned out to be my biggest ally!

We lead Ayelet's family through our house out to the garden. Mrs. Cohen surveys the damage, then turns to my grandmother and speaks to her in Arabic. Sitti's eyes light up.

Before long, the two of them come up with a plan and we get to work.

We dig channels to drain the standing water away from all the plants. We mound dirt around all the exposed roots in the rows, so they'll have new areas to grow while the beds dry out.

Baba and Mr. Cohen venture out into the wide-open space with the wheelbarrow and come back with a load of sticks to stake the plants upright. Sara and Tal gather the pieces of the grape vine trellises, and Mr. Cohen helps my father put them back together. Salim splashes in the puddles until he's covered head to toe in mud.

We fall into the rhythm of digging and replanting, digging and replanting. We work side by side all day in the breezy, warm weather, saving everything we can, and Sitti's garden slowly comes back to life.

My grandmother has tears in her eyes again, but this time, they're the happy kind.

She gives her thanks to each of us with a quick hug or the pinch of a cheek. When she gets to me, we stand eye to eye for a moment, then she leans in close. She presses her lips firmly to my forehead and holds them there.

I know she's left her crimson smear on my forehead, on my heart, and I don't ever want to wash it off.

When the sun dips below our backyard fence into the wide-open space, we look around the garden. Our job is done. It's not the same as it was before the big Texas storm—it's changed—but Baba says the surviving plants will grow tall and strong.

Mrs. Cohen bends her head toward my grandmother as she tells her stories about her parents and grandparents' life in Iraq. When Sitti nods and squeezes her hand, any tension that's left falls away. They talk about what they have in common, instead of what might pull them apart.

Baba's face has softened, no longer cut in hard lines and angles. He and Mr. Cohen talk quietly as they work: about the storm, about their jobs, about living in San Antonio. They talk about what they have in common, too.

They talk about us.

I remember one of my father's favorite proverbs—one hand cannot clap by itself.

Our families need each other in more ways than just this garden, on this day. We need each other to begin again here in Texas, to tell a new story.

We need each other to dream a new dream.

I meet Ayelet's happy eyes in the late afternoon light, as our parents talk and work together. Could this be the friendship between our families we've hoped for?

Thirty-Nine

Monday morning, there's a buzz in the halls. Rumor has it that Hallie's flinging words again but this time, they're not aimed at me. Apparently, the Sapphires botched their Elite Showcase in Dallas over the break for the second year in a row when Waverly messed up her routine.

Hallie's furious. Her ugly words bounce off the lockers in between periods and soon enough, they swarm. I hear hurtful things about Waverly all morning like *she doesn't belong* and *what a loser*. I wonder if she was dropped from the Sapphires' group chat like I was.

At lunch, Waverly sits by herself in my old corner of the cafeteria. Her food goes untouched. Her head hangs toward the table and her stick-straight hair falls over her face. Her shoulders rise and fall, then she starts crying.

I thought I'd stay mad at her forever, but I ask my friends, "Shouldn't we invite Waverly to sit with us?"

They look at me like I must be out of my mind.

"Ayelet, we got a second chance at being friends," I say. "Shouldn't Waverly get one, too?" Her eyes get big and she bites her lip.

Esme's plain annoyed. "I'm not even on first chances with that girl!" she snaps.

"Esme!" we all say.

"Why is she still trying to be friends with those mean girls anyway? Hasn't she learned? Just look at her!"

Every pair of eyes in the cafeteria watches Waverly shuffle over to the Sapphires' table. But Hallie doesn't talk to her—she ignores Waverly like she's not even there.

Like she's out for good. Like she's left on the school steps all alone.

I know that feeling. I understand why Waverly's still trying, perfectly well—she thought she and Hallie were friends, until Hallie decided they weren't.

That afternoon while I'm sprawled on my bed doing Sudoku puzzles, there's a knock at our front door. My mother exclaims, "Waverly, how nice to see you!"

Within minutes she's standing at the entrance to my room, her eyes red rimmed like she's been crying for days.

I walk over to her. "What?" I say, trying to sound mad.

But I'm surprised—my mad's turned back to sad again.

"I'm just here to say sorry, Yasmeen," she says really fast.

"Okay, you did," I say, and start shutting my door.

Her face crumples. It literally scrunches up so much that I'm worried she won't be able to breath out of her perfectly sloped nose.

She sputters, "I'm so sorry for everything, Yasmeen. I'm so sorry for the way Hallie and the Sapphires treated you . . . the way I treated you. I don't know why I still do what she says. We've been best friends forever but she's so mean now! I didn't know . . . I didn't know how much it hurt. That's not even true! I knew it hurt and I just lied to myself. I'm just so sorry!"

Waverly stands in the hall and cries.

Maybe she feels awful about how she treated me, but maybe she wishes she were braver than she really is.

I know that feeling, too.

And maybe just like me, she was on a runaway train and the person she lied to the most was herself.

I move into the hall with her, and she looks at me with a question in her big Texas-sky eyes.

My eyes answer her question with a *maybe*.

I say, "Hey, Waverly, come out back with me. I was just about to check on my grandmother's garden."

I don't tell her that I understand what she did to me. I don't tell her it's okay. I don't tell her that all's forgiven.

Those things are going to take some time.

But the maybe in my eyes means that maybe with me—Waverly can begin again, too. Maybe she can hop off the train.

By the end of the next week, you'd never guess that a big storm had ripped through San Antonio. Everyone's soggy yards dried up in the bright sunshine and the raging river in the wide-open space became a trickling little creek again.

My father explained that all the water flowed far underground into a giant aquifer, a vast subterranean lake that feeds our city's water supply. He says now we'll have plenty of water for the long, hot summer.

Sitti's vegetable garden dried out, too, and then it flourished—just like the Garden of Eden. But so did the weeds; they're threatening to take over.

After school, my grandmother perches on her stool in the middle of the garden and supervises while Sara and I weed. She even persuades my mother to help.

I pull some tall, prickly weeds out between the vegetable plants and chunks of dark, heavy soil cling to their sprawling roots. Pretty soon the beds are filled with big, gaping holes.

"This garden, you cannot believe!" my mother complains, yanking on a weed next to the lettuces. She's put on one of her least fancy outfits and a pair of flats, since she doesn't own any sneakers.

Her sleek hair frizzes and tangles and her makeup runs down her chin in the warm Texas sun. She has a thick stripe of mud across one cheek, but we don't tell her, since it would only make matters worse.

"We need more assistance!" she cries.

So I text Ayelet and Waverly and not a half hour later, they come to help and bring their mothers with them.

I'm a little worried about putting Ayelet and Waverly together.

Since Waverly came over and apologized, she's been trying extra hard to be my friend again and I'm letting her. I just hope Ayelet will let her try, too. And maybe then I can work on Esme.

Waverly chatters nonstop the whole time we're gardening, just like she always did. "Did your grandmother plant this whole garden by herself? Are you sure this little yellow flower will turn into an actual tomato? Who knew digging in the dirt was such a blast? Everyone, worm alert!"

Ayelet gets increasingly annoyed. She rolls her eyes when Waverly's not looking, and she bites her lip harder and harder until I'm worried it might bleed. Whatever she's thinking, I'm sure it isn't very nice. Finally, she looks like she's about to lose it.

"Hey, y'all!" Waverly says, "I didn't know that you could eat squash flowers! How . . ."

Ayelet takes a big scoop of dirt, walks up behind Waverly, and pours it over her head.

Waverly stops chattering and blinks the dirt from her long eyelashes and says, "What the . . ." and then whips around with a scoop of dirt and does the same to Ayelet.

For a minute, I hold my breath while my friends stare each other down, covered in dirt.

When they point at each other and both start laughing hysterically, I exhale. So do our mothers.

Then Waverly and Ayelet both grin and scoop up more dirt—and I'm covered, too.

I turn to Ayelet after Waverly and her mom leave. "Thanks so much," I say.

"For what?"

"For giving Waverly a second chance."

Ayelet shrugs and reaches over to brush some dirt off my shoulder. "She's actually pretty nice when she's not hanging out with Hallie and the Sapphires."

Forty

A few days before Easter, I walk into the kitchen after school as my mother's chopping another big pile of parsley and onions. She winks. "You have something important on the counter from the mailman."

"Thanks, Mama!" I say, grabbing the thick, glittery envelope and stealing up to my room. I shut my door and carefully peel up the back flap of the envelope.

A big, beautiful main card layered in deep purple and silver paper invites me to Ayelet's bat mitzvah service at her synagogue the second weekend in May, and a smaller card invites me to a party later that night at a fancy hotel. There's a third card to mail back to the Cohens with response spaces that say, "Enchanting! I'll be there!" and "Sorry to break the spell."

Ayelet explained her big weekend to me. Friday night for Shabbat, her family will go to their synagogue for services with their out-of-town relatives and close family friends, where she'll get up in front of everyone and receive a bat mitzvah blessing. After that, the Cohens will host a big dinner for the family back at their house. Mrs. Cohen has been baking and freezing challah for weeks.

Saturday morning, Ayelet will lead her entire congregation in prayer and chant from the Torah, the Jewish Bible, which is written in Hebrew. She'll also give her d'var Torah, which means a word of Torah: it's the lesson about the portion of the Torah she chanted. She's been writing it all year.

Then Saturday night is the party we've all been waiting for.

She and her mother have planned a big dance in the hotel ballroom with a DJ and a super-yummy dinner buffet. And Ayelet's invited the whole grade since Mrs. Cohen said that school year parties should include everyone, even though Ayelet might not have wanted to invite a few people.

I'm so excited. First, I text Ayelet.

> **Me:** I got it!
> **Ayelet:** 🎉 🎉 🎉
> **Me:** Can u come over?

Ayelet: Not today, it's Passover!

Me: 👍 Have a great holiday!

Next, I text Waverly.

Me: Did u get Ayelet's invite?

Waverly: 👍 So excited!

Me: 🎉 I hope I can go!

Waverly: What? Of course ur going!

Waverly: Yasmeen?

Suddenly, I'm worried. Sitti's garden has helped bring Ayelet's family and mine together, so my father will let me go, won't he?

I just have to figure out the right way to ask him.

After dinner, I bring Ayelet's invitation down to our living room where my parents and grandmother sit on the sofa watching the news.

Sitti cross-stitches and tsk-tsks under her breath. "Who are these people, making headaches?" she comments, and my mother nods. Her English has gotten so much better since she started her classes.

I stand next to them and clear my throat. "Baba . . . I got an invitation today for Ayelet's bat mitzvah in a few weeks. Can I please go?"

My mother nods to my father as I hand him the

invitation. He takes his time reading it, then he gives me a long, steady look. "You wish to go to Ayelet's service as well, in the synagogue?"

The synagogue.

It hadn't occurred to me that *this* is what he'd ask about. I'd been so worried about Ayelet's dance party that night with the boys from our grade, including Carlos.

Words fly out of my mouth. "Of course I want to go! Ayelet has worked so hard! You should see all the prayers she has to learn! And her d'var is going to be awesome!"

I ramble on and on, then wonder if I've said too much. I quiet down.

A wave of recognition settles on my father's face. It's like he's remembering something important buried deep inside.

He looks up from the invitation. "I had a Jewish friend once, such a long time ago in Jerusalem . . . Gabriel."

Baba had a Jewish friend named Gabriel? This is the first time my father has told me he had any Jewish friends, at all.

"Gabriel had a bar mitzvah, I remember. That is for the boys, you know. Bar means 'son of' and bat means 'daughter of.' But my father said I should not go to the synagogue for my friend's bar mitzvah." He looks away. "Who knows? Maybe they would not have let an Arab boy into a Jewish synagogue in such hard times. It does not matter now."

306

Baba explains that Gabriel lived on his street. They were exactly the same age, and they played sports together every day after school. He laughs. "They could not keep us apart! We were a pan and a lid, too!"

I sit down on the couch, stunned. The way Baba usually describes his childhood, it seems like Jews and Arabs only hated each other—that they were never friends. But just like I've already learned, nothing is ever what it seems.

"What happened to your friend Gabriel, Baba?"

My father sighs. "Well, it was hard for us to remain friends as we got older, we had pressure from all sides. It was best we moved on." He says quietly, "I hope my friend Gabe has had a good life."

I sit still, not knowing what to say or do next. *My father had a Jewish friend once named Gabriel. They couldn't keep them apart.*

Only they did.

Baba passes the invitation back to me. He holds up his hand, and for a second, my heart sinks because I think our conversation is over.

But then he says, "It is settled, Yasmeen. You will go to Ayelet's bat mitzvah. It is an important rite of passage for her, and her best friend should not miss it."

I try to hold my tears back, but they come anyway. My father is my ally, too.

The currents of the Holocaust and Nakba carried his friendship with Gabriel away, but they won't carry mine. My friendship with Ayelet is going to be different—we have a new story to tell.

Forty-One

The rest of April flies by into May. Before I know it, the Math Lab city-wide competition is finally here.

Each middle school team holds preliminary rounds of the competition during their regular Math Lab sessions that week and only two teams will go on to the finals on Saturday.

Mr. Cohen can barely sit at his desk while we work our challenge problems on Monday and Thursday afternoons. He runs his hands through his wispy hair and paces the room a few times until Ayelet says, "Dad!" and he sits back down.

When the buzzer sounds each day, he drops our finished problem sets in big envelopes, then sends them off so the judges can score them.

I'm sitting in advisory Friday afternoon when Principal Neeley's voice sounds over the school intercom: "Attention, Forest Hills students! Kudos are in order! I've just received word that our Math Lab is going to the finals at the Jewel of the Forest Auditorium tomorrow! They're taking on our biggest school rival, Shadow Glen!"

Mrs. Shelby lets out a *whoop! whoop!* and comes over to hug me. Waverly gives me a big high five.

Esme, Ayelet, and I practically float around the track that afternoon, talking about how cool it is that our school got this far, imagining what it will feel like if we take first place tomorrow.

And at dinner, I'm not even the least bit annoyed when my mother serves me mjaddara.

The next morning, I come downstairs, and my entire family is assembled in the kitchen and ready to go: my mother with her jingly bangle bracelets and click-clacking heels, my grandmother with her long Palestinian dress, my father with his slacks and a video camera hanging from his neck, my sister with a book tucked under her arm, and my brother with his Hot Wheels cars.

I smile. My family looks exactly how they always look, and that's perfect. I like them just the way they are.

We all file into the minivan to head back to the Jewel of the Forest Auditorium, the scene of my sister's regional spelling bee win. It's kismet, but as we get closer, I start worrying that fate won't be on my side this time.

My stomach starts winding into knots as usual, but I try to ignore it.

When my mother turns around from the passenger seat and gushes, "It is such good luck to be at the Jewel, habibti, yes?" I force a smile.

She's on cloud nine, and I hope I'm not the one who brings her back down to earth.

I squeak, "I sure hope so, Mama!" and rub my queasy stomach.

When we get there, my family joins all the other families in the foyer until the main doors open. I find my teammates and make nervous chatter, rattling on about anything and everything, trying to calm my nerves.

But it doesn't work. My nerves only get worse. Pretty soon, I'm eyeing the bathroom, wondering if I'll keep my breakfast down.

A big clock on the wall strikes 10:00 a.m. and we all file inside.

I walk to the desk I'm assigned to between Esme and Ayelet, and immediately sense the pressure rising—the air in the room almost vibrates, fuzzy in my ears.

The expectations from both my parents and Mr. Cohen seem overwhelming all of a sudden.

I know my parents think I'll win the individual

championship and confirm what they've always thought was true—that I'm a math genius. And though Mr. Cohen has pinned his hopes for the individual win equally on both Esme and me, he says I'm the new math wizard that will finally help Forest Hills pull off the team win.

What if I disappoint my parents? What if I disappoint Mr. Cohen? I managed to catch up on my Math Lab homework over the last few months and I'm sure I helped get us to the finals, but what if that's not enough?

My family positions themselves front and center on the bleachers next to Mrs. Shelby, Mrs. Cohen, and Tal. "Meenie! Meenie! I over here!" Salim tries to get my attention.

I give him a shaky smile back.

Esme waves at her father and Carlos. She whispers, "My dad's so excited about this competition, Yasmeen. I sure hope I make him proud."

I look at Mr. Gutierrez's smiling eyes. He hasn't taken them off his daughter, even once. "I don't think you have to worry, Esme," I say. "Your dad seems like he's really proud of you already."

A judge walks to the podium. He leans into the microphone and explains that competitors will have an hour and a half to work six challenge problems.

Though each one will be much shorter than our tricky unicorn and potion problem, Mr. Cohen says they'll be just as difficult. He's coached us to show all our work since there's an elaborate system for scoring each answer and he wants us to get as much partial credit as we can.

A buzzer sounds and the competition begins.

The minute I start working, I feel a familiar shift. My worries fade away and my stomach calms down. Everything makes perfect sense. I answer problem after problem, my pencil flying across my paper.

I finish in an hour and twenty minutes and sit back, relieved. Maybe I'll do well after all. Maybe I am a math genius!

I know I should check for mistakes since I have time to spare, but I can't help but look around.

Sitti's knitting, of course, since she brings her big bag of colorful yarn everywhere. My mother's scrolling through her phone with her shiny red finger. Baba's holding Salim on his lap and they've both dozed off. The red light on his video camera flashes—he's probably filming the floor in front of him.

The only person who catches my eye is Sara, who looks up from her book and gives me a big thumbs-up.

I give her a thumbs-up back.

The time's-up buzzer jolts me from my thoughts. "Pencils down, Math Lab competitors," a judge announces.

Ayelet sighs and looks at the ceiling. "Thank you! Another year of Math Lab is finally over!"

Esme and I exchange nervous smiles.

While the judges score our problems, we're allowed to stand and stretch, but we can't go far from our assigned seats.

Esme tells me she doesn't know how she did, even though she finished before I did. Ayelet tells me that she didn't finish, but she doesn't really care. Honestly, I'm not sure how I did, but I suppose I'm glad it's over, too.

Finally, the judges finish scoring, and we sit back down for the results. "Families, thank you so much for coming to today's competition," one of them says from the podium. "First off, these kids are all so great at math. Please give our amazing students a round of applause for how hard they've worked!"

My hands get clammy. There's something nagging me about the third problem. Then it hits me. I made a critical mistake—I should have used a matrix.

Hopefully, I'm not the only one.

The Math Lab coach from Shadow Glen announces the individual winners for her school first. The students get up one by one to accept their awards. Even though it only takes a few minutes, it feels like forever.

Then the podium passes to Mr. Cohen to announce our school's individual winners.

I steal a glance at my family. Now that the big moment has arrived, they sit forward on the edge of the bleachers, technology ready. My mother has her phone poised to snap a picture of me with the first-place ribbon, and my father's video camera blinks in my direction. My grandmother puts away her knitting and Sara shuts her book.

I wipe my hands on my pants, but they just keep sweating. Mr. Cohen's voice sounds even more fuzzy and far away.

He looks from Esme to me, and says, "Forest Hills is doubly charmed this year. We have two exceptional math students who've really pushed each other to do their very best work. Plus, these girls couldn't be better friends. They've been neck and neck in their challenge problem assignments, and today's competition is no different. They are true math wizards!"

I glance at my family in the bleachers—they're half out of their seats for a standing ovation.

"I'm proud to announce that today's first place individual win goes to Esmeralda Gutierrez, with Yasmeen Khoury finishing in close second!"

Esme squeals and runs up to the podium. Ayelet squeezes my arm and whistles.

I follow Esme to the podium in slow motion as the crowd rises. When I finally get there, she throws her arms around me. Mr. Cohen shakes both our hands and gives us our awards.

I steal a second glance at my parents. I'm worried they're disappointed. I'm worried I'm not the girl they thought I was—again.

But I don't need to worry at all. They're still recording

the moment with big, happy smiles.

So, I give them a big, happy smile back.

Mr. Gutierrez and Carlos are the last to sit down. They clap and clap, and Esme's father has tears in his eyes. He couldn't be prouder of his daughter—the real math genius.

I give Esme a big hug. Neither could I.

The Math Lab city-wide director announces the team winner, and it's our school, Forest Hills! We all cheer. Our school hasn't won by just a hair this year—we've won by way more than that.

While the families mingle at the refreshments table, Esme, Ayelet, and I sit on the bleachers munching on cookies and watching Salim race across the auditorium. "That little guy is super fast, Yasmeen!" Esme says, laughing.

I nod to my parents and laugh with her. "Maybe Salim's genius is something they never thought about!"

"You know, you came really close, too, Yasmeen," Esme says. "Without you, our team didn't stand a chance!"

Ayelet finishes her cookie and nods.

"Thanks, Esme," I say. "You did great. Your dad was so proud of you . . . and I know your mom would've been so proud, too."

She smiles and nods. "My education means so much to my dad. One of our biggest dreams is that I'll go to college in America and become an engineer like he wanted to be."

That night, I can't stop thinking about my friends Esme

and Carlos. I can't stop thinking about Mr. Gutierrez's standing ovation for his daughter and the pride in his eyes.

When my Dreamer friends fall asleep at night, I wonder what language they dream in—Spanish or English?

Maybe it doesn't matter what language you dream in, after all. Maybe it's only important that you dream.

Forty-Two

Ayelet texts me in a panic a few days before her bat mitzvah.

> **Ayelet:** OMG! What if I forget my
> prayers? What if no one likes my d'var?
> **Me:** Ur going to be great! No What Ifs,
> remember?
> **Ayelet:** Ok! No What Ifs. What would I
> do without u?
> **Me:** What r best friends for?

Before I met Ayelet and made my first Jewish friend, I didn't know what a bat mitzvah was all about. But now that I've watched how hard she's prepared I realize how important this weekend is for her.

Saturday morning, I put on a dress like I'm going to St. Anthony's. Waverly's mother carpools us to Ayelet's synagogue, and my mother's going to pick us up after her service is over.

We follow a big group of families up a walkway to the tall, front doors of the main sanctuary. I stand at the entrance taking it all in—the synagogue seems the same and different from my church.

They both have soaring ceilings filled with still, quiet air; they both have hard floors where your shoes make *tap, tap* sounds as you walk to the pews; and they both seem like places where you could ask for something you really, really need.

But Ayelet's synagogue doesn't smell like St. Anthony's; there's no strong incense that soaks into my skin and clothes. And unlike my church, the sanctuary's modern. Instead of facing forward, the pews form a semicircle around a big platform with a podium in the middle of the room where Ayelet will lead her congregation in prayer and give her d'var.

I'm stuck at the entrance. I've never been in a synagogue before. I don't think anyone in my family has. I'm the first.

I scan the crowded sanctuary for a good place to sit. It looks like most of our grade is already here, except for Hallie and a few of the Sapphires, who sent their response cards back to Ayelet with a big fat *X* over the space for "Sorry to break the spell." Ayelet said it didn't bother her one little bit.

"Yasmeen? C'mon!" Waverly grabs my hand. "Look, there's Esme and Carlos. And Ayelet's friend Lauren with her boyfriend. Let's sit with them!"

We scoot beside them in the long pew behind Ayelet's family. Mrs. Cohen turns around and gives my hand a squeeze, and Mr. Cohen says, "It's magical that you're here, Yasmeen!" Tal turns around and gives me a small wave.

Their kind eyes reassure me—yes, I should definitely be here.

Ayelet walks to the center podium and stands next to her rabbi, who's the teacher and minister for her congregation. He begins the service, then sits down a short while later and Ayelet takes over.

She stands proud on the platform the whole time, leading everyone through the prayer book. She doesn't look nervous at all. Her sandy-brown hair is swept to the side with a gold barrette, and she wears the tallit that she showed me, a colorful prayer shawl with a Hebrew blessing written on it, over a beautiful new silk dress. Every so often, she looks around her congregation and smiles.

I follow along with the English translations, since I have no idea what any of the Hebrew means. I'm surprised that the prayers are really familiar. A lot of them talk about one

God, which my family believes in, too.

Two women open a long curtain on the sanctuary's front wall and unroll a large Torah scroll on the podium for Ayelet to read. She chants her verses like a song and the melody of her voice echoes high into the sanctuary's ceiling. When she's finished, her parents rush up to congratulate her and the congregation yells, "Yasher koach!"

Waverly asks, "What does that mean?" and I shrug. An older woman across the aisle taps me on the arm and explains that it's a way to say, "Good job!" but that it literally means, "May you be strengthened."

Yasher koach, I repeat in my heart, *May you be strengthened*. I say it for Ayelet, and then for her family. I say it for my family, and all of my friends. Then I say it for me.

It seems like the perfect prayer.

Ayelet waits for the congregation to quiet, then she gives her d'var Torah.

Just like the articles she writes for the Forest Hills paper, her lesson today is no less impressive and no less passionate. She holds the attention of the room, seeming far older than a girl who's in seventh grade.

When she's done, she tells them about the girl she chose to honor on this special day, the girl in the black-and-white photo that has stayed taped to her dresser mirror all year— Hannah Stein.

Ayelet reads a letter she read to me in her room last

month, where Hannah asks her cousins in the United States to send for her family during the Holocaust. But as the congregation already knows, our country wasn't accepting Jewish refugees. Hannah and her family died in a concentration camp called Auschwitz.

While she tells the story that's become etched in my heart, sadness washes over all of us. I hang my head and try not to cry.

I think about how Hannah never changes. She never turns thirteen, like us, or finishes middle school. She never has a first crush.

She only looks like she did in the photo—a beautiful girl with light, piercing eyes whose shoes barely touch the ground, whose hands are folded forever, just so. She dies like so many others during the Holocaust, just because she's Jewish.

But today at Ayelet's bat mitzvah, Hannah seems like she's with us. I feel her spirit in the room, and I'm sure other people do, too.

I lift my head and look around. A young girl opens and closes her prayer book. A mother holds her son so tight that he looks like he's getting smooshed. The older woman across the aisle from me starts to cry, so finally—I do, too.

My heart squeezes tight, and I understand: sadness is sadness and loss is loss. They're the same for everyone, no matter how or where they happen.

I think about the Holocaust and the Nakba—tragedies that flow like a raging flood in a storm, uprooting everything in their paths—and I start to pray. *There has to be a way for us to escape the flood, I just know it. If we can't escape, what will happen to us then?*

Suddenly, I'm pulled under and swept away like the little trees behind our house whose roots did not hold. I can't breathe.

Then Ayelet says, "I made a best friend this year named Yasmeen Khoury," and air fills my lungs.

"She's half Palestinian and half Lebanese, and before I met her, I thought that Arabs and Jews could never be friends. I thought we'd stay enemies forever. But now I know . . . friendship changes everything."

The whole congregation sits forward to listen, and our eyes meet.

"Yasmeen and I are like a pan and a lid," she says, standing before them. "We fit together perfectly."

And just like that, I have something to hold on to. I won't be washed away in the flood. I'm rooted, just like Sitti's new garden, right where I am.

Forty-Three

"This party's amazing!" Waverly and I scream when we get to the hotel ballroom later that night.

"I know, I know!" Ayelet screams back. "Didn't my mom do an incredible job?"

Big, mirrored balls hang from the ceiling and cast multicolored, twinkling lights over the walls. Balloon bouquets in the shapes of silvery stars sit at the centers of each of the dinner tables.

I look around the ballroom and laugh. Ayelet's bat mitzvah party theme is *magic*.

The tables have signs that say, "Magic Wands, Black Cats, Miraculous Magicians, Flying Broomsticks, and Crystal Balls," and there are little cards with everyone's names on them to tell us where to sit.

Waverly and I pick up our cards. I'm seated at the very front of the room near the dance floor at a table called "The Wizards."

Ayelet giggles. "So maybe I'm still *a little* into magic like my dad!"

She's wearing glittery eyeshadow and dark mascara, and she's pulled her hair up into a sleek, high ponytail. She twirls to show us her party dress. It's deep purple like her invitations and it has a silk wrap that looks almost like a magician's cape.

I'm wearing my first party dress, too—a shiny emerald satin that complements my dark skin and hair—and my first pair of real heels. Last weekend my mother surprised me with another shopping spree. She winked. "A special day needs a special dress, yes? But nothing showy!"

I see Esme and Carlos across the room and leave Waverly with Ayelet.

"Hi, Esme!" I say, giving her a big hug.

Carlos shifts from foot to foot and takes a tiny step forward, like he wants to hug me, too. I shoot my hand toward him. He holds on to it for longer than just a hand-shake, and I let him.

Esme punches his arm. "Like I said, gross!" Then she darts to the buffet table.

The seriousness of the synagogue service has softened. Now, with the colorful lights and loud music, we're ready to celebrate Ayelet's big accomplishment.

Carlos and I follow Esme to the buffet. After we've all found our tables and devoured everything on our plates, the DJ takes the stage.

For a lot of us, tonight is our very first dance.

We stand in a big pack near the tables and shuffle around each other for about thirty minutes, not knowing exactly what to do. Then, Ayelet's friend Lauren grabs her hand and yells, "I love this song!" and they spin to the middle of the dance floor.

Waverly finds me and Esme and grabs our hands. "Look at those two! We've gotta support them!" she says, and before we can say anything, we're dancing, too.

The music pushes everything from my mind. I move to the beat just like I learned in my Magic Is the Night dance practices. By everyone's nodding and smiling, I must be doing it right.

We dance and dance until the DJ announces, "Please clear the floor for the hora!"

A song called "Hava Nagila" begins to play. Everyone holds hands in a large circle, and Mrs. Cohen grabs mine. Ayelet sits on a chair in the middle of the dance floor and her uncles hoist her up high. She looks a little scared at first, but as we all dance around her faster and faster, she throws her head back and laughs.

When the hora is over, the DJ plays a slow song to give

everyone a chance to rest, and most of the dance floor clears.

Carlos finds me in the crowd and shifts from foot to foot again. "Did I tell you that you look really nice, Yasmeen?" he says.

I shake my head.

"Umm, well you do. Wanna slow dance . . . with me?"

"I don't really know how," I sputter. "But sure!"

Carlos slips his hand in mine again and leads me back on the dance floor. He puts one hand around my waist and his other hand holds mine tight. We sway back and forth for a few minutes, then he says, "Yasmeen, I've never met anyone as cool as you."

"Me, cool?" I shake my head again and my hair falls into my face. He unclasps my hand and pushes it back.

"There, now I can see your face," he says. But even before tonight—I already knew—Carlos really sees me.

"You won't forget me this summer when I'm in Houston visiting my abuela, will you, Yolanda?"

I look up at his goofy grin. *Forget Carlos? Not a chance.*

"My name is Yasmeen, Carlitos, and don't you forget it," I say, tossing my hair like Nadine does.

He whispers, "Not a chance," echoing the words in my heart, and then he spins me around the dance floor.

When the party's almost over, I look at my friends' smiling faces. So many good things have happened since

I moved to San Antonio, when I was so sure that nothing would work out at all.

Waverly and I are beginning again, and my competition with Esme turned out to be a friendly one. Ayelet and I became best friends, and now our families are friendly, too. And Carlos, I know all his dreams will come true someday, and they might just include me.

With seventh grade almost over, I just have one more thing to worry about—my Magic Is the Night performance. With a whole lot of practice and a little kismet, it will end up fine, too, *won't it?*

I push my worries away. There's time for that, but not tonight.

Tonight is bringing its own kind of magic—the magic of having friends in San Antonio, Texas, a place I never thought I'd belong.

I run over to the big group of kids in the middle of the dance floor, and we all throw our hands up at once as balloons cascade from the ceiling for the very last song.

Forty-Four

It turns out Sitti's garden can grow enough vegetables to feed a small neighborhood. By the middle of May, it's clear that even with my mother and my grandmother's superior cooking abilities, they can't cook them all.

"These vegetables are coming out of our ears!" my mother complains.

Sitti beams with pride.

We start bagging the extra vegetables for a few of the neighbors in our cul-de-sac, and they're beyond excited.

They tell other neighbors about my grandmother's garden, and before we know it, people start calling the house. *"Could your grandmother please spare some cherry tomatoes? Does she have any green beans or summer squash? What about some more of those delicious cucumbers? I've never tasted anything like them!"*

Overnight, Sitti's garden becomes the talk of the neighborhood, and she's the star. Everyone hopes for a delivery of fresh summer vegetables, and we're happy to help out.

But even though Waverly and Ayelet and their mothers have been coming over to help us a few times a week, it's not enough. We can barely keep up with harvesting and bagging all the vegetables.

So, I text Esme after lunch on a Saturday and she tells her father about Sitti's garden, and then the real expert arrives. Mr. Gutierrez pulls up in front of our house with Esme in his shiny truck full of gardening supplies, ready to help.

Ayelet and Waverly pop over, and Sara invites a few of her friends to help, too.

We all work in the garden side by side, weeding and harvesting, bagging and delivering. With our big group effort, we don't let a single vegetable in my grandmother's garden go to waste.

While we're kneeling in the rows, my friends and I play the game What If, just for fun.

"Can we play, too?" Sara asks.

"Sure," I say. "But whisper, okay?"

What if you accidentally call your teacher Mom or Dad in class? What if a boy asks you to be his girlfriend? (Everyone looks at me. Esme pretends to gag. Sara giggles.) What if we'd all never met?

The last What If seems unimaginable now.

Esme's dad leaves for a while and comes back with a truckload of mulch for the planter boxes. He brings Carlos over to help, too.

My mother keeps a close eye on him, and Sitti laughs at his goofy smile and pinches my cheek. My father shakes his head and tries to ignore all of it.

Carlos keeps to the edges of the garden and works extra hard. He goes to the truck and gets his lasso to teach Salim how to capture his ride-on fire truck, which my little brother has decided is a make-believe horse.

My mother steals glances at us the whole time like she knows something. But what she knows, I know, too. Carlos is handsome and kind, just like my father, or as I tell my friends—he's really cute and nice.

When our work is done, Mr. Gutierrez assures us that the new mulch will help the beds stay moist in the hot summer sun and will keep them from being muddy if heavy rains return. The mulch will also help prevent the fast-growing weeds.

Sara runs inside and comes back with her Spanish dictionary. She leafs through it, then taps his arm. "Muchas gracias por . . . por . . ." She keeps leafing.

"You're very welcome, Sara," Mr. Gutierrez says with a smile.

"Sara," Esme says, "would you like me to give you some

Spanish lessons this summer when I get back from Houston?"

Sara nods and gives Esme a hug. "Yes!" she says, and skips off.

My mother looks at everyone's happy, tired faces and winks at me. "What if all of you stay for a picnic in the garden?" she says. Then she walks past Carlos, who's the last to stop spreading mulch. "And *you* can stay, too."

I laugh. Nothing gets past my mother, Mrs. Myriam Khoury. She's full of surprises lately, now that she's my ally. Or maybe she was always my ally—and I'm finally starting to see her, too.

The Saturday of Memorial Day weekend, there's another neighborhood potluck. This time, it's in our cul-de-sac. Judging by the sheer amount of cooking in our kitchen, my mother's still a little confused about the one-item rule for this kind of event. I text Ayelet.

Yup, she says. *There's epic cooking going on at my house, too!*

Baba and Mr. Cohen gather tables and chairs from our neighbors and set them in the middle of our cul-de-sac. Mrs. Cohen covers the tables with bright patterned fabrics, and Ayelet and I place comfy embroidered cushions on each of the chairs. Sitti adds the finishing touch—little brass cutout lanterns from her shipping container.

When we're finished, our eating area looks like it's been

transported from Jerusalem, except for the backdrop of Hill Country–style houses.

Ayelet bites her lip and raises an eyebrow at me. We're thinking the very same thing, since that's what best friends do: *Will our neighbors like it?*

"Mama," I say, "don't you think it's all a little too . . . different . . . for a potluck?"

She smiles and waves her hand across the tables. "Everyone likes this Middle Eastern style," she says. "It is just as good as Hill Country style!"

Mrs. Cohen and my grandmother smile and nod.

And of course, they're right. When our neighbors arrive, they're really excited. They tell us that in all the years of Oak Forest potlucks, this one's the best.

Waverly's mother exclaims, "It's like we're in Greece!"

In addition to the food our neighbors bring, my family and Ayelet's put out a full buffet: baba ganoush, hummus, lemony roasted cauliflower, a giant chopped salad from everything in my grandmother's garden drizzled with tangy tahini dressing, and my mother's secret za'atar spice mix with olive oil. We've even fried up falafel, crunchy brown on the outside and soft and sandy-colored on the inside, to put into the pockets of homemade pita bread.

Sitti stands by the buffet, smiling and shaking hands with everyone as they fill their plates. It's almost like this is her party, a chance to display her food and culture in this strange American city she's landed in.

The neighbors who've been getting vegetable deliveries are excited to finally meet her in person. When one of the fathers goes back for a generous second helping of baba ganoush, my grandmother pinches his blushing cheek.

Everyone eats until they're stuffed, then the adults rest and talk while we play Capture the Flag in the front yards.

My mother lights the little brass lanterns, and Mrs. Cohen passes around desserts while my grandmother serves her strong Arabic coffee. Sitti becomes a fortune-teller, examining the coffee dregs in our neighbors' cups for signs of good things to come.

On a night like this, of course she finds them.

My father gathers some of the men at the edge of the party for a smoke from his nargila. My mother passes colorful scarves out to the women and girls and we tie them around our hips. She plays Arabic music from her phone as loud as it will go.

I teach Waverly and Ayelet some moves from my Magic Is the Night routine, while Sara helps direct. Chloe and Kayla inch over to us, and in barely a whisper, ask if they can dance with us, too.

I take in their wide, nervous eyes and shuffling feet. Their rounded shoulders and the way they hug their arms to their sides.

Maybe it's the magical night, or maybe I'm sick of

holding on to things that should be left behind, but I hand each of them a scarf, then we shimmy and sway to the music together.

When the lanterns burn out, our neighbors take their empty potluck dishes and head home. Mr. and Mrs. Jones give us big hugs and tell us "Greek Night" should be an annual Oak Forest tradition.

Waverly rolls her eyes. "Gosh, Mom and Dad! Don't you know anything? The Khourys are Palestinian and Lebanese, and the Cohens are Israeli!"

Ayelet and I just smile.

Finally, it's only my family left cleaning up with Ayelet's family. We carry the leftover food inside and stack the tables and chairs on the sidewalk to be picked up by our neighbors tomorrow.

When there's one table left, we sit down to rest under the big night sky. We talk about our successful potluck and about the school year and Math Lab. We talk about the summer to come.

Our parents speak in English, then drift to Arabic, and then Baba and Sitti switch to speaking in Hebrew with the Cohens.

I've never heard these sounds in my father's and grandmother's voices. They're a little like the familiar sounds of Arabic: languages that flow like water, streams joining other streams as they wind to the ocean.

Sara's eyes pop wide, and she turns to Tal. "Thanks for teaching me Hebrew at the bus stop, but it looks like I have some teachers at home now, too!" Everyone laughs.

But even in the gift of this day, our hearts remember the faraway place that holds a piece of who we are, where there is still so much suffering. We talk about the conflict that never ends. We talk about how lucky we are, safe in San Antonio.

Baba's voice breaks with emotion. He says, "It is hard to imagine that there is still war, on such a night."

Mr. Cohen's eyes meet my father's eyes in understanding, and he nods—yes.

I look up at the big Texas night sky, filled with a million stars. The North Star seems so close right now I could almost reach up and touch it. And I know—we are all wishing upon the same stars tonight—Ayelet and me, our families, and the people in Gaza and Israel, so very far away.

The wish in my heart rises to my lips. I whisper, "Maybe peace will begin here, with us."

My father draws me into a hug and whispers back, "From your mouth to God's ears, Yasmeen. From your mouth to God's ears."

Our families eventually head back into our houses. Sitti retires to her room, and Sara to hers. My mother puts sleepy Salim to bed and then joins me at the big picture window in our living room.

Baba and Mr. Cohen have stayed outside on the curb, talking quietly under the streetlight. They shuffle from side to side. They put their hands into their pockets and then bring them back out again. Sometimes, they meet each other's eyes. Sometimes, they look away.

We watch them and we wait. I hold my breath and hope that our magical night won't end.

Finally, Baba smiles and extends his hand and Mr. Cohen clasps it. They shake hands a little longer than is necessary, and I exhale.

Such small things—a smile, a handshake—wouldn't stand out among most neighbors, but between my father and Mr. Cohen, they mean so much more. Maybe they mean that when the next war or the next flood comes, our families will keep reaching for each other with another chance.

Maybe, we can keep holding on.

Tears slip from my mother's eyes, and I reach up and wipe them away. I say, "Mama, Baba has honor even without any land in Jerusalem."

She nods her head—yes.

Forty-Five

My father and Sara fly to Washington, DC, on Sunday afternoon for the National Spelling Bee.

By Monday, my mother's a nervous wreck. She click-clacks around the house, tidying and cleaning the whole morning while we wait for my sister's written first round to end.

Sara's second round will be aired on national TV this afternoon. We're so excited!

I sit at the kitchen table with my grandmother, practicing cross-stitching. She tells me that this type of Palestinian embroidery is called tatreez, and that each design carries a special message.

After I learn the basic stitches, Sitti teaches me to make little white flowers in the shape of stars. And once

I've mastered those, she unfolds long panels of fabric covered with stitching canvas from her big bag and lays them across the table. They're in the shape of a thobe, about my size.

The top of the bodice has a big brown square with a green vine woven along it. Inside the square, there are boxed rows of plants, some with bright-colored flowers and some with tiny vegetables.

My heart squeezes. "Which garden is it . . . the one here, or in Jerusalem?"

She pinches my cheek and says, "Both," then she points to the vines on the square. "Please put your jasmine flowers here, Yasmeen."

The dress is for me.

I hug her tight. "Shukran, Sitti, shukran," I say, then get to work on my flowers.

Finally, Sara's second spelling bee round begins. My mother, Sitti, and I sit hip-to-hip on the living room sofa to watch the broadcast, while Salim runs his Hot Wheels cars along the windowsill.

"There she is!" I say when Sara's called to the microphone, and we all hold our breath while she spells her word onstage.

But her answer is incorrect. *Ding!* The judge hits the bell and spells the word correctly for her. Then my sister shuffles offstage.

My heart sinks. "Mama, is it all over?"

She nods. "Sara will need a very big pick-me-up when she returns, habibti."

A short while later, I hear the funny faraway ringtone on Baba's laptop, and I leave my mother and grandmother on the sofa and run to his office to get it.

We huddle close together so Sara can see all our faces at once.

Baba's face fills the screen. He says, "Hello, family!"

My sister slumps next to him with red-rimmed eyes and a swollen, pink nose. My father pats her head as he talks. "Congratulations to our Sara for an excellent showing at her first National Spelling Bee!"

"We are so proud of you! You are amazing! You will do even better next year!" we all tell her at once.

She nods her head and manages a small smile. "Yasmeen, will you help me with my flash cards for the sixth-grade spelling bee?"

I don't miss a beat. I give her a big thumbs-up and say, "Next year, Sara, I've got your back."

When Ayelet and I get on the bus the next morning, Chloe and Kayla make their way from the back seats and slide into the bench behind us.

Kayla says, "Mind if we sit up here with you? It's super bumpy back there."

"Yeah," Chloe chimes in. "It even makes me carsick sometimes."

Kayla gives me a long look. "We had so much fun at the potluck Saturday night, Yasmeen—with you and Ayelet and Waverly."

Chloe nods.

"And we . . . we just wanted to say we're so, so sorry . . . about the texts and the awful way we treated you . . ."

"Yeah, we're sorry about everything," Chloe says. "We were pretty big jerks."

Ayelet and I look at each other, and I can tell we're both thinking the same thing again. It felt good and right to give Chloe and Kayla a second chance at the potluck. This feels right, too.

"So . . . ," Kayla says. "Is it okay if we sit here with you?"

I nod my head. "The back of the bus is really smelly from all those fumes!"

A few stops later, Waverly hops on the bus and sits down with us. Then we all talk and laugh the whole way to school.

We're standing on the Forest Hills steps waiting for the bell to ring when Hallie's face appears in the main doorway. Her eyes dart from me to Waverly, to Chloe, Kayla, and Ayelet, and then back to me again.

At the beginning of the year, I might have been the one standing by myself, watching other girls chat and laugh.

But now Hallie is. Her nostrils flare, her face gets red, and her chest puffs in and out until she finally storms into school.

In math class, the second Mrs. Shelby turns to the board, Hallie hisses something I thought was all in the past. Something I hoped was just history. "It says on the news that your people are *dangerous*. We don't want you at our school."

My teacher whips around. Now her heel is tapping. "What did you say, Hallie?"

Hallie crosses her arms over her chest and pinches her lips together.

Mrs. Shelby pushes the button on the intercom. "Please tell Principal Neeley that Hallie is on the way," she says in a steely voice.

Hallie thrusts her chin out and shoots up from her desk. She throws her things in her backpack while Mrs. Shelby watches and waits. The whole class stays extra quiet.

Then Hallie gives me the meanest look I've ever seen as she huffs out the door.

Right away, What Ifs bubble back up with a vengeance, even though I thought they were over now.

What if my kismet is over? What if Hallie convinces every-one at school that what she said is true? What if my new friends believe her?

The whole rest of class, I try to push my worries back down. I try to pretend that what Hallie said doesn't matter to me anymore. But I'm out of practice.

I sink down in my seat: maybe words that hurt always matter.

I'm a mess by the end of math class. Mrs. Shelby tries to catch me on my way out, but I'm already at a full sprint. I rush to the bathroom and hide in a stall until the second period bell rings.

It doesn't take long for Hallie's mean words to bounce down the halls. It doesn't take long for the gossip to start all over. It doesn't take long for me to feel like I don't belong again—that I'm unwelcome at this school.

At lunch, I rest my head on the cafeteria table. "Maybe it will blow over like last time," I mumble to my friends.

Esme says, "Maybe I can help it along, Yasmeen. I'm good at it, trust me!"

I lift my head. "That's okay, Esme." I don't want her to get in trouble.

"It'll probably blow over by tomorrow, Yasmeen," Waverly says. "And if it doesn't, seventh grade ends on Friday and you won't have to see Hallie all summer!"

Ayelet snaps, "Blow over, Waverly? What about next year in eighth grade? It's not okay for Hallie to keep bullying Yasmeen!"

Then she repeats what she said to me in her bedroom all those month ago when she told me about Hannah Stein. "Waverly, real friends stand up for what's right if something bad is happening! They have your back!"

Waverly's bottom lip quivers and her blue eyes cloud over. Then she stares at Hallie the rest of lunch, completely silent for once.

All I know is that the last day of seventh grade can't come soon enough.

And before long it does. Friday afternoon, Ayelet and I walk the track for the very last time. Esme runs laps around us, Carlos plays soccer with his teammates on the field near the gym, and the Sapphires practice some dance steps at the far end of the field. But really, since it's the last day of school, everyone's just goofing around.

Ayelet and I talk and talk, and never seem to run out of things to say.

I tell her all about Sara's big year at her spelling bee competitions, and we remember Esme's Math Lab win and the pride in her father's eyes. I tell her about my family's trip to the stables with Carlos and Mr. Gutierrez to meet Butterscotch. We talk about my grandmother's garden, and how so many friends have helped it thrive. We run through all the details of Ayelet's amazing bat mitzvah weekend together. Then I tell her how much I love dancing with my Magic Is the Night troupe, now that I've got the hang of it.

And I start to feel better. One mean bully can't take away all that.

But as we near the far end of the field, Hallie tries. She snickers and points at me, cups her hand, and whispers. Some of the other girls join in, too. Then as we get closer, she leads the entire Sapphires drill team onto the track.

I can tell right away—this time, things are different. Hallie seems extra bold in her mean girl pack. It's the last day of school, and we're out of earshot of any coaches or teachers. And out here, there won't be any cyberspace texting record to get her in trouble. She's going to try to put me in my place once and for all. What does she have to lose?

"Just keep walking," I tell Ayelet. "Pretend like they're not even there."

Her eyes flash hard, and she nods.

But we can't. They walk toward us and stop in a line across the track right in front of us.

Hallie rushes up to me with her fists clenched tight. "I hate you! Because of you, Principal Neeley says I can't be the Sapphires team captain anymore!" she spits out. "Everything was so much better before you came! Why are you still here? Next year, we don't want you at our school!"

Waverly steps out of the line of Sapphires. Her fists are clenched, too.

Ayelet scoots closer to me and lifts her chin. "Hallie, you're the one who no one wants here anymore, not Yasmeen!"

Esme catches up to us, her breath coming in sharp

bursts. "Why don't you repeat what you said to my friend," she hisses. "Dare you."

"Hey, I've got this," I say to Ayelet and Esme, and they nod.

Hallie keeps spitting. "Did you forget how to speak English? I said, why are you still here? When are you going *home* to wherever you're from?"

"I am HOME!" I yell right in her face. "And I BELONG here just as much as anyone else! I'M NOT GOING ANYWHERE!"

Hallie flinches and steps back. She grabs Waverly's arm. "Come on!"

But Waverly shakes her head. "No."

Hallie pulls harder. "Waverly, I said come on!"

I reach for Waverly's other arm, then I notice her clenched fists again and the anger in her big sky-blue eyes. My friend needs to know that she can stand up, too.

So I drop my hand, and wait.

And Waverly stretches as long as her mattress.

But not in the way I expect. She says, "Hallie, I know deep down you don't want to say such mean things. I know you don't want to be such a bully. You weren't always like this."

For a second, Hallie looks confused. "What are you *saying*, Waverly?" she screams. "I mean every word!"

Waverly's eyes rest on me for a split second, then she says, "I'm giving you a second chance, Hallie, if you still want to be my friend. But you have to say sorry for what you said about Yasmeen . . . and me, too."

Hallie explodes. Her face turns strawberry-colored just like her hair. "I'm not sorry for anything!" She gestures to the Sapphires. "I know you feel the same as us!"

Waverly doesn't back down. "I never felt that way, Hallie. I just went along because we were best friends. But we're not anymore. I don't want to be friends with someone who says such hurtful things. I don't want to stand up for a bully."

Then she points to the Sapphires. "And I don't think they want to stand up for a bully, either."

Chloe takes a deep breath and steps out of line. "Hallie, what we called Yasmeen is terrible and wrong. She's my friend."

My heart skips a beat. *Is this really happening?*

Then Kayla steps forward. "Yasmeen's my friend, too . . . I really like her."

Hallie's face flames bright red. She gestures to who's left. "Come on, Sapphires!"

But only a few girls follow her as she huffs back to the gym. Almost the whole team stays with us!

I've learned a lot about second chances since moving to San Antonio: for them to work, someone has to be brave enough to give them, but someone has to be brave enough to accept them, too.

I guess Hallie's not brave enough to do either.

"Too bad for Hallie I caught it all on video!" A deep voice booms behind me. I spin around to find Carlos standing there with his entire soccer team. He waves his phone. "I'm sure Principal Neeley is going to love seeing her in action!"

I laugh and look at Ayelet. "Maybe she *is* the one who won't be at this school next year!"

Ayelet says, "Well, Waverly, it looks like your team needs a new captain!" and Chloe and Kayla both grin and nod.

Waverly flashes her sunniest smile ever. "Guess what, y'all? Some of these eighth graders are heading to high school! What do you think, Yasmeen and Ayelet? Wanna try out for the Sapphires this summer? Sure beats walking the track!"

I smile. "You never know, anything could happen!"

Ayelet shakes her head. "I'll pass. But if you try out, Yasmeen, I'll cheer you on!"

Carlos laughs. "I'm heading to Principal Neeley's office right now!" Then he takes off across the field with his team. Halfway there, he turns around and smiles his goofy smile and calls, "Later, Yasmeen!" and my heart skips another beat.

Everyone starts giggling, even Esme. They look at me like they know something. But what they know, I know, too.

Carlos is more than just my friend now.

Waverly turns to Ayelet, Esme, and me. "Sapphires' practice is definitely over. Would you mind if my team walks the track with you until gym class ends?"

Esme takes the lead. "C'mon, you slowpokes, try and keep up with me!" she says, and we all laugh.

I look around at the big group of girls who surround me—the girls who had my back—and a giant, warm, happy feeling rushes through me.

What more could an almost eighth grader who started a new middle school clear across the country even ask for?

Not very much, but maybe for one more tiny thing: for kismet to be on my side for my Magic Is the Night performance next week, so I can keep riding this wave.

Forty-Six

That night after dinner, my mother calls up the stairs, "Yasmeen, Sara! Yallah! We are going on a family outing!"

Sara and I look at each other and groan—*a family outing?* We know what *that* means.

When we come downstairs, the rest of our family is ready to go on another walk around the neighborhood. Our mother pats her stomach and announces, "We will walk off our dinner!"

Sitti nods and pats hers.

"I've already walked today," I protest. "Around the track during gym class with all my friends. We walked really far."

My mother looks at me, perplexed. "Yasmeen, what are you saying? You can never breathe enough fresh air, yes?"

She has a point.

My grandmother sticks her foot out from beneath her long dress, and grins—she's wearing a brand-new pair of white sneakers, just like our father's. Our mother has on a pair of sneakers, too, but hers are silver and studded with rhinestones.

Sara and I smile at each other. Where in the world did she find *those*?

As we stroll around our neighborhood, the houses that once looked nearly the same to me look a little different now.

There are things I didn't see before. Our neighbors with the triplet boys have a bright yellow door and the older couple next to us has a rocking bench for two on their front porch. The Cohens' house has the biggest climbing tree on our cul-de-sac.

Maybe things that seem too different or too much the same at first start to come together after a while, if only you look a little closer.

I can't help but wonder again how my family appears—if we still look as different to our neighbors as we did when we arrived—or if they're looking at us a little closer, too.

If we blend in just like everyone else now.

My answer comes in small doses—a wave here or there and a shout hello, a neighbor stopping his mower to shake Baba's hand.

And I realize: one of my biggest What Ifs—whether or not my family would ever belong here in San Antonio—is no longer a question at all.

Sunday after services, we have our last Magic Is the Night dance practice before our big performance. My troupe runs through each of our routines twice from start to finish without messing up once. Even Nadine seems impressed! All our hard work has paid off. She says we're more than ready for the main stage at the Texas Folklife Festival.

I sure hope she's right.

My mother and grandmother take me to Mrs. Haddad's house for my last fitting on Wednesday and Sara rides along. I can't wait until we can dance together next fall. From all our *Just Dance* sessions, I can already tell—my little sister's going to be a natural.

A faded yellow sticky note on Mrs. Haddad's front door says: Min fadlik—come on in!

This time, I'm not sulking and wishing I were somewhere else; my mother isn't dragging me along. I push the door open and lead the way.

Inside, we find a familiar scene. Young girls walk into Mrs. Haddad's dressing room and emerge in their brightly colored costumes as Magic Is the Night dancers. They twirl in front of their mothers and grandmothers to whistles and clucks. They compliment each other's choices.

The excitement builds.

Mrs. Haddad's assistant makes sure each hem is even, each top secure, and each midriff nearly covered.

My mother nods approvingly, and ignores Mrs. Haddad when she repeats, "If they go home and adjust before the performance, what can I do? These girls can sew!"

When it's my turn to change, I'm not nearly as nervous as before. This time, my fitting really does feel like a ladies-only party.

I step out of the dressing room in my peach costume, and my mother breaks down in tears. Sitti smiles ear to ear, fanning her flushed face. They beam as I twirl in the kitchen like the other dancers, while all the ladies cluck for me.

Sara gushes, "Yasmeen, you look like a princess!"

I smile. *Maybe I do.*

As I take my costume off, I catch my face in the three-way mirror. The girl I see isn't the same one I saw at my first fitting, so many months ago.

This girl stands braver and taller. She holds her head high. Her pale peach costume complements her dark skin perfectly.

She's the right kind of pretty to me.

I blink, and the day of my performance is finally here.

Saturday morning, I come downstairs to find my whole family at the kitchen table, smiling. My mother practically sings, "Tonight is the night we have all been waiting for! You cannot believe! *Everyone* is coming."

"Who's coming, Mama?" My voice gets tighter and higher, not sounding like the confident girl in the mirror at all.

"Do not worry, habibti! You always worry! Our *friends* are coming!"

My heart pounds in my chest. "Which friends?"

She tsk-tsks and gestures out the kitchen window. "Our neighborhood, of course!"

"You invited *our neighborhood* to the Folklife Festival . . . to see me dance?"

My mother waves her hand in the air to swat my worries away. "Yasmeen, everyone in our neighborhood loves this style of Arab dancing, especially since our very successful potluck."

I take a deep breath and try to steady my heart. There is no use arguing with my mother, Mrs. Myriam Khoury. Plus, it's already done. She invited all our friends.

There's nothing I can do now, but dance.

"I'm going back to my room to rest for a while."

"Good idea, you will need your second wind."

I head up to my room just as my phone *ding, dings*. I can't believe it—it's Dina.

Dina: Yasmeen! I finally got a cell
phone! I can text u!
Me: OMG! But I'll miss video chatting
with u!
Dina: Hold on! We can still do that!

We hang up and my phone rings, then Dina's smiling face fills the little screen all the way from Detroit. I flip my phone around and show her my Magic Is the Night costume hanging on a hook outside my closet.

"Wow," she says. "It's so beautiful."

"I know, right?" My heart swells with pride.

"Your mom invited us to your performance, and I wish we could come but it's a little far away. Good luck, Yasmeen!"

"Thanks! I wish you could come, too, Dina, but I'll send you my father's video!"

She nods, and then her face lights up. "I nearly forgot—I have breaking news!" She puts on her most serious newscaster face and tells me that at the end of the school year, she and Nabil became regular study buddies. Then she breaks into giggles and glances away.

I smile and wonder if Dina knows what I already know. But if she doesn't—I'm sure she'll figure it out really soon.

Then I tell her what happened on the track my last day of school with Hallie and the Sapphires, and how my San

Antonio friends all stood up for me. She gets a little quiet, so I ask, "Are you okay?"

Her lips quiver. "Will we always be best friends, Yasmeen?"

I think about my old friend in Detroit, and my first Texas friend, my Dreamer friends, and the best friend I never thought I'd have—my heart has room for everyone.

"Yes, Dina! We'll just be best friends from 1,489 miles away."

After we hang up, there's more texting. I laugh—Dina loves emojis. Hearing from her is just what I needed.

I touch my beautiful peach costume and stand at my window looking at the big Texas sky. Another wish in my heart rises to my lips. I say aloud, "Please let me remember my steps, please help me not mess up."

I hope someone is listening.

And more than anything, I hope I won't break the wave—especially now that almost everyone I care about is coming to watch me dance.

That afternoon, we speed out of our neighborhood to the Texas Folklife Festival.

Kind of: my father drives exactly how he always does— very slowly.

My mother taps her fingernails on the dashboard, and I check the time on my phone over and over. I catch my father's eyes in the rearview mirror. "Baba, can you please, *please* speed up?"

And miraculously, he does! He steps on the gas and our minivan flies forward to the speed limit. But he doesn't go over—he says there's a limit for a reason.

We all cheer, and for once, we're not late.

The festival grounds are set up a lot like the rodeo, with lines of booths selling food and goods from all the cultures that immigrated to the great state of Texas.

Members of our church staff a food booth with a long charcoal grill in the back. People line up for hummus and tabbouli, baba ganoush and spiced, grilled meat. My mouth waters, and Salim jumps up and down. "Yummy hamburgers!" he says.

Baba pats his head. "We will eat after Yasmeen's big performance."

As we wind our way through the crowd to the main stage where I'll perform, we pass other dancers in their traditional costumes: boys dressed in charro suits paired with girls who wear flowing tiered skirts and frilly white tops; Chinese lion dancers carrying the animal masks that disguise their faces; and German folk dancers wearing suspenders and white knee-high stockings.

Then there's me, in my Magic Is the Night costume. It falls soft on my skin and shimmers in the afternoon light. It fits perfectly because it was made just for me. And I realize—it's the most favorite thing I've ever worn.

We find my stage, then I wait with my dance troupe and the boys' dabke troupe in the back while everyone crams into a tall set of bleachers out front.

I peek around the corner. Lots of families from our congregation are here and sure enough, all our friends from the neighborhood came to watch me, too. The family with the triplets is here, trying to keep them quiet with dripping ice cream cones. The older couple who lives next door is here, talking with Mr. and Mrs. Jones. Chloe and Kayla sit next to Waverly, and of course Ayelet, Esme, and Carlos are here with their families as well.

My family's front and center, my father already videotaping the scene. Salim calls from my mother's lap, "I over here, Meenie! I over here!"

I wave and blow him an air kiss.

As soon as I step back around the corner, the music for our first number begins to play. Nadine shouts over the familiar beat, "Yasmeen, you're up!"

I lead the front row of dancers to our places and the rest of the troupe cascades in behind me. We fill in at arm's length until there isn't an empty space left on the stage. I turn my head side to side to check our line, and smile. Sylvie's on one side of me in the front row and Nadine has taken the other spot next to me!

I point my toes and hover my leg in front of me. One of

my hands rests on my hip, and I fly my peach scarf high above my head with the other.

The music builds and builds as I move in unison with my troupe. I remember all the steps to the dance I know by heart. We ride the wave together—like *magic*—and our cymbals make the sound of a thousand gold bangles.

I spin and spin, catching glimpses of the people who have come here for *me*—Ayelet Cohen, the best friend I was never supposed to have, with her family; Waverly Jones, my first Texas friend; and Esmerelda Gutierrez, with her proud father.

I see Mama, my biggest ally, smiling ear to ear, and Sara dancing with Salim next to the bleachers. I see Sitti, regal in her traditional Palestinian thobe, and Baba, whose mind and heart have flown back to us.

There's even Carlos, the dreamy cowboy who likes me, clapping in time with everyone else. He smiles his goofy smile, and I know it's just for me.

These people are the family I was born to—immigrants with traditions and histories they carry with them, that make them who they are and make me who I am, too. And they're the friends whose friendship changed everything—including me.

When I stop spinning, my mind and heart fly back to me from a faraway place. All this time, they had been in Detroit, not San Antonio. Now just like Baba, they're finally where they belong.

Sometimes what you want most is not what you get, and what you need is something you never expect. Sometimes home is the place you never thought it would be. And sometimes everything changes, even when you didn't want it to.

But thank goodness it does: it changes for the better. That's the magic, and that's the dream come true.

Y isn't for Yvette, or Yvonne, or even Yolanda. *Y* is for Yasmeen—Yasmeen Khoury. I'm an Arab American girl from Texas.

Later that night, after I've danced my heart out and the magic comes to an end, I go downstairs to write another sticky note before bed.

My mother's supply has dwindled, but there's one left.

I write my message and stick it in the middle of the refrigerator where my whole family will see it.

San Antonio = home

Author's Note

This book, while not autobiographical, draws from my experience as the daughter of a Christian Palestinian father who was born and raised in Jerusalem. He lived in Israel until immigrating to the United States, where I was born. Just like Yasmeen, my family moved from the Midwest to Texas when I was young, and I attended a Maronite church where I was in a dance troupe. And, I had two left feet!

While I didn't make a middle school best friend like Ayelet, I did make a Jewish best friend when I was eighteen, who later became my husband. Being a part of a Jewish family inspired me to write a story for middle grade readers about the power of new beginnings between Palestinian Arabs and Jewish Israelis.

Maybe just like Yasmeen and Ayelet, there are people in your lives who seem too different to ever become friends. It's my hope that you relate to this story and that it encourages second chances at friendship. We are all wishing upon the same stars. Peace can begin anywhere. It can begin with you.

Acknowledgments

To my wonderful agent, Peter Knapp, thank you for championing my writing and this debut.

To my amazing editors at HarperCollins Children's Books, Megan Ilnitzki and Toni Markiet, thank you for your many thoughtful readings of this story, and for helping me find its center.

To my team at HarperCollins—designer Laura Mock, art director Amy Ryan, production editor Lindsay Wagner, marketing manager Vaishali Nayak, and publicity manager Aubrey Churchward—thank you for making my book the very best it can be.

To my talented cover artist Fathima Hakkim, your breathtaking artwork is a dream come true.

To the folks at Austin SCBWI and the Writers' League of Texas, your programming has been invaluable.

To Bethany Hegedus, I honestly could not have written this story without finding the Writing Barn. The amazing space you created helped me remember the stories of my childhood.

To Writing Barn faculty, Christina Soontornvat and Carolyn Cohagan, your novel courses gave much-needed

shape to my process. Thank you for your enthusiasm and encouragement of the early chapters of this book.

To attorney Karen Crawford, thank you for patiently answering all my questions about Dreamers and immigration.

To my husband, Lowell, my first and best reader, thank you for everything, but especially for calling me your love.

To my sons, David, Isaac, and Daniel, when I write the words of my heart, I write them for you.

To my sister, Jeneen, your love and support mean so much to me. Thank you for reading anything I send your way, and for always encouraging me to keep writing.

To my father, Jacob, thank you for telling me your stories. They were not always easy to hear, but I listened. They are my stories, too.

To my mother and the rest of my family, when I write about kids and families who love each other no matter what, you are my inspiration.

To my dear friend Raman, who has cheered me on for most all my life, having you in my corner makes trying anything, even writing a book, seem so much less scary.

And to the dancers at St. George Maronite Catholic Church, my peach costume still hangs proudly in my closet.

31901067778862